LAURA LUKASAVAGE

Moonlight Destiny

First edition

ISBN: 978-1-956994-19-3

Editing by Ashley McLeod
Editing by Marlena
Cover art by Laura Lukasavage
Editing by Josie O'Brien

This book was professionally typeset on Reedsy.
Find out more at reedsy.com

To anyone having a hard time in life. Whether it be work, love, loss, or something greater, know that life is full of ups and downs, good and bad, happy and sad. Life can never knock you down as long as you keep moving and focus on the happy. Remember something better is always around the corner.

FOR THIS CRAZY THING WE CALL LIFE

Lastly, to my Aunt Ginny, who fought her battle with grace. As I write this, as of last night, she was placed on life-support. Praying for more time.

Life isn't like a book. It's not fantasy or make-believe. It's not all romance, smiles, and happy times. It's work, it's hard, it's long and filled with heartache, loss, and death. But life is also beautiful and we must remember to embrace the good along with the bad, for without the bad the good wouldn't be as fulfilling.

LAURA LUKASAVAGE

Contents

Acknowledgments

I want to personally thank anyone who has continued along this journey with me. My readers and reviewers, you are the reason I continue to try to better my writing and make each story better than the last. Here's to what's to come.

To all who believe in me and help me to be able to achieve my dreams, each book takes me one step closer to the end goal.

Finally, to my wonder team of editors, Ashley, Josie, and Marlena, who without my written work would be a mess and anyone who helps me spread my word, I appreciate you all.

I

Part One

For my Aunt Ginny, and all the souls close to my heart I have lost. For my readers, anyone who's ever loved and lost or known true pain or suffering. This story is for you. Hold on tight and try to enjoy the ride.

Chapter 1

Angela

Sorrow squeezes my heart tightly as I watch my grief-stricken Alpha from a distance. His shoulders are hunched forward. His sadness is evident.

We may have won this battle, but not without some heavy losses. We must ensure their sacrifices are not in vain.

Serenity gave her life so another could live. She insisted they were vital for us to triumph in the final battle, and we were the only thing standing between the preservation or end of our world. If Vladimir's army won, we wouldn't be safe. No one would. Serenity knew this and paid the ultimate price, believing, 'One life can't outweigh the lives of many.' By giving up hers, she gave us a fighting chance. She was the bravest of us all.

Jocelyn…her absence has already affected everyone in the pack. Her kindness set her apart; a heart like hers was hard to come by. A trait Aaron learned and Amberly inherited from her. Since their family was reunited, she slowly became the beating heart, keeping them all grounded. I fear what's to come in her absence.

It has been only four short hours since the battle ended. Our new reality, without those we love, is beginning to sink in. More than ever, we need to remain strong and united if we are going to survive the imminent battle. It is the only way to truly honor those we have lost.

I stand quietly in the shadows, watching Aaron gently place Jocelyn's body on their bed. Kneeling on the floor at her side, he never releases her hand. Even from this distance, I notice his gentle and slow movements as he reaches out to brush the hair away from her pale face.

I quietly creep closer, knowing that startling a wolf in a moment of grief could easily turn deadly.

Placing a loving kiss on Jocelyn's forehead, Aaron whispers, "Rest, my love."

Now, only a few feet from their bedside, I move into the lamplight.

"Aaron."

"What is it?" His broken voice takes me back many years to one of our darkest times. It is a tone I prayed I would never hear from him again.

Pausing briefly, I choose my next words carefully. "I wanted to see how you were. What can I do?"

The heartbreak Aaron felt all those years ago, believing his daughter and the love of his life were murdered, turned him into a cold version of the alpha we have come to know and admire. It took him many years to put them and their absence in his rear view, but now I see that same sorrow pulling him back down into the pits of despair.

I move closer, hoping to give him some kind of comfort even though I know there's nothing anyone can do to ease this pain. I can't imagine his sorrow, and I pray I'll never have to.

Ignoring me completely, Aaron addresses Jocelyn once more, "I'll wake up soon."

My heart stops dead in my chest. He can't really think he's dreaming. I read something long ago about how when life's events become too much for the mind, it messes with your reality. If Aaron's mind were ever to play him like a fiddle, I guess now would be that time.

"Aaron."

"What do you want?" He growls.

I take an involuntary step back. In a pack, your alpha is to be respected, and what he wants or says goes, no questions asked. However, right now, I

4

can't think of him as only my alpha. Because if I do, he will be lost to us, and the pack needs him now more than ever. I need to find a way to get him out of this room.

"We need to talk."

His tone is fuming with his annoyance. "About what?"

"I was hoping we could go for a walk."

Smiling for the first time, his gaze returns to Jocelyn as he brings her hand to his lips. He places a soft kiss on the back of her wrist before placing the hand beside her on the bed. "I'll be back soon, my love."

Facing me, he mumbles. "Let's go."

He turns and disappears out the door almost too fast for my eyes to catch, leaving me to follow after him. We exit the cave, and the brisk night air hits me hard in the face, waking every sense in my body. I take my place beside my Alpha hesitantly, knowing this conversation isn't going to be an easy one.

"You're not acting like yourself," I say in almost a whisper.

"I wish to wake up now, so whatever you need to say, please say it. I want to return to my family."

"Aaron. You're not…" I take in a deep breath. "You're not dreaming."

"This is a horrible nightmare, a trick that my mind is playing on me. It's the fear of the battle coming to our door in a few hours. I've thought of nothing else since Amberly told us about Vladimir. I've feared losing my family all over again, and so that's all this is. My subconscious is playing on my deepest fears."

I turn away from Aaron before speaking. Taking a deep, nervous breath, I decide it's best to come out with it fast. "Vladimir came. He was already here. Jocelyn jumped in front of a blast meant for Aidan." I look back at Aaron before saying the next words, "She died saving your son."

Rage fills the atmosphere between us, warming the chilly air. It takes everything in me not to step back. I know if I do, things will only escalate.

The veins in his neck become more noticeable as he turns on me in blind anger. "You're lying!"

I reach out in hopes of comforting my leader, my friend, and my adoptive

5

father. But he takes a step back. Just far enough for my hand to fall, returning to my side.

"I'm sorry. I wish I was, and I wish there was a way to break the truth to you in a gentler way, but sadly, there isn't."

Without warning, his legs give out, sending him dropping to his knees with a gut-wrenching thud. I struggle against the urge to drop down next to him, knowing he needs some distance for my words to sink in.

Falling forward, his hands land on the earth as his body begins to convulse. His head flies to the heavens as a growl, followed by a deep cry of pure anguish, escapes his body.

I take a step back, trying to hide the pain I'm feeling for him as I watch the realization of what he's lost hit him.

My eyes open wide as I see his teeth growing, and a realization takes hold. He's changing. His howl subsides, but the tears continue to run down his cheeks in a waterfall fashion as he peers at his hands to see that they are now sprouting fur.

Sorrow fills my heart as I watch my alpha on his knees, howling at the sky. I feel his heart breaking as if it were my own. This man, who has been the only father I've ever known, is shattered. I want to comfort him, but I know nothing will help. Not now. He's lost the love of his life, not once but twice, in one lifetime.

I choke back the cry forming in my throat, and tears begin to trail down my face as his shift begins to take hold. Closing his mouth, he lowers his head to look back at the earth, staring in confusion at his half-human, half-wolf hands.

His agony has become too much for him to take, making it impossible for him to control his shift.

I watch as his agony becomes my own, knowing there's nothing I can do. My eyes never leave him, even as he completes the shift. Aaron is gone. Now, standing in his place is a giant gray wolf. His eyes are unfocused and sad. My heart drops to my stomach as I gaze at him. All that's left is the wolf, and I know there is only one thing he needs to do. Run. To escape his new fate, at least for a little while.

"Go," I whisper. "But come back to us. We need you." Thinking of something, anything that might reach him before he disappears. "Your children need you."

His eyes tell me he's registering my words as he nods and turns away. Moments later, he disappears into the forest, leaving me alone with one thought: How will we make it through this?

Chapter 2

Amberly

The battle didn't go how I had hoped, not by a long shot. Serenity died saving Troy, and I couldn't be more grateful for her sacrifice. I only wish there was a way I could repay her for what she's done. I don't think I could have made it through one night if I had lost both my mother and him.

My mother.

Her loss has already become more than I can handle. Her absence is everywhere I look, causing memories to replay in my mind, but the one I want to shake is the one I can't get rid of.

The scene plays on repeat in my mind to the point of insanity. I watch as Vladimir raises his hand, sending his spell toward my brother, but I'm not fast enough. The spell hits her, sending her to her knees, and I watch the light leave her eyes. A day I had never thought about came way too soon. With her loss, I lost my will to fight.

I know the next battle is already at our doors. I can barely breathe, let alone fight, and a huge part of me doesn't want to. For the first time, I want to die, and I don't care if that is my fate. My life had so much light and hope ahead, and now it's shattered, all gone in a moment.

My mother and I were never close. Most would say I couldn't stand the woman, at least not until we came here. Here is where I truly found her. She became the woman I always wanted and needed. She had just got her light back, and now she's gone. For the first time in my life, just when I finally had everything I ever needed to feel whole, the rug was pulled out from under me. Everything was ripped from me the moment her eyes closed for the last time.

Taking with her my will to fight.

If losing my mother has taught me anything, it's that time waits for no one, and nothing is promised. I only wish I learned this lesson another way.

Chapter 3

Julian

Aidan actually took my side. Who would have thought the two of us would ever see eye to eye on anything? I still don't trust him completely, but he did the right thing when it mattered most. I know it wasn't easy for him; I could see it on his face. But he knew, just like I did, that it had to be said. It's hard to believe that not too long ago, he was our enemy, and now he's the love of my life's brother and our ally.

Having him around hasn't been easy. I'm always on edge watching him, praying Amberly is right to trust him and bring him here. For all we knew, he could have been part of Vladimir's end game, but after recent events and the look on his face as their mother lay dead on the ground at his feet, I know I was wrong.

In his short time here, I have noticed a change in him. Tonight, for the first time, he let down his guard with everyone.

Who knew all it took was smores? I laugh to myself.

Well, smores and his family, which is now shattered.

Defeated, I forcefully ran my hand over my dirt and blood-covered face. Tonight's events have left us vulnerable in ways I wish I didn't need to think about. We lost Serenity and Jocelyn, and now Amberly has disappeared. I wish there was something I could do or say to take her pain away. I remember all too well how crippling the loss of family can be, and knowing Amberly is now going through that kills me.

I was never one to focus much on the good in the world because I never felt life owed me anything, and if it did, I didn't think I would get it. I was used to the pain that love caused, so I remained distant from as many people as possible. Angela and Aaron fought like hell until they penetrated my metal walls, but no one else had been so lucky, not until Amberly.

I showed everyone the angry side of myself, someone that no one could possibly love. Then, slowly, the people around me became family, and now I find myself exactly where I never wanted to be again.

A man with everything to lose.

Two battles behind us, one battle left, and I fear the worst is still ahead of us. Sighing, I remove my hand from my face and continue walking as my mind races.

Serenity said to win this coming battle, we need to be united, and we couldn't be further from it. How are we going to fight after today's loss?

We can't. Not like we are now.

"How am I going to fix this?" I ask the darkness around me.

I push the door open in one swift move and glance around the pitch-black room.

No Amberly.

Not that I'm surprised. I don't know what I expected. I knew her room was the last place she would be found at a time like this. I walk over to her bed and sit down on the edge. I take off my shoes and filthy shirt before running my hand through my mangled hair.

"What am I going to do?"

I can't let her heal her mother. That's not an option. It's not worth losing her, and we all agree. Well…everyone except Amberly. I lay my back flat on the bed, releasing a long breath I didn't know I was holding. Closing my eyes, I run through different scenarios in my mind.

Bringing Amberly flowers.

Nope.

Having a run together as wolves.

Nope, that could end badly.

Having a long talk.

Not a good idea.

I shoot up into a sitting position as the answer hits me hard in the face.

I run from the room faster than a bolt of lightning. Shoes and shirt long forgotten.

Chapter 4

Aidan

I've looked everywhere for what's left of my family, but my father and sister are nowhere to be found. It's like they've just disappeared. I sigh in defeat, turning to head back inside, hoping to find them in the morning. As I make my way back to my room, I pray that all we need is some time alone. Despair is an evil thing; it will take over if you let it.

But I refuse to let despair win. Not over me, and sure as hell not over my family. We will find our way out of this.

I may not be my sister's favorite person right now, and if I were in her shoes, I wouldn't want to see me either, but I can't leave her alone. Not now. I may not have grown up with our mother, but I feel her loss all the same, and I know stopping Amberly from healing her was the right thing to do. It was the hardest decision I've had to make since coming to the cave with Amberly. I could take the hate stares and the words whispered about me in the dark. I could even take not being accepted by my parents. But Amberly, the only person I've ever needed was her, and now, I feel I might have lost her. That thought alone kills me inside. She's the reason I'm becoming a better man. I know I'm royally messed up, and I've done some unforgivable things, but in the end, she didn't look at me with hate or disgust. She looked at me as I was. Simply her brother. That was until I sided with her ass of a boyfriend and told her she couldn't heal our mother.

I take my first step inside the cave, and my forehead collides with someone else. I stop and rub at it feverishly.

"Damn, you have a hard head," Julian groans.

"Speak for yourself."

He places his hand back to his side at the same time as I do. "I didn't come to argue."

I smile before moving around him. "Smart."

I don't make it three steps before his words hit me in the back. "I think we can save her."

Stopping in my tracks, I turn back to him slowly. My expression urging him to continue.

"I think there might be a way to bring back Jocelyn."

Hope fills my chest before I can shove it back down. "How?"

Running his hand through his hair in a desperate gesture, he answers. "Don't get your hopes up. I'm not sure it will work."

"Will you just spit it out?" I say, trying to hold my composure.

"I was thinking how Amberly has the power to heal."

Anger fills my body as I cut him off, "We've already had this conversation. I'm not letting her do it."

Exposing my back to him once more, disgusted that he would even consider letting my sister do that, knowing what it would mean for her. For someone who claims to love her, he isn't showing it.

"I wasn't talking about her."

Stopping, I release a long sigh. "Then who?"

His voice is so low that I almost don't hear it. "You."

Turning toward him, I say my next words slowly. "What do you mean, me?"

He takes two steps in my direction and adds, "You and Amberly are twins."

I roll my eyes at the obvious. "Yeah, and?"

A low growl forms in Julian's chest, causing me to smile. "I'm saying if she has the power, there may be a chance you do too?"

Now I'm annoyed.

At myself.

I mean, why didn't I think of that?

Closing the distance between us, I slap his shoulders with my hands. "You, my friend, are a genius."

He smiles smugly. "Who? Me?"

I laugh. "Don't let it go to that big head of yours."

"I don't have a big head."

I drop my hands, shrug, and turn away. "Whatever you say."

"I don't." He says in a whiny tone.

"Let's go try out this idea of yours."

I look over my shoulder to see him nod in agreement before he walks past me. Following him, I push down the hope that's trying to rise to the surface. We don't know if this will work. I hope that it will, but I don't want to get my hopes up only to have this fail.

Looking at Julian's back, I hesitate before asking, "Do you know what to do?"

"Not exactly."

I clench my fists, trying to keep my tone neutral. "Then how are we going to try this?"

He stops walking. "I'm hoping Johnathan and Aayda will be willing to walk us through the process."

"You mean the people who just buried the woman who had this gift? You want to go and talk to them about this right after she died saving that kid?"

I hear him release a breath. "That kid has a name." Turning toward me, he continues. "And I'm hoping that because it was Jocelyn and because it will help Amberly, they will be willing to."

"Fingers crossed, I guess."

"Plus, if you can bring your mother back, then you can bring back Serenity, so it would benefit them to help us."

"I never agreed to do that," I mumble.

Looking at me with uncertainty, he asks, "You're telling me you wouldn't bring her back, too?"

I shrug, "Why should I? I mean, who is she to me? Why would I give my life for someone who isn't blood?"

I catch him rolling his eyes, which causes a growl to form in my throat. That makes him smile.

"Did you ever think if Serenity was alive, Amberly wouldn't need to use her power? Serenity didn't want her to use it in the first place. So if she was alive, and someone died, and she knew Amberly would use her power, I think she would step in and do it instead. So if you think about it, genius, in the long run, it would be better to have her around, don't you think?"

Ignoring his comment, I add sarcastically, "Whatever you say, *bruh.*"

Julian scowls at me, and I can't help but laugh.

"What's so funny?" He asks, annoyed.

"You. Only you," I mumble, walking past.

Chapter 5

Julian

I knock on the door as gently as possible, suppressing my eagerness. I hear hushed footsteps as they approach, and the door slowly opens. Johnathan looks at us with worry-filled eyes.

"Can I help you boys?" Johnathan whispers.

"We hope so," I answer slowly.

As Johnathan follows my gaze, I glance at Aayda sleeping on the bed before stepping forward. Aidan steps backward so Johnathan can exit the room. Once in the hallway, he looks us over with uncertainty. Aidan is covered head to foot in dirt and blood. A nice cut above his eyebrow runs across the top of his head, plus a few bruises forming on his cheek and chin. He's definitely a sight. As for myself, I don't doubt I look just as bad as he does, plus I'm shoeless and shirtless.

"Boy, where are your clothes?"

Looking down at myself, I mumble, "I, um, I was in a rush."

"I can see," he says to me before turning his attention back to Aidan. "So, what brings you to my door at this hour?"

"We…I mean, I was hoping," I sigh. "I had a thought."

I look at Aidan, hoping he will chime in. From the look on his face, I know I'm in this alone.

"What is it, Julian?"

"I was thinking how Amberly and Aidan are twins. So wouldn't he have the same powers as his sister?" I ask in a hopeful tone.

"Not necessarily."

Aidan throws his hands wildly in the air around us. "See, I told you. Let's go, this is pointless."

"Hold on a moment. What's pointless?" Johnathan asks.

"I was thinking maybe Aidan had the power to heal."

"Oh, I see. You were thinking he could bring back his mother?"

I nod.

"It's a possibility. But you must know, it's a small one."

The desperation is apparent in my voice. "I'm willing to try anything." I turn to Aidan, pleading. "Aren't you?"

A moment of silence lingers before Aidan simply nods his head.

"So be it. I will try to help you. But like I said, it's a long shot."

Aidan and I nod in understanding before we take off in the direction where we know Aaron is keeping Jocelyn. Holding my breath, I pray to anyone listening to please let this work. I fear if it doesn't, we will stay divided in the impending battle, leading to our defeat.

Chapter 6

Cole

"Where are we going?" My tone fills with annoyance.

Annabeth turns in my direction before smiling at me, "Home."

"Why?" I ask, confused. "There's nothing left for us there."

Facing forward, she takes her next steps and offers, "To gather the others?"

Snarling, I ask. "What others? No one is left."

"That's where you're wrong," Annabeth replies before quickening her stride.

"Then please enlighten us. I think we deserve to know what's going on."

Henry jumps in my path. "You would be smart to watch your tone boy."

Annabeth places a hand on her husband's shoulder, unphased. "Thank you, Henry. But you must understand his uncertainty. He does not know."

Celine moves next to me. "Doesn't know what?"

Annabeth's smile widens. "Vladimir had a backup plan. Just in case."

"You mean, in case he failed," I say, cutting her short with a grin.

Annabeth's smile disappears. "He was a wise man. You're best to remember that."

"A wise man that got himself killed," I mutter in defiance.

Henry raises his hand, ready to strike, but my sister moves to stand in front of me before he can land a blow. His hand hovers in the air, ten inches from her face. His cheeks turn a deep crimson.

"You best back away from my brother," Celine warns.

Henry backs away with a groan, cradling his hand in the process. My sister isn't one to mess with. Unlike most witches, she doesn't need her hands for most spells. We may be twins, but my sister is far stronger than I'll ever be.

"Henry, do compose yourself," Annabeth says in a scolding tone.

"Yes, dear."

Celine turns her attention to Annabeth, or Anna, as I like to call her. "You were saying. The contingency plan."

"Oh, yes." She turns away and begins walking again. "Vladimir was always searching for the seven."

"Seven what?" I ask.

"I know he told you the story about the seven reincarnated originals," Annabeth offers.

My sister and I nod.

"And he told you when you find the seven good, the seven evil are always born around the same time. This is how we come to know hard times in history. Whenever there has been great war or darkness or long moments of peace, that was because they were alive. There can never be less than fourteen. The good seven cannot be here without the evil seven. It's the universe's way of maintaining the balance."

We nod again.

"I'm sure Vladimir didn't tell you that the two of you are of those fourteen souls."

"What?" Celine and I blurt in unison.

"Vladimir searched high and low until he found as many as possible."

My head is spinning. I always thought they were simply stories.

"He found you and many of the others," she snarls. "However, Aaron and his pack beat him to a few, and some were born in Amberly's village, but by the time he learned about them, it was too late. The wards were already up."

"Wards?" I ask.

"Her mother put them in place to keep everyone safe. Only her blood can enter unless she lets someone in. Otherwise, no one can get inside."

"So, Vladimir was kept at bay," Henry says. "Until they surfaced."

"You mean when she left the village in search of her stupid father," Celine's tone is pure distaste. "Stupid girl."

"Stupid indeed," Anna continues. "That simple act 'uncloaked' her and the rest of the seven, for lack of a better term."

"Huh," I mumble confused.

I see her annoyance as her eyes fall on me. "They would have been hidden from Vladimir if they had remained inside that village. Once she left, so did the rest of them, and he was able to sense and locate them."

"Stupid girl," my sister repeats, as Anna replies again, "Stupid indeed."

"So other than Amberly's group and us, where are the rest of the fourteen?" I ask.

Anna's smile takes over her face. "Back at the foundation."

"Home?" Celine's tone sounds skeptical.

Anna nods. "He hid them."

"Where?"

"We will show you," Henry adds as he continues to push us further.

The air around us turns thick with the silence. My sister's eyes connect with mine, and I see the fear and uncertainty in them. If what they say is true, then the war isn't over, and Celine and I aren't safe.

The forest seems to grow darker with each step. Creatures lurk in the shadows, watching us with their white and yellow eyes. I have no doubt that if it were only my sister and I, they would come out from the shadows, and we would have another fight on our hands.

Chapter 7

Aidan

My palms are sweaty as I lean over my mother, unsure where to begin. Looking over my shoulder at Johnathan, I hope he understands the question in my eyes.

"Get comfortable," He says.

Groaning, I pull a chair over to the bed and turn to him once more for direction.

"Place your hands on her."

Looking at her unmoving frame, I reluctantly place my hands on her forearm, which is thankfully covered by a thin blanket. The cool temperature of her body is barely noticeable through the material.

"Now, I need you to close your eyes and clear your mind."

Lines form across my forehead, "Are you for real?"

"I know in this situation that's hard to do," he says, expression full of compassion and understanding.

I cut him short. "You think."

Ignoring my outburst, he continues, "If this is going to work, that's the first step you need to take."

I close my eyes and release a long breath. "I'll try."

My heart beats a mile a minute inside my tight chest. It feels like my muscles and organs are closing in around it, making each breath harder than the last. Someone places a hand on my shoulder, offering much-needed support. The gesture helps ground my nerves.

"Relax. Slow, shallow breaths." Johnathan's voice is calm.

His words make focusing easier, and I do as he says. In through my nose, out through my mouth. Repeat.

After doing this a few times, my heart begins to calm. I wiggle my fingers before placing them back on my mother's stiff arm.

"Please, let this work," I mumble to myself.

Trying to clear my mind is a lot harder than I thought it would be. The same thoughts keep going around in circles. How Amberly needs her mother, and hell, if I'm being honest, so do I. Our family has just found each other. This can't be how it ends.

"You've got this," Julian says from somewhere in the room.

Sweat drips down my forehead as I try to concentrate on nothing but my mother.

"That's it," Johnathan praises.

I take in a slow, deep breath between my teeth. Letting the cool air hit my throat and then my lungs, waking me up. Surely, if I can take a life, I can bring one back. I hope my past hasn't taken away a gift that could be our only hope.

"Now. Picture her as if she were alive and well and right in front of you. Reach out for her."

I see her smiling face looking at me as tears begin to form behind my closed eyes.

"You have it?"

I nod.

"Now picture reaching for her, placing your hands on her, and imagine pulling her through the veil and back to her body."

I nod.

I see myself reaching for her, but the further my arm stretches, the more she moves away from me.

"Mom. Take my hand."

She shakes her head.

"I can't," she says sadly.

"Yes, you can. I'm right here. I've come to take you home."

Her smile is so bright. "My son. I am so proud of you."

Confusion and uncertainty surround me. "What?"

"I can see the man you will soon become, and I know you will be there to take care of your sister."

I try to hide the surprise in my voice. "Of course. Always."

"You can't see it now, but I do. Stay close to one another. Amberly will need you now more than she knows."

I feel her slipping from me. Panicking, I reach out, begging.

"Mother, take my hand, please!"

Tears shine in her bright eyes. "I'm sorry, my son. But this is not a power you possess. Even if you did, I wouldn't want my child doing anything that would hurt them. Even if you didn't feel the change or the toll it took on you for bringing me back, I would. Make sure Amberly understands this. I could never put myself before my children. You are both grown and have one another. That is more than a mother could hope for. Please help her understand. Help her to grieve. You will need each other."

Her pleading tone makes me agree.

"I need her to understand that I'm at peace, and it makes my heart soar to know you are both safe and have each other at last."

"I don't know what to do. Things feel so dark here without you."

She stretches her hand out for mine, our fingers inches from each other. "I'm so happy I got to know you. Don't let your past define you; your future is full of light. Follow that light, my son, with your sister beside you, and you will both be fine."

I feel the truth in her words as they lift the shadow of darkness hanging over me.

"The coming battle won't be easy. As long as you are all united, you will make it through, and I promise there will be many happy days ahead."

My energy quickly pulls back, and when I look up, she's gone. My eyes open, sending a tsunami down my cheeks as I whisper one word.

"Mom."

"What happened?" Julian asks hysterically.

Ignoring him, I look down at my mother and whisper, "I will make you proud."

Johnathan addresses Julian's question. "It didn't work."

"What? I don't understand. I really thought this was the missing piece. I believed he could do it."

I bend over to kiss my mother lightly on her forehead before standing and facing the men in the room. "There is nothing we can do. She's gone."

"Don't say that!" Julian yells.

I turn to Johnathan. "I spoke to her."

Their eyes widen.

"She told me I don't have the power to bring her back. She told me she's happy and at peace."

"This can't be it." Julian stumbles over his words.

I turn to him with sympathy and understanding that I didn't have before. "There is nothing to be done. We must focus on mending the rift between everyone. Starting with Amberly. She told me we would make it through the battle ahead, but only if we were all united."

He cuts me off, "Only if we are all united. I know."

"So, let's go find my sister. I have a promise to keep."

Chapter 8

Amberly

Being alone is both calming and deafening. On the one hand, I don't have anyone annoying me. But on the other hand, I have too much time to think, and my mind goes to dark places.

How do you say goodbye to someone you've had your whole life? Someone who taught you to be who you are. I'm too young to be without a parent. Too young to be in these life-or-death battles and to see only death around me.

I'm too young to be fighting and taking lives. Too close to turning into exactly what Vladimir wanted. This isn't a life for anyone, let alone someone so young. How did we get here? How did this become my reality?

I'm trying to think back to before all this happened, before my life changed so drastically when my biggest issue was growing up without any family other than my mother.

Now I'm alone, once again.

Surrounded by people I barely know.

This is all my fault. I wanted so badly to feel like I fit in. So badly to understand why I felt something was missing in my life. I needed to put the puzzle pieces together, even if it meant going against my mother's rules. I wouldn't listen, and now she's dead. And I have no one to blame but myself for her loss. Vladimir never would have found me, and we would have never learned the truth if it hadn't been for me leaving our village.

At the same time, I never would have found my father, the pack, or Julian. If I could go back, would I have chosen differently? Honestly, I don't know.

As the sun rises, the sky changes to a beautiful mix of orange, pink and purple. The trees are my only protection from the rays. I take notice of the little animals emerging from their homes, searching for breakfast. Ignorant of the blood that now stains the earth floor. The bodies that still lay where they were slain only mere hours ago. The smell of smoke, fire, and death fills my nose, and tears fill my eyes.

"There you are."

Julian's voice sounds far away as my heart pounds in my ears, and my vision begins to blur. I turn around to see Julian and my brother walking toward me, wishing they would turn around and go back to where they came from. After today, I don't want to see either of them. Of course, the first time they get along is when they decide it's for the best to let my mother stay dead. How ironic is that?

"I don't want to talk to either of you." The words barely make it out of my mouth.

"Well, that's too bad." My brother's tone is final.

"Please, just leave me alone," I mumble before turning my back to them once more.

He shakes his head. "Not gonna happen, sis."

I sigh before moving into a standing position. If they won't go, then I will. I walk past them and don't stop. I notice their wide eyes before their mouths drop open, but I don't stop walking. The more distance I put between me and them, the better.

Julian's voice comes from behind me, "Oh my God, Amberly."

Annoyed, I turn back toward them. "What?"

Moving to stand in front of me, he gently takes my arm in his hand. "Why haven't you started healing?"

I look down to see the ten-inch-long wound on my arm. I shrug, answering, "I don't know."

He turns his attention to Aidan, panic clear in his eyes.

Pulling my arm away from him, I say, "It's not like this hasn't happened before. Relax."

His eyes plead with me. "That was back before you wanted to accept who you were. This. This is different." He says while pointing at my arm.

"How so?" Aidan asks.

"If she's not healing, there are only a few reasons why."

Aidan rolls his eyes. "Which are?"

"One. She doesn't want to heal herself," Julian offers while looking in my direction.

"Not that. I honestly forgot all about my cuts."

Julian sighs. "Two would be that they used something magical to inflict the wounds."

"Possibly," I answer in an uncaring tone.

"And third?" Aidan asks.

Julian's eyes look at me like he's searching for something, "Third would be if the weapon used was poisonous to shifters."

Trying to recall the fight, the pounding in my head grows. Then I remember the knife that Vladimir's man so eagerly wanted to use. Taking his time as he repeatedly ran the blade over my skin. Suddenly, I'm finding it hard to swallow.

Could Vladimir have been more prepared than we thought?

How careless had I been? I should have known better, but no, I had to go into that fight all cocky. What if he did use a poisoned blade? Do I really care anymore? Wouldn't I have felt more of the effects by now if that's what was causing me not to heal?

As if on cue, the pain intensifies around the cuts on my arm and face, making it almost impossible to breathe, and my hand flies to my throat without warning.

"Amberly." My brother's voice rings in my ears.

My vision begins to blur as my temple pounds away like a drum, sending a ringing through my ears. I was so angry and distracted by my loss that I didn't notice what was going on inside my body. Not until now, when it might be too late.

The feeling of lava in my veins begins like a fire, causing my skin to burn. I rake my nails over my skin as Julian and Aidan lunge for me.

"Amberly, stop!" Julian screams, grabbing my arms in a vice.

"It burns!" I scream.

Julian's eyes widen as he looks at Aidan in a pleading manner. I can clearly see that neither of them has a clue what to do.

"What's wrong with her?"

Julian whispers, "I think we go with option three."

Chapter 9

Troy

I hear Amberly's screams long before I see Julian and Aidan running with her through the door. They are practically carrying her. Sweat drips off her face in heaps.

"What's wrong with her?" The worry is evident in my tone as they race toward me.

"She's been poisoned," Julian snarls.

"How?" I ask frantically.

"In the battle, the man who attacked her had a dagger, and I'm fairly certain he laced the blade."

Afraid of the answer, I ask, "With what?"

Julian slows his steps and places Amberly gently on the ground. His gaze falls on me, sending a chill over my body. If looks could kill.

"I believe it's wolfsbane," he whispers.

"What is that?" I ask, having never heard of it before.

"It's a poison that's only deadly to us shifters."

"What can we do?" I ask hysterically.

Julian picks her up in one fast movement and heads off in the direction of her room, leaving us all to follow in his wake. We pass Logan, Amara, and Angela along the way. They take one look and fall in step behind us.

Logan asks first. "What's going on?"

Offering my answer in a whisper. "Julian thinks Amberly's been poisoned with…" I pause to look at Aidan for clarification, "…what did he call it?"

Without looking in our direction, he snarls out, "Wolfsbane."

Angela's gasp makes my head turn so fast that I almost give myself whiplash.

"Wolfbane is deadly to our kind." She whispers.

"So he said."

"How long?" she pauses, and her face turns to pure concern as she moves up next to Julian, "This didn't happen in the fight, did it?"

Julian nods.

Her pace slows, "Oh my God."

"What?" I ask as anxiety sets in. Everyone slows their steps, waiting for an answer we're not sure we want.

Angela's gaze is full of worry. "It's been too long."

"What does that mean?"

Amara speaks for the first time. "She's not going to die, is she?"

I glance at her in horror at the question.

"I don't know. No one has ever survived after being exposed this long," Angela mumbles.

"We still have time." Julian's voice is firm and determined.

Angela's voice is full of pain when she replies, "Julian, I don't–"

His glare silences her. We walk the rest of the way to Amberly's room in silence. Once there, he gently lays Amberly on her bed. Somewhere along the way, she fell unconscious. Staring down at her unmoving body, my mind flashes back to Jocelyn.

"We can't lose her, too," I whisper to Logan.

"We won't."

Julian turns to Aidan with sheer determination on his face. "Go find your Dad. We're going to need him."

Angela steps forward hesitantly, "You won't find him."

Julian whips around to her, "What do you mean he won't find him? Where is he?"

"I don't know."

Julian takes two long strides until he's standing in front of her, and even from this distance, I can feel the heat from his anger radiating off of him. My protective instincts make me want to step in front of her, but Logan's arm stops me. I glance over at him as he shakes his head at me, his eyes never leaving Angela.

"How can you not know?" Julian's tone is hostile.

"He shifted."

His face changes to one of worry, "You mean…"

She nods sympathetically.

Julian turns his back to us, "This isn't good."

Aidan looks at Angela, asking, "What's going on?"

"Your father is in a lot of pain," Angela begins.

Aidan scoffs at her words, "Aren't we all."

"I'm not belittling what anyone is going through."

"Sounds like you are to me."

Angela takes a slow breath. "I only meant…"

"To protect your leader. I get it," he says in a heated tone.

"You've only shifted once, Aidan. You don't understand."

"Then make me," he snarls.

Logan takes a protective step forward. This situation is escalating fast and not in a good way.

"Just like any magical creature, our powers are attached to our emotions," she says slowly.

"Duh."

Logan moves to stand next to Angela. His expression is defensive. "Why don't you shut up and let her get the words out."

Aidan reluctantly closes his mouth, rolling his eyes before turning away.

"Your father lost all of you once already. He barely made it out of his grief the first time around."

"Poor Daddy."

Logan's look silences him.

Angela continues, unaffected by Aidan's hot demeanor, "Losing Jocelyn. It was too much for him. So, his wolf took over. It made him shift. He had no control."

"Okay, and…"

She looks unsure of his question. "And what?"

"Like Julian said, we need him. So can we go find him or something?"

She shakes her head sadly. "It's not that simple."

Taking a cautious step forward, I sigh. "Angela, there has to be something. Anything. Amberly needs him."

"Maybe one of us can sniff him out."

Aidan erupts into laughter. "Sniff him out." He grabs his abdomen. "Now that's a wolf joke if I've ever heard one."

Julian launches toward Aidan and grips his shirt in his fists. "You done?"

"Just getting started," He snaps back, the anger in his voice rising.

Julian releases him with a shove. "This isn't helping. Stop being a dick and help, or leave. I don't care which."

Logan's voice breaks through the silence. "Julian's right. We've all been through a lot, and tension is running high, but we must come together and focus." He pauses briefly, looking at Amberly, "She needs us to."

"What do you need me to do?" Aidan mumbles.

Julian addresses everyone. "Angela, you're going to stay here with me since you're the closest thing we have to a nurse. We are going to attempt a blood transfusion, praying that will be enough to hold her over. Troy and Logan, I need you to grab some things for us. I'll give you a list in a moment. And Amara, I need you and Aidan to go look for Aaron."

"Are you crazy?" The words fly out of my mouth before I can stop them.

Julian's glare silences me, but not Aidan.

"Why? Are you worried I'll hurt your little girlfriend?" He says in my direction.

Amara shrinks into the shadows, lingering by the door.

"You did not too long ago, yet I seem to be the only one here besides her who remembers that fact."

"Trust me, I didn't forget, and I never will," Aidan spits out, his teeth bared.

Julian's yell echoes through the room. "Enough! Aidan and Amara are our only options. They can both shift and smell him out." Looking at me, he continues, "Unless you learned to shift recently and forgot to share with the rest of the class."

I shake my head, defeated.

"I didn't think so."

Aidan comes to stand in front of me. "I'm not happy about my past, but I'm trying to make up for it. I don't need people like you throwing it in my face every chance you get." He walks to the door and stops. "I'll bring her back exactly as she left. You have my word." His gaze falls on Julian. "We will find my father and be back as soon as we can. Keep her heart beating until then."

"That's the plan," Julian whispers. As Aidan and Amara leave to look for Aaron, he kneels beside the bed, taking Amberly's hand in his.

"What do you need from us?" Logan asks.

Angela places a hand on his shoulder. "I'm going to need you to find a few buckets and rags. I'll also need a few bags of saline, and bring some water and food. It's going to be a long night."

Julian looks over his shoulder at her. "What about.."

Cutting him off, she adds, "I have those in my room. I'll go grab them and be right back."

He nods.

Logan grabs me by the arm, pulling me toward the door. We exit in a hurry, but not before each of us takes one last look back.

Chapter 10

Aaron

I try to focus on something, anything other than the loss of my mate, which puts me in this current situation. But my mind can't. I keep seeing it play on repeat. Vladimir. Our children in the line of fire. One second, Jocelyn's there next to me; the next thing I know, she's falling to the ground in front of our children's feet.

I was too weak to protect her, to protect our family.

It should have been me.

A deep, angry growl rises from within my chest, sending birds and squirrels hiding in the bushes to emerge and scatter. I know I need to shift back; I'm the alpha, and I don't have time to wallow in this crippling grief. But I can't shift back into my human form. I've tried many times. My wolf is too broken, angry and ashamed, and we both feel that our pack is better off without us. The only thing I've been good at doing since this battle began is losing people. Half the pack has died in the last two battles, and being their alpha, I should have trained and protected them better than I did.

It's all on me.

I'm the one to blame for everything that's happened. All the loss, pain and heartbreak. When Amberly first arrived, I didn't know what to think or how to react. I couldn't believe that my family was still alive. All this time, they were out there, and I never knew. All the time we lost... my heart hurts just thinking about it. Amberly's first word, first steps, first everything. Then there's Aidan. How could I not know Jocelyn was pregnant with twins?

When Amberly finally found me, I should have done more to protect everyone. We waited too long, got too cocky. And now, because of it, we have lost so much.

I have failed in every way a man can't afford to. I fell short on everything we are meant to provide, and now it's time to admit what needs to happen.

It's time for a new pack leader.

Chapter 11

Aidan

Every time I glance back at Amara, she's hugging herself and looking anywhere but in my direction. Releasing a breath, I wish there was something I could do to make her feel more comfortable around me. I've owned what I've done. All the horrible things in my past; I regret it all, but I can't change it or take it back. All I can do is try to make amends.

"Amara, it might be safer up here than back there by yourself. We don't know what state my father will be in or what else could be lurking in these woods."

I hear her pick up her pace, and I slow down so she can catch up. She still stays a few feet behind me, staring at her feet.

"Listen," I start, clenching my fists nervously. "I wanted to say how sorry I am. Nothing I say can justify what I did to you and the others in the camp, but I'm trying to be a better person. I'm trying to make amends. I won't hurt you. I know you might not believe that, but you won't ever come to trust me unless you give me the chance to prove myself."

As she tilts her head up, her eyes connect with mine for the first time, and I see how scared and unsure she is. I do my best to make myself look less intimidating. She rubs her arm nervously, then comes to stand next to me for the first time since we left the cave. I offer her a smile, but she faces forward without returning it.

Oh well, progress is progress. Better than nothing.

"Aidan?"

Surprised, I hesitate for a moment before acknowledging her, "Yes?"

"You were right when you said nothing you say can justify what you did, but I've been wondering…"

She turns quiet once more, and I know I need to push for her to continue. "What?"

"Why did you do it? Why did you follow Vladimir and do the things you did?"

* * *

I face forward, thinking about all the horror of my past, the things I did and why. I could say it's because of my upbringing, but that isn't entirely true. Yes, Vladimir raised me and trained me to be tough, brutal and even deadly, but until recently, he had been like a father to me. And for that reason alone, I was always trying to please him. Any child would do almost anything to make their parents proud of them, right? He was all I had. But he was dark, evil, and closed off. I tried everything to get him to open up and let me in like a normal father would, but nothing worked. Not until I thought like him.

I knew the only way to get recognition from him was to be like him. I hated the idea, and it took me many years of torturing, killing, and being like him before it became second nature, and I started to do those same things without a second thought. It was like that for a long time until I learned the truth. Once I knew the truth about Amberly, things shifted and seemed to make sense. I always wondered why I had to work so hard to be like Vladimir. If I was his son, some of who he was should have been instilled in me at birth, and I wouldn't have to work so hard. But I wanted to be anything but like him.

Then I found Amberly, and the moment my eyes locked onto her, that darkness that had taken over my life and clouded my judgment for so long just shattered. I found myself sneaking out to see her as often as I could. Each time, the darkness became less than before. When I wasn't with her, I would think about what she was doing and who she was with. I wondered if she knew about me and if we were alike in even the smallest of ways. All I could think about was meeting her. She changed my whole perspective on everything, and the things I had done made me sick to my core. It still took until she was in our camp with Vladimir threatening her life for me to really change, but that was a different fear. I didn't know if my parents wanted me. If they gave me away so willingly at birth, then why would they want anything to do with me now, after all the evil I had done? Would they ever want me? For that reason, I wanted Amberly to stay with me and Vladimir until I had to choose between the two, and then the real shift happened.

* * *

I shake the thoughts from my mind, realizing her question had made my mind drift. I glance in Amara's direction to see her staring at me intently, and I realize I haven't answered her yet, lost in my thoughts.

"That's a good question. However, my answer is a bit complex."

"I'm all ears," she mumbles from next to me.

"Okay," I sigh, "So answer me this—what would you have done to make your parents proud of you?"

She's quiet for a moment before her answer comes.

"I never had to try to be more than who I was to make them proud. What's your point?"

Must be nice to have a normal family. Or a real one. Vladimir wasn't my father, so I guess it makes sense that I had to work for it. When I came to live with Amberly and my parents, they welcomed me with open arms, even knowing what I had done. I guess that's what a real family and unconditional love is like.

39

"I grew up thinking Vladimir was my father. Being nothing like him only angered him, and his wrath became more harsh as the years progressed. He was always trying to mold me, to make me more like him. He was never happy with me; all I ever craved was his approval. To be told, just once, that he was proud of me. I turned off my humanity and did ungodly things just to hear those words, but they never came." I peer down to see her looking at me with sadness in her eyes.

"I can't change what I've done and hate myself because of it. If it wasn't for Amberly, I don't think I would have ever walked away from him and what I was doing, but I'm trying to be better. It's hard. I'm used to being angry and inflicting fear and terror on those around me to get what I want."

Lightening the mood, she giggles, "Yeah, I've noticed."

We continue walking silently, allowing me to hear the forest noises around us. I never used to enjoy them. I didn't care enough to. Hearing little feet running across the stones and leaves covering the ground makes me think more of family. Knowing these creatures are just like us, they need more than themselves; they need others to survive.

The sun begins to lower in the sky, casting a beautiful reddish light against the trees. Everything has looked and felt so different to me recently, and it's an amazing feeling. I can't believe what I let myself turn into, all for a man who stole me from my family.

We walk in silence for another half a mile before Amara breaks it, turning to look at me.

"You know, if you want everyone to like you, you might want to try to stop being so strung out."

"What do you mean?"

She pauses, and I can tell she's unsure if she should say what she's thinking. She's still afraid of me and how I'll react.

"You can say it. I won't bite," I offer with a smile.

Her gaze remains uncertain, so I add, "I promise. I want to hear what you are going to say. I just need more of an explanation."

Looking forward again, the corners of her mouth turn into a smile, "You come off as obnoxious and cruel sometimes. I get that's how you were brought up and that being that way allows you to protect yourself, but you can let that part of you go. You don't have to be closed off and guarded. Not with us."

The sincerity in her words is evident, and I don't doubt what she says. I wish it were easy. I've been like this for my whole life, and changing how I react to those around me, especially other males, is going to take some time and a lot of work. I know it will be worth it, though. Like my mother said, we need to be united if we are going to survive this next battle, and I'll do anything to keep my sister and those she cares for safe. If I need to change how defensive and obnoxious I can sometimes be to mend the rift between all of us, then I'll do my best.

"Thank you," I whisper.

Amara comes to a stop abruptly, causing me to do the same.

"Did you just say thank you?" Shock and awe fill her expression.

I laugh, "Yes."

Amara smiles before beginning to walk again. "There may be hope for you yet."

We walk in silence once more for a few hours. I'm just about to say we should stop for the night when I hear it — a deep, heart-wrenching howl. I turn to Amara, whose eyes are wide.

"You heard that, right?"

She nods.

"You think?"

She nods again, "I guess there's only one way to find out."

I feel Amara's hand on my arm as she moves behind me, and I can tell she's nervous about what lies before us.

"Don't worry, I'll go first. Just stay behind me."

"Okay." She whispers.

We slowly move into the bushes. Creeping forward, I move the branches aside as quietly as possible because if it's Aaron and he's unhinged, we don't want to startle him. And if it's not him, we don't want to be noticed. I move aside the last few branches before a giant grey wolf comes into view. I have no doubt that it's him. Now that he's in eyesight and I can sense him and his despair, it almost cripples me. There's only one thing left to do. Figure out how to get his attention without him attacking us.

Chapter 12

Angela

Logan and Troy took around twenty minutes to get everything I had asked for. By the time they walked back through the door, I already had Julian hooked up to Amberly and their blood flowing.

Logan moves beside me, taking my hand in his, "How is she?"

"She's a fighter."

He squeezes my hand lightly, "Will she survive?"

I look into his pained eyes, afraid to answer his question. He had known Joycelyn his whole life; she was their leader. He almost lost Troy last night, and now he might lose Amberly. I don't want to be the one to cause him more pain than he's already feeling. How can you tell someone you care about that there is a high possibility they are about to lose someone else they love? I wish I could do more for Amberly, but if there were, I would have done it already.

His next words come out as a whisper, "Be honest with me."

I look back in Amberly's direction, unable to face him with these words.

"I honestly don't know. Her wounds haven't healed at all, and she's lost a lot of blood. The poison ran through her body for hours, causing damage to her heart and other organs. Because of the poison, they can't heal. Then there's the fact that she might not want to survive."

He pulls me lightly until I'm standing in front of him. "What do you mean she might not want to survive?"

I sigh before my gaze returns to Amberly's unconscious body. Sweat pours off her as she gasps for air.

"She just lost her mother, and none of us would let her do the one thing that could save her. She's angry at us, and her mother is gone."

"She would never just give up," he offers sternly.

Releasing another long breath, I reply, "I know you've known her your whole life, but shifters are different from witches. Now that she's shifted and accepted that side of her, things are different. We feel things differently than you do; everything is more intense for us, as we are technically two beings inside one body."

"What does that mean?"

"We are part human but also part wolf. They both have a mind of their own," I explain.

Confusion becomes evident on his face, "I didn't know that matters?"

"Her wolf side feels things just as deeply as her human half, but on a different level. Like with Aaron, his wolf took over because the grief was too intense for his human side to handle. I feel Amberly's wolf will be no different."

"But again, what does that have to do with her giving up?"

I pull him closer to the door, not wanting Julian to overhear our conversation.

"If Amberly has already given up, I have no doubt her wolf won't be far behind." I try to speak as quietly as possible. "If they both don't want to live anymore, then her wolf side won't come to heal her wounds or push the poison from her body. Instead, it will do the opposite."

His eyes connect with mine, and I see the worry my words have brought. "Meaning?"

"Instead, it will fight to keep it in."

Logan's eyes widen as he looks back at Amberly. "What can we do?"

"I don't think there's anything to do besides what we've already done. She's unconscious, and I doubt she would listen to any of us right now even if we tried."

44

We stand in silence by the door for a few minutes before I break it.

"I need to do a few more things here to make sure she is okay until we get Aaron back. How about you go to my room and try to relax? I'll be there soon."

Panic sets in his eyes, "I don't want to leave either of you."

I touch his arm, reassuring him, "There's nothing more you can do here, and I'll be coming to join you shortly."

I can tell my words have no effect on him, and I know the only way they will is if he feels like leaving this room helps in some way.

"I could really use something to eat. Maybe you could get something together and take it to the room so it's there for me when I'm done here."

A small smile creeps across his face, letting me know he knows full well what I'm trying to do. He leans over and kisses me lovingly on the forehead.

"As you wish. I'll see you soon," he whispers before heading for the door.

He turns around, catching my eyes before glancing at Amberly on the bed one last time before exiting the room. I release a breath, hoping it will take at least some of the stress of the last few days with it. I turn toward Julian and Amberly, and all the stress and worry remain.

What are we going to do if she doesn't wake up?

Amberly has come to mean so much to all of us in the pack in such a short time. If I'm being honest, it has nothing to do with how powerful she is, and that we need her to make it through this fight alive, or even that she will one day be our pack's alpha. It has to do with who she is. She's the kindest, most thoughtful and loving person I've ever known. I shouldn't be surprised since her father is the same way.

Aaron.

I turn to the door, hoping he will walk through it. I stare at it for I don't know how long before I snap out of it. I move next to Julian and take a seat.

"How are you doing?" I whisper.

I know it can't be easy to see his mate like this. Our wolf side searches hard for our mates our whole lives, some of them never finding each other. Then there are fated mates, like Julian and Amberly, who are foreordained, and their bond is stronger than anything. It's a lifelong attachment; some might even say their souls are bound to one another. I can't imagine watching Logan like this, wondering if he would live through the night. Not so long ago, Amberly watched Julian die, and it nearly killed her. I don't know what he will do if she dies because there will be no one to bring her back like she did him.

I wish I could do more for them both, for Julian's sake, the packs and mine. Losing Amberly would shatter us all in a way I feel we wouldn't recover from. She has become the heart of the pack.

Julian turns his gaze on me, his hand never leaving Amberly's. His eyes are red and glassy, and I know he's barely holding it together. I place a reassuring hand on his shoulder as my heart shatters for him.

"Oh, Julian."

He turns his attention back to his mate. "I can't lose her, Angela. I won't survive it. I don't know how she did it when she thought I was dead."

"If I'm being honest, she was a mess." I smile lightly.

Wiping the back of his hand across his face, he replies, "I don't doubt that, but she would have gotten past it."

"I don't know about that."

He turns in my direction once more.

"Why do you say that?"

I sigh, not believing how naive he is.

"Julian, she was so broken. All she could do was cry; she never left her room, she didn't eat."

A small, sad smile creeps across his face. "Yeah, but that's normal."

"Nothing about it was normal. She was beyond broken; she was shattered. I think if you didn't wake up, she wouldn't have made it past a few more days."

I didn't think it was possible, but his eyes turned sadder with my words.

"I can see how strong your connection is, no matter how much you both tried to deny it at one time or another. You need each other. You're only half of who you should be without the other."

His free hand finds mine, "Is she going to wake up Angela? I need you to be honest with me." I can see the torment all over his face.

"I wish I knew. It's not only her body and mind taking a beating, but her heart, too. Every part of her is hurting and broken." I remove my hand from his and place it on his shoulder. "If anyone can get through to her and make her want to get through this, it's you. You're her other half, her soul mate. Call to her. She will hear you." I move into a standing position, making my way to the door.

"I'll be back in a few minutes to check on you both. Make sure to keep drinking. I'll see if someone with the same blood type can switch with you. You can't lose much more blood."

Julian remains silent as he pushes the hair off Amberly's face. With one last look at the two, I exit the room.

Chapter 13

Logan

My eyes are heavy, and I have to pry them open when I hear Angela enter the room. My gaze falls on her as she moves toward me, a smile growing across my face.

"I'm sorry, I tried to be quiet," she whispers as she makes her way to the bed.

I move into a sitting position. "No need. I want to spend some time with you. We need it after the last few days."

"I couldn't agree more," she says, sinking to sit on the corner of the bed.

She begins to untie her shoe as I move to stand in front of her.

"Here, let me."

She leans back with a smile. I make quick work of removing her shoes and socks. I look into her eyes, taking in her appearance for the first time since the battle ended. She's covered head to toe in dirt, blood and cuts, just like the rest of us. Her hair is a knotty mess, and bruises are forming all over her body.

"I already got my shower; it's time for yours."

She moves closer toward me, "Trying to get me undressed already, I see."

"Always." I whisper.

"But you're right. I do need to wash away the last twenty-four hours," she sighs, standing from the bed slowly.

She begins to remove her shirt with a wince, sending me to her side.

"Let me do it."

I grab the shirt, pulling it up and over her head in one swift, gentle motion. I try to keep my eyes focused on hers, but I'm having a difficult time doing so.

"Thank you," she whispers.

"You're welcome."

Without warning, she closes the last of the distance between us, throwing her arms around my neck. She pulls me down until our lips are touching, and I can't stop the moan from escaping my lips. She tastes like raspberries, blood, and sweat, and I love every bit of it. As our tongues weave together, the events of the last day leave my mind altogether, and there's only us here and now.

I grip her hips in my hands, squeezing lightly at her burning skin, causing a deep growl to emerge from inside her chest. I move my hands to cup her ass and, in one swift movement, pick her up until I feel her legs wrap around my midsection. Her heat rests against me, nearly sending me over the edge. I walk us slowly toward the shower and remove her legs from around my waist. Once her feet touch the ground, I separate our lips and arms to find her pouting up at me.

I chuckle, "You need to shower."

The skin above her nose wrinkles, "Do I really smell that bad?"

I laugh so hard I almost lose my breath, "No, beautiful, but you need one nonetheless, and if we keep this up, you won't be getting a shower for a while."

She shrugs, "I'm okay with that."

I smile widely down at her, "Well, I'm not. Shower. I'll be waiting for you when you've finished. We can continue this after you eat."

I turn away and head for the door.

"Fine, be that way," she says sarcastically behind me.

I close the door and lean back against it, closing my eyes and releasing a long breath.

That was harder than it should have been.

I laugh to myself. This woman is going to be the death of me.

* * *

"So, where were we?" Angela asks in a seductive tone.

I look up to the bathroom door to see her wearing nothing but a towel. Her beautiful raven hair is dripping wet, hugging her body as her yellow-brown eyes bear down on me, full of lust. My arousal instantly returns as I look at this beautiful woman and wonder how I got so lucky.

She walks slowly to the bed and looks down at me.

"You should eat; it's getting cold," I utter, choking on the words.

I know she hasn't eaten anything in hours, and that's more important right now.

She laughs as she moves to straddle my lap, instantly making me hard. I'm in over my head here. She leans down until her lips find mine, sending a wave of desire crashing through my veins. My hands find her hips once more and squeeze, not so gently this time, causing Angela to moan against my lips. I feel her hands leave my body, and a second later, her towel is hanging over my arms, causing me to sigh.

This woman is now officially naked on top of me. How the hell am I supposed to think clearly? I never put my shirt back on after my shower, so when she lowers herself down to me, her nipples press against my skin, causing my body to react instead of my brain. I flip her onto her back in one swift movement, causing her to gasp. I look down into her eyes before speaking in a lustful tone.

"You're killing me, woman."

She smiles devilishly at me before whispering, "I want you, Logan. Is that such a bad thing?"

A rumble forms deep in my chest.

She runs her hand down my chest, leaving goosebumps in its wake. "I know you want me. Is it too much to ask for us to get lost in each other just for a little while?"

She doesn't wait for my response before crashing my lips to hers once more. I quickly become lost in her smell and touch, letting the world fall in around us until we are the only thing left.

Chapter 14

Julian

I'm half asleep when I hear her calling my name. I open my eyes to find a confused Amberly staring back. I move to rest my hand against her scorching skin.

"You're awake," I whisper.

She glances around the empty room. "What happened?"

"Your brother and I had to carry you the rest of the way home."

Her eyes widened slightly, "I passed out."

I nod.

"For how long?"

"A few hours."

She nods in understanding before trying to move into a sitting position. She fails miserably and winces in pain, followed by a deep cough.

"Where is everyone?" She asks, still struggling to stay upright.

"Your brother and Amara went to look for Aaron. Troy, I'm not too sure where he disappeared to, but I'm pretty sure Angela and Logan shut it down for the night. But I should go get her now that you're awake."

I move to disconnect us, but she stops me.

"Don't."

"She would want to know you're awake."

"And she will. I just need a few minutes of quiet before all hell breaks loose again."

I nod my head in understanding.

She places her head back on her pillow. "Did Angela figure out what's wrong with me?"

"She agrees that you were poisoned."

Closing her eyes, she releases a long sigh. "Does she know what I was poisoned with?"

My throat goes dry before answering, "She thinks it's wolfsbane."

I squeeze her hand lightly, relieved she's finally awake and talking to me. I never thought I'd hear her voice again.

"Is there a cure?"

"We think your father should know of one, which is why we sent them after him. But for now, Angela wanted to try to flush out what she could."

"And, cue the blood transfusion," she laughs lightly. "At this point, we probably share the same blood."

I smile down at her as I ruffle the hair on the top of her head. Her eyes open, and my heart contracts as they connect with mine. To think I could have lost her; I still could lose her. My heart hurts just thinking about it. This woman lying here has saved my life in every way someone can save another person. She's my reason for being. Without her, I'm lost, running through life with a compass that doesn't work. She points me in the right direction.

I know we need to talk about the elephant in the room, but I'm so afraid she will stop talking to me altogether, and right now, I need her. I need to hear her voice, feel her touch. I need to know she's still alive and with me. I can't imagine my life without her in it, and once all this mess is behind us, I plan to make her mine in every sense of the word. I wanted to ask Aaron for his blessing, but with recent events, I feel it would be unkind. I've wanted to ask Amberly to marry me for some time now, but first, there was the fight, then I died, she was taken, and then another battle, and then Aaron stated how he wanted to marry Jocelyn, and I didn't want to step on their moment. If there's one thing I've learned, it's that life is too short, and you should make sure the ones you love know how you feel about them and do everything you can to keep them close.

Marriage has always been important in the pack, and I already feel like we've been doing things backward, so now I want to do right by her. I only hope she will accept and doesn't feel it's moving too fast or that she doesn't stay angry with me about last night's decision. There's one thing I will never apologize for, and that's protecting her. Healing her mother would have only put her one step closer to death. I pray that one day she can understand that.

"Julian."

"Yes?"

She pauses for a long moment before speaking again, "I'm sorry."

"For what?"

She squeezes my hand lightly. "I don't want to be angry anymore."

My heart jumps gratefully in my chest. "You don't have to apologize. You had every reason to be angry with us."

"And you had every reason not to want me to do what I was thinking. I won't lie and say I'm okay with it, but I understand."

I bring her hand to my lips. "I hate seeing you hurt, and I wish I could change what happened, but I will never stop doing what I need to do to keep you safe. I hope you can understand that. We won't always agree, but no one ever does."

A tear escapes her eye, and as I move to wipe it away with my thumb, she erupts into tears.

"My heart hurts so much," she cries out.

I pull her to my chest gently. "Baby, I'm so sorry. I wish I knew how to take the pain away."

Her hands grip the fabric of my shirt as she buries her face in my chest.

"I don't know what to do without her. I don't know which way to go now. I feel like I just got to know my mother, and now she's gone."

I place my chin on top of her head as I hold her tightly. "I know it's not easy, and the journey ahead is hard, but I also know she will be there with you every step of the way and that she wouldn't change a thing. She died protecting her children like any mother would."

"My family was finally whole, and now…" She breaks into sobs again.

I hold her to my chest, wishing nothing more than to make her pain go away. If I could take it from her, I would. I remember all too well what it's like to lose your family. I wouldn't wish it on anyone, especially not someone I love. I remember how lost and angry I was for so many years after Aaron found me. I didn't make it easy on him or the pack, but no one gave up on me. I would never abandon her, even if Amberly pushed me away and didn't talk to me for years. It would kill me to be without her, but I would be there when she needed it. I'm so thankful that I don't have to go without her anymore, but seeing her like this, knowing how much she's hurting, it's crippling. What are you meant to do when you can't help or protect someone you love from heartbreak?

For now, I need to do what I can to keep her strong physically until I can help her be strong mentally. I ate before she woke up, so I'll unhook from the transfusion and grab her something to eat once she calms down. Now more than ever, it's important to keep her body sustained with what it needs.

Chapter 15

Cole

We walked for what felt like years before we finally returned to the place we call home. We are the only ones left now. Well, other than the people Anna claims are asleep inside the walls. The rest of our family joined Amberly and her pack of delinquents. As soon as our father turned to dust, they betrayed his life's work.

He wasn't a smart man, and I would have done things differently than he did, but he was our father. He saved and raised us, so the least we can do is avenge him. Right?

I'm so lost in my head that I almost walk into the back of Celine, not realizing everyone has stopped walking. I peer around her to see Henry and Anna standing in front of a brick wall.

"Henry, I'm going to need your help to bring it down," Anna says.

Celine moves forward, "Let me."

Before anyone can protest, the room begins to shake. I fear my sister sometimes doesn't recognize her own strength, and it may one day lead to our end. But I trust today isn't that day, and she won't bring the building down on our heads.

In mere moments, I see the cracks forming in the brick and seconds later, the wall begins to cave in on itself, creating a cloud of dust that causes everyone but my sister to cough up a lung.

"Finished," Celine says in a happy tone.

I wave my hand around in front of my face, hoping to clear the air enough to breathe and see if what Anna claims about the walls is true. Once the smoke clears, I note what looks like five bodies. I strain my eyes, trying to make out something more. It takes me a few moments longer than I would like before I can tell that the bodies consist of three women and two men inside the brick walls. I take a few steps closer until I'm standing directly in front of Anna and Henry, the brick wall now under our feet.

"They seem dead to me," I say to no one in particular.

I tilt my head to the side, looking at one of the women. I squint my eyes and move as close as the wall will allow me to. The woman's hair is the color of fire, bright and inviting.

As if on cue, one of the men begins to move, causing me to stumble a few steps back as Anna laughs.

"It has begun." Anna sings happily.

Chapter 16

Aaron

I smell them before they emerge from the bushes.

I growl deep in my chest, letting them know to keep their distance. Two humans against one wolf. I could take them, but I'm tired and not in the mood for a fight. Lucky for them, I've already had my fill for the day.

The male of the two takes a step closer, but he's smart and cautious with his movements. The female stinks of fear. I release another growl, causing her to take a few steps backward.

The male turns to her slowly, keeping his eyes focused on me. "No, don't move."

He turns his attention to me completely once he sees his companion standing still.

"Aaron."

I look around for another human, but no one shows. I sniff the air, searching for another scent, but come up empty.

Hold on.

What's that?

Something smells familiar, another wolf, one of my blood. I sniff the air once more until I realize the smell is coming from the human standing in front of me.

"Dad." The male pleads, still focused on me.

He says the word like it's foreign to him.

Is he talking to me?

He moves slowly closer, lowering himself to my level.

"Amberly's been poisoned, and she needs you."

Why does that name sound familiar to me?

"She will die if you don't come with us now."

His words cause an ache in my heart that I don't understand.

"You need to change back. Your pack and children need you."

The fog of confusion begins to disappear slowly from my mind. I shake my head lightly before looking back and forth between the two humans standing helplessly in front of me. They look as lost as I feel confused.

The girl takes a cautious step closer, her voice soft as she speaks to me. "Aaron, time is running out. Amberly has been poisoned with wolfsbane, and none of us know how to heal her. You are her only hope. You need to shift back into your human form."

I take a few steps backward as the memories come rushing back into my mind. Jocelyn and our children. The pack. Losing Jocelyn and Amberly, only to find them once more almost eighteen years later. Learning I have a son. A battle. Watching Jocelyn die in front of me. My grief, so intense and crippling, and finally, my shift.

I have to go back.

A long howl escapes me before I fight like hell to shift back to my human form. My daughter needs me, and I'll be damned if I let her die too.

Chapter 17

Aidan

One second, I'm staring at a large gray wolf, and the next, I'm looking at my father's naked form. I turn toward Amara, reaching out my hand. She pulls the clothes from the bookbag on her shoulder and hands them to me. I turn my attention back to my father as I slowly take a few steps forward.

"Aaron?"

My weary hazel green eyes lock onto his onyx ones, and the struggle is apparent in his gaze. He's having a difficult time staying in his human form. He doesn't say a word before returning his eyes to the ground. I move closer until I'm an arm's length away. Aaron looks up at me as his expression turns to one of fear, and he scurries back away from me once more.

His tone was heavy with fear, "Stay back. It's not safe. I'm not safe."

I move forward again, slower than before. Amara's voice calls out from behind me.

"Aidan."

I ignore her, closing the distance between my father and me, once more offering him the clothes in my outstretched hands.

"Here. Take the clothes."

He glances up at me, and I can see the internal struggle he's experiencing all over his face. His entire body radiates with nervous energy.

"Dad, take the clothes, and I'll go back and join Amara until you're ready to talk."

It takes him a second, but he nods in agreement before snatching the clothes from my hands and turning away from me. I do as promised and retreat back to where Amara is waiting.

"Are you crazy?" She snaps at me once I'm at her side.

"We don't have time to do things the slow way, and it's better I take the chance than you."

A small smile creeps across her face before she hits me in the chest.

"Just don't do it again."

I laugh, nodding in agreement.

We wait silently for, I don't know how long, and then Aaron emerges from the bushes, rubbing his hands over his face.

I take a step in his direction. "Are you ready to go?"

He nods.

I turn to Amara, who looks unsure. "Let's go."

Amara stops me as I start to walk off in the direction of the cave.

"Don't you think we should give him a little more time? I mean, he doesn't look altogether there."

I glance back at him. "He will be fine. The walk will do him good and clear his mind. By the time we make it home, he will be his normal self again."

She folds her arms over her chest. "Remember that conversation we had earlier?"

I smile, "Vaguely."

Her arms drop to her sides once more. "Aidan, I'm serious."

"I'm sorry. Yes, I remember, and I know what you're going to say, but it will already take us at least a day to get back to the cave. We can't shift because we can't take the risk he won't change back. We can't afford to waste any more time."

Her eyes lock with mine, showing her understanding as she nods.

"Just don't push him too far. I know getting back to Amberly is important, but we can't lose your father in the process. You might be able to live with that outcome, but I don't know if she can."

Her words hit me hard. I've waited a long time to be reunited with my family, but she's right. Losing my mother has taken a toll, and I know losing Aaron would do the same. But losing Amberly would shatter me. Amara's right. I need to think differently than I am. Amberly needs our father, and on some level, so do I.

I turn back toward him. "You okay to walk?"

He answers with a whisper. "Yes."

"If you need us to slow down or if you need to take a break, just say the word."

He nods before walking past us and heading deeper into the forest, leaving Amara to look back at me. I place my hand in front of us.

"After you."

She laughs before following Aaron, "You seem different."

"What do you mean?"

Facing forward, watching my father, she answers, "It's just, the version of you I knew when we were with Vladimir was different from the version of you that came back with Amberly. But now... this version of you," she gestures at me with her hands, "I kind of like him. I could actually see us being friends."

"Friends, huh?"

"Is that so hard to believe?"

I look forward, my heart tightening in my chest as I swallow my saliva, which feels like acid going down my throat. "Well, I did torture you and do things I'm not proud of. I guess it's just hard for me to think of someone forgiving me for my actions, let alone willing to be my friend after the fact."

She crosses her arms over her chest and replies, "Honestly, if you were still that guy, I wouldn't. But who you are now isn't that same person. I've been watching you closely since you came back with Amberly, but more so since the battle. And you're different. I can see the struggle inside of you and how hard you are trying to be better and keep that darkness at bay. I can see what you want and need clearer than maybe even you can, and I see you slowly making the changes in yourself in hopes of obtaining them."

"And what is it you think I want or need?"

Her eyes lock with mine as she smiles, "A family, friends, maybe even someone to love. You want what everyone wants but need and crave it more since it's something you've never really had until lately. Being with Amberly and your parents for this short time made you realize it wasn't just something you wanted but something your soul deeply craves, and it makes you the best version of yourself in the process."

"Well, I dare say, Amara, it seems you have cracked the mystery that is me." I laugh.

She hits my shoulder with her own and grins, "Don't worry, your secret is safe with me."

I smile back before we look to my father and fall in step behind him with one thought in mind. To make it back to my sister and pray our father knows how to save her life.

Chapter 18

Cole

I place the last unconscious body on the ground next to the others before standing. My eyes move down the line until they rest on her. I thought Vladimir had killed her, and I find myself grateful that he didn't.

"Bro, stop staring."

I turn around to look my sister in the eyes.

"Sorry, I..."

She cuts me off. "I know what you were doing."

I sigh before looking away from her. She never liked Sage. I can't say I blame her, but there's always been something about Sage that I can't seem to resist.

"She's no good for you. I don't know how many times I need to tell you."

"Apparently, once more." I smile at her.

"It's not funny, Cole. You're nothing like her."

"You mean I'm not a killer."

"And I hope you never have to be."

"You really think we'll make it out of this without killing?"

Celine turns away from me and the bodies that are spread across the floor. Without a second thought, I approach her.

"I'm sorry. I didn't mean..."

"I don't want you to be like me or her. You're better than we are," she cuts in, her voice a mix of anger and sadness.

"Don't say that."

"You are Cole, and if anyone is going to make it out of this alive, I'm going to make sure it's you," her stare cuts into me. I know what she's thinking, and I wish I could do something to remove the thoughts from her mind.

"It wasn't your fault, you know."

She looks at me, surprised. "What wasn't?"

"He didn't give you a choice. It was you or her. You know that, right?"

I think back to a little over a year ago. It was the day Vladimir learned Amberly was still alive, and Aidan had been sneaking away to see her. He was so enraged that he went on a beating spree. He beat all of us in the camp until he had a better idea. He wanted to watch us fight each other. To the death. He said, 'What better way than for the weak to get weeded out of the herd.' His exact words still stick with me.

"Only the strong belong here, and only the strongest will win this war."

He laughed as he watched two at a time fight to the death. My sister had to go up against a friend she had known since they were children. It wasn't an easy choice, but she knew it was kill or be killed, and so did Serena. Serena came out guns blazing and didn't give my sister a choice; she had to fight back. The only reason I didn't have to fight anyone to the death was that, by the time my turn came, Vladimir had grown bored of his new game.

"It doesn't matter. What's done is done," Celine mumbles.

"You can't let that hold you back."

She turns on me fast. "I don't."

"And what if we have to kill in this fight? What are you going to do?"

"You won't have to kill anyone."

I laugh lightly. "You can't promise that."

"Yes, I can because I'm getting us out of here."

Her words take a moment for me to register. She can't mean what I think she does.

"You're talking about leaving?"

She nods.

"Anna and Henry will never allow it."

She laughs. "They couldn't stop me."

I look back at the bodies on the floor. "What about them?"

"That's the problem. I don't know if I can take on all five of them, plus Anna and Henry. I'm strong, but I'm not that strong."

"Then what's the plan?"

"We are leaving here tonight before they wake."

I look to the exit. "And where will we go?"

"You're going to think I'm crazy."

My eyes open wide as they return to her. "You can't possibly think we can go there."

"Why not?"

"Celine, we are evil. Did you not hear what Anna said? Seven evil and seven good, and as far as I know, the seven good are already together. Which makes us the enemy. They will kill us on sight."

"I don't think they will."

My sister has damn near lost her mind. She can't be serious. Can she?

"And why is that?"

She looks at me with a grin plastered across her face. "Because without our help, their golden child will be dead in a matter of days."

"Amberly?"

She nods.

"What do you mean she will be dead?"

"Jax cut her up with his poisoned blade before she killed him, and I doubt they know how to cure wolfsbane."

"You're banking our lives on that."

Her eyes fall on me, but she doesn't have a chance to reply before Anna and Henry enter the room.

Anna stands over the bodies of the last of our family. "It's almost time."

Henry nods. "Yes. It won't be long now."

Celine moves to stand next to them. "How long until they wake?"

Anna replies. "Only a matter of hours now. You two should get your rest. It's grown late, and we need everyone at their sharpest."

Celine moves closer to Anna. "How do you expect to win a war with only them and us? They have over a hundred fighting on their side, at least."

Her eyes turn to my sister as her smile widens. "Oh, dear child, it is not only us."

My eyes widen. This can't be good.

"We have called the rest. They will be here in a few days, and then we will take the final battle to their doorstep."

The words leave my mouth before I can stop them. "Who's coming?"

Henry answers this time. "Witches, warlocks, and demons by the hundreds."

My heart sinks to my stomach as my eyes rest on my sister, who seems just as worried as I am.

So much for that plan.

Chapter 19

Angela

I leave Logan asleep in my bed as I make my way to check on Julian and Amberly. Last night was amazing and just what I needed, but I've been gone much longer than I said I would or planned to be.

Logan is one of the sweetest men I've ever known, and I never imagined I'd be lucky enough to find someone like him. It's been hard trying to make time for our relationship and connection to grow when we seem to be fighting for our lives every other day, so last night was a nice change of pace, and I think we both needed it.

I push the door open as quietly as possible when I hear voices from inside. I enter the room to find Amberly awake and alert, speaking with Julian.

"Amberly, you're awake."

Julian turns around to look at me. Happiness fills every line of his face.

"She woke up a few hours ago. She seems to be doing well, considering."

I move closer to them, checking the fluids and blood lines.

Amberly places her hand on my arm. "Thank you for saving my life. Yet again," she laughs.

I smile down at her. "You never need to thank me. I'm just glad to see you awake, and you can repay me by not getting yourself into this kind of situation ever again. Deal?"

"Deal." Forcing a smile, Amberly moves almost into a seated position.

"How is Logan?"

"He's doing fine. I told him to try to get some rest. There is nothing more he can be doing right now, and he could barely keep his eyes open."

Amberly relaxes her shoulders against the pillow with a sigh. "Did you get any sleep?"

"I got enough."

Her eyes catch mine, "You're no good to anyone if you aren't getting your rest."

I place a reassuring hand on her shoulder. "You need to focus on yourself right now. Stop worrying about everyone else for once. We will be fine."

"You know Amberly," Julian chuckles lightly. "It isn't in her nature. She's always worrying about everyone else first."

I walk to the table nearby, where a pitcher of water and a few cups sit. Pouring a glass, I carry it over to Amberly. Offering the refreshment with a smile, I say, "I know it's hard right now, but what everyone needs is for you to get well. We don't stand a chance in this war without you. Focus your strength on healing. Everyone else will follow."

Chapter 20

Amberly

I feel like I've been run through with a flaming sword and run over by a mack truck. I can't recall the last time I felt this exhausted. Being poisoned sure takes a lot out of you.

Before I woke up, I was somewhere dark, and I remember feeling alone. I stood in the darkness as my memories flooded over me. The further the memories went into my life, the more intense they became until I fell to my knees and broke. Then I remembered the loss of my mother and the still impending battle, and I didn't know if I wanted to wake up.

Then I thought about my brother and everything he had been through. I knew he needed me; I could feel it through our twin connection, and I couldn't leave him alone to find his way in this new life without me. My brother deserves better than that. Then, my father crossed my mind, and I was quickly reminded of how I wasn't the only one who lost my mother. I tried putting myself in his shoes, and that's when Julian moved to the center of my mind. I remembered what it had felt like to lose him.

I couldn't breathe. Every inch of my body hurt, and I no longer wanted to live in a world where he didn't exist. It took everything in me not to give in to the grief. And right now, my father is feeling the same thing. I couldn't leave him alone to face that. I thought about all my friends, both old and new, and how I would be leaving them to fight this war without me. A war that started because of my brother and I, and should therefore end with us.

Ultimately, it was the love I felt for my family, friends, and mate that pulled me from the emptiness of my grief. I would be lying if I said I was okay with everyone stopping me from saving my mother.

Did I agree with it?

No.

Did I understand why they did it?

Yes.

If it were one of them, I wouldn't want them to take the chance either if it meant it brought them closer to death. It's a hard choice, but I understand it on both sides. I'm not ready to give up on the chance that I could see my mother again, but right now, I need to focus on keeping everyone else I love alive. And to do that, I need to figure out how to get this poison out of my system and get back on my feet.

"Angela?"

My voice sounds horrible, almost like I have a dying bird in my throat.

Angela turns away from Julian to smile at me. "Yes?"

"What can we do to get rid of this poison?"

Julian sits back down in the chair next to the bed I'm occupying. "We are waiting for Aidan and Amara to return with your father. He should know something more about how to reverse the wolfsbane. If anyone does, it would be him."

"We can't wait for them," I whisper.

I feel the poison moving through my blood, growing closer to my heart. I'm getting weaker, and soon, we won't be able to do anything to remove it.

Angela's eyes widen. "Are you…"

I cut her off, not wanting to make them worry more than they already are.

"What about Johnathan and Aayda? Maybe they know something about this? Or maybe there's something in the journals?"

Julian jumps up from his seat, smacking himself in the head. "Why didn't I think of that?"

I giggle. "That's why you're the pretty one."

He smiles down at me. "And you're the brains."

I smile. "Damn straight."

He leans down, kissing me on the forehead before placing ours together and whispering, "God, I missed you."

"I love you," I whisper back.

Angela turns away from us. "Okay, love birds. I'll leave you two to it and go see if they know anything."

Julian stands up once more, turning to face Angela. "Actually, let me go. I want you here with her in case something happens or Aaron gets back before I do."

"You sure?" Angela asks nervously.

Julian looks back down at me. "Yes. I'll be back as soon as I can. You hang in there."

I nod with a smile. "I'll do my best."

He leans down and kisses me softly, sending a warmth I've missed running through my body.

"You better do better than your best. I don't plan on losing you until we have many years together and we are both old and grey. I love you. I'll be back before you realize I'm gone."

He turns and walks out the door without another word. Once the door clicks closed, Angela turns her attention toward me.

"Okay, spill."

I smile, playing dumb as I shrug. "I don't know what you mean."

"Amberly, what's going on?"

I sigh, pausing only for a moment. "I can feel it."

"The poison?"

I nod. "It's moving through my blood faster now."

She looks at me, confused. "I don't understand; the blood transfusion should have slowed it down and taken some of it out, at least."

"I can feel it getting closer to my heart. We are running out of time."

She places her hand on mine in a reassuring manner. "We will figure this out. We aren't going to lose you."

"You can't promise that."

She nods. "Yes. I can. I refuse to give up on you. You're stronger than anyone here, and you will beat this like you beat everything."

"Even a cat only has nine lives," I joke as I move to lie down, placing my head back on my pillow. "I was hoping to return home when all this was done."

Angela squeezes my hand gently. "You will."

I smile.

"What about your people back home? They have magic. Maybe someone there will know what to do or how to heal you. Plus, it couldn't hurt to have them around for the coming battle."

My eyes widen. "I don't want my people fighting in this battle. My mother's magic still protects them, and I would like to keep it that way. If none of us can escape this, I want them to, at the very least. It's bad enough that Logan and Troy got sucked into my mess."

"Do you think that's how the people in your village would feel? Do you think Logan and Troy regret coming here to find you?"

"Even if they can't admit it or say it, I know they had other plans for their lives than the turn I took them down, and I would give anything to protect them and not have them be part of this. It's bad enough that I lost my mother, and there is a good chance we will lose many others in this final battle. If there is one thing I have control over, it's protecting my village, and as its leader, I refuse to pull them into this."

She nods. "I understand."

"I knew you would," I say with a smile.

"But Amberly, you need to believe we will make it through this together. I don't plan on any of us dying. We are strongest together and will come out the other side together."

"I hope so. I know we will give it our all. But before Julian returns, I need to ask something of you."

I see the fear forming in her eyes, and I know she has an idea of what I'm about to ask her.

"I need you to find something, anything, in the journals that can help us win. Something to protect everyone, even if it costs me everything. As long as I know you all make it out of this battle alive, that will be enough for me."

She places her hand lightly on my arm.

"Amberly, we will find a way. But I won't let anything happen to you if we can help it. I want us all coming out of this together, and that's what we need to plan for. Nothing short of that will work."

I nod, even though I'm not sure if that will happen. I know the chances of everyone making it out alive are next to impossible, but I will do my best to make sure as many of us as possible survive in the end. No matter what I have to do to make that happen.

Chapter 21

Logan

"We're back."

I hear his annoying voice echo through the hall.

I left the warmth of Angela's room to check on Amberly, but I guess fate had better ideas for my time.

I turn around to see Amara, Aidan, and Aaron entering the cave.

"How long were we gone?" Amara asks as they approach.

"About a day and a half," I mumble back.

Aidan turns to face her, "Made better time than I thought."

Aaron moves in front of them. "How is she?" He looks broken as the words leave his lips.

I throw my thumb over my shoulder. "I was just about to go check on her."

Aidan gestures with his hand. "Lead the way, wizard boy."

I bare my teeth at him but say nothing as I turn away and head down the hall, but not before taking note of Amara's facial expression toward Aidan as he smiles back with a shrug.

Amara moves next to me as we continue down the hall.

"Do you know where Troy is?"

"Honestly, no. I haven't seen him since we got the supplies for Angela."

Her expression turns to one of worry.

"What's wrong?"

"I'm just worried about him. Losing Jocelyn and now Amberly. I think it might be too much for him."

I smile reassuringly at her. "Troy is stronger than he seems. Believe me, I've known the kid our whole lives. I know he's feeling lost and sad, like we all are. I'm sure he just needed some distance."

"Maybe you're right, but I'm going to see if I can find him and let him know we are back. Give my love to Amberly, will you?"

I nod as she turns down the other hallway. Now that the space next to me is empty, Aidan decides to fill it.

"Can I help you?" I sigh. I don't need his lip right now.

"Nope."

I roll my eyes.

"So, let me get this right. You're supposed to be Amberly's best friend and ex-lover, and you haven't checked in on her once since we left?"

If I was a wolf, I'm sure I would be growling at him right now.

"She's been well taken care of. I know her better than you do, and she doesn't like crowds or people worrying about her."

"What you mean to say is you were too busy getting laid to make sure she was okay."

I come to a dead stop and turn in his direction, livid. I feel heat on my face, and I know I'm about to lose it.

Aaron moves to stand in between us. "Can you two not do this right now? I would like to make sure my daughter is still breathing, if you don't mind."

Aidan and I look at each other before our faces and stances soften, and we take a step back from one another.

"Sorry," we both say at the same time.

He nods and turns to me. "So, what room is she in?"

"On the right."

I begin moving back down the hallway, trying to brush off how much Amberly's so-called twin gets under my skin. I honestly don't know why he's still around. Amberly has always been a good judge of character, and I understand he's her brother, but the dude is nothing but trouble.

Chapter 22

Aidan

When we enter the room, I stop dead at the sight before my eyes. Amberly is awake and sitting up, talking with Angela. I was preparing myself for the worst, so seeing her awake and alert has my mind buzzing.

"You're back," Amberly says in a weak voice.

Logan and I move to the side to let Aaron pass. He moves to the bed and drops to his knees, placing his head in Amberly's lap as he begins to sob violently.

"I'm so sorry. I should have been here."

Amberly smiles and rubs our father's head, trying to reassure him. I take a step forward but stop myself.

"Where's lover boy?" I ask no one in particular.

Angela turns in my direction. "He went to speak with Johnathan about a cure."

I turn to Amberly, "I'm going to go hunt him down. Two heads are always better than one," I wink.

She laughs weakly. "Don't take too long."

"Be back in a jiff," I say with a smile.

Logan chuckles. "A jiff, really?"

I growl in his direction before heading for the door. I hear the last of the conversation before I make my exit.

"So, do you know how to remove the poison?" Logan asks Aaron.

His voice is broken when he answers.

"No, I'm afraid I don't. Wolfsbane is hard to come by. It was destroyed a long time ago, so the packs were never taught what to do if poisoned by it because we never thought we needed to know."

I close the door behind me, knowing that Johnathan looking for a cure is our last hope to save my sister. I run toward their room as my heart beats wildly in my chest.

I refuse to watch my sister die.

I will not watch her die.

Chapter 23

Julian

"I wish I had thought about the journals possibly having an answer for us about the wolfsbane; it honestly escaped my mind," Johnathan says as he stressfully rubs his face.

"We didn't think of it. Amberly woke up and mentioned it." I rub the back of my neck, embarrassed. "I should have thought of it since the journals have been under the same roof as me for almost my whole life, but I think we just forget about them since no one has really read them in our lifetime."

His eyes find mine as he smiles sadly. "We all had other things on our minds. Understandably, the journals were not something we immediately thought of as an answer."

Not wanting to focus on it more than I have to, I decide to change the subject.

"How is Aayda doing?"

"As good as can be expected."

I nod.

"If there's anything I can do…"

"Thank you, but you have something more important to deal with, and we all need to get ourselves ready for what's coming next," he cuts me off quickly, wanting to change the subject.

Johnathan turns away from me, opening a cabinet door. When he closes it again, he turns to me with a decent-sized box in his hands. Closing the distance in a few short strides, he offers it to me.

"Here is everything you will need. The journal marked *Healing* is the one where you'll find what you're looking for."

Surprised, I stare at him. "When did you bring them to your room?"

"When we learned Serenity was sick, we wanted to cross off every hope of there being a way to save her. Aayda remembered the journals, and Aaron didn't hesitate to bring them for us to look over."

I glance down at the box in my hands, "I take it you didn't find anything?"

"Not that could help in her situation. But that doesn't mean there isn't an answer for Amberly."

I nod my head in gratitude, "Thank you."

He waves me off with his hand. "No need. Just get her better. We need her for what's coming."

I turn toward the door when someone knocks loudly.

Johnathan's brow raises. "Now, who could that be?"

I whisper, "Good question."

He opens the door, revealing an out of breath Aidan.

Aidan looks past Johnathan toward me, "Did you get it?"

My heart plummets to my stomach. "Is she okay?"

"She's fine, but she's getting weaker."

I turn to Johnathan once more. "Thank you again."

Without another word, Aidan and I take off down the hall, leaving Johnathan to stare after us.

I'm running as fast as my legs will carry me. The thought of losing her takes over my senses, nearly crippling me. I bust open the door to have everyone's eyes fall on me. I notice Aaron's eyes are bloodshot and puffy.

I move past him to find Amberly's eyes closed. Dropping the box to the ground, I move to her side.

Angela speaks as I reach Amberly on the bed. "Tell me you found something."

"Johnathan gave us the journals. One of them has to have something to help her," Aidan says from behind me.

I place my hands on Amberly's shoulders, trying to wake her.

Aaron's distraught voice sounds far away, "It's no use. Without a cure soon, she won't make it."

My eyes fall on him. "How long do we have?"

"Hours."

Angela breaks my trance, lightly placing her hand on my shoulder. "Julian, did Johnathan give you any idea where to start?"

I pull back from Amberly as tears escape my eyes. I rub my face violently before turning to face her. I drop down to the box, remove the pile of books inside and place them on the ground, searching for the one Johnathan mentioned.

"He said to look in the book of Healing," I mumble, trying to keep my emotions under control.

Aidan, Angela, and I work through the pile of about twenty journals.

Aidan holds one up. "Got it."

He hands it to me without another word. I flip through it, quickly scanning each page until I come across the entry I was looking for.

Wolfsbane

**There is only one known cure for the deadly poison.
Wolfsbane is only deadly to shifters; everyone else is immune. If the poison infects you, you will first notice by your breathing turning labored. Shortly after, you may feel like your skin is on fire. Within one to three days, the infected will become unconscious. No one has survived longer than a week with this poison in their system. Once the infected becomes unconscious, it is a matter of hours before the effects take them.
You can slow down the symptoms by the transference of blood or an ice bath, which will thin your blood and slow the poison.**

Aidan's voice pulls me from reading. "Anything?"

Annoyed, I reply, "It's telling me everything we already know."

Angela's hand returns to my shoulder, knowing my frustration is building. "Skip to the end; sometimes, the most important things are at the end, if not the beginning."

The calmness in her voice helps me to push down my anger and nervousness. I do as she says, running my eyes over the lines.

The only way to cure someone of the poison is with the Subcinctus.

My heart pounds in my chest. "Here! It says there's only one way to cure it. We need to find something called the Subcinctus."

"The what?" I hear Troy's voice for the first time in days.

When I look up, everyone is staring at him. I don't know when he and Amara joined the group, but at least now we are all here.

Looking around the room at everyone, Troy asks, "Do we have any idea what that even is?"

Everyone seems almost as confused as I am, except for Aidan, who moves to stand next to me with a look of recognition on his face.

With a sigh, he says, "The word is Latin. It means shifter. But, when Vladimir spoke about it, he said it was also called the 'Alpha's amulet.'"

Aaron jumps up and begins pacing immediately after the words leave Aidan's lips, leaving Amberly's side for the first time since I entered the room.

"Do you know what that is?" Angela asks him.

"I've heard of it, but we were told it was a myth. Like a lot of things lately, I guess it wasn't," he whispers, still pacing.

I slam the book closed, standing in frustration.

"Well, that figures."

Angela moves closer to me, but I back away from her outstretched hand.

"Julian, calm down. We will figure something out," she says to him.

I drop the book back down on the ground with the others, throwing my hands in the air, defeated.

"Don't you get it? There is nothing else. It says it right there," I point angrily at the books on the ground, "In that damn book. It's in black and white for everyone to see. The only way to cure the poison is with this amulet, or whatever it is. Something that no one knows anything about, other than believing until this very minute that it was another myth."

My legs turn to jelly as I slump to the ground, defeated.

Troy turns to Aaron, "You don't know anything about it that might help? Something that someone might have said. Even myths have stories told about them."

"The only other thing I remember was that my father said that if it did exist, it would need to be kept hidden," Aaron responds, rubbing his chin as he thinks of the past.

"Why?" Asks Troy.

"Because it does a lot more than just cure you of poison."

"Like?"

He answers Troy slowly, his eyes slightly closed as he struggles to remember. "It can... heal someone of any life-threatening disease, illness, or element. It also gives the wearer temporary powers over other shifters."

"Meaning?" Troy continues with his one-word questions, ones that we're all asking in our heads.

"It means that if they are in their animal form, they can make a shifter do anything."

Angela's eyes widen in worry. "Anything?"

Aaron replies, "Yes. It was also said that there was another amulet. One that would give the person wearing it an unseen armor that nothing could penetrate. But again, these were myths."

"If I know anything, there's always some truth to the legends and myths. As I'm sure everyone in this room now thinks in the same way. Everything we have grown up believing was only a story isn't," Aidan says.

Putting my head in my hands, I mumble, "We can't just sit here and do nothing."

Troy is the first to reply. "And we won't."

Amberly shoots into a sitting position, followed by a coughing fit, sending us all running to her side.

"Slow breaths," Angela whispers while rubbing circles on her back.

Amberly's lips move as I kneel next to her, but nothing comes out. I pick up the cup of water on the table beside her and put it to her lips. She drinks it greedily before smiling and trying again to speak.

"They're coming."

Aaron stands tall. "Who?"

Her eyes fall on her father as a weak smile forms on her face.

"Don't be afraid. They mean no harm. They have what we need."

Without another word, Amberly's eyes close once more.

"Ly," Troy says, his eyes desperate as he calls her by his nickname for her.

I stand slowly, my eyes drifting from Amberly to the others surrounding me.

"Well, it appears we are expecting some visitors. I suggest we go and welcome them."

Chapter 24

Cole

"How much further?" I ask Celine.

"It's right over this hill. We were just here a few days ago. Your sense of direction is horrible," she laughs.

We were lucky enough to sneak out when everyone was asleep and, thankfully, haven't been followed. I can only hope those at our destination don't kill us on sight.

"You still have it?" Celine asks over her shoulder.

I pat the bag slung over my shoulder, and she smiles, facing forward once again.

Celine said we would need the Alpha's amulet to heal Amberly, but she wouldn't tell me where she got it. Or its partner. From our teachings as children, I think the other amulet was called 'Mighty's Protection.' It was said to offer the wearer a shield that nothing could penetrate. God only knows if these things even work.

Celine points off to our left. "There it is."

I pause, looking in the direction where she is pointing.

"Maybe we should think about this."

She grins over her shoulder at me, coming to a stop. "What's wrong, little brother? You aren't afraid, are you?"

"Only the stupid wouldn't be. There are hundreds of them, and only two of us. And we are their enemies."

"Not anymore," she says with hope in her eyes.

I sigh as she takes a step forward. I know nothing I say will make her turn back.

"But they don't know that, so what's to stop them from attacking us?" I'm still not moving, my hands wrenching at the bag on my shoulder.

Glancing over her shoulder, she tells me her plan. "We knock and then back away from the entrance. Keep our distance. When they emerge, we tell them we are here to help save Amberly."

"And what if they still don't believe us?"

She turns and points to the bag I'm carrying.

"Then we show them what we've brought for them."

As if on cue, four bodies emerge from the cave entrance, causing Celine and I to take a few steps back.

"Moment of truth," I whisper.

She rolls her eyes at me before looking forward, about to walk toward the cave.

I reach to stop her, "Celine."

"They can't see us from here. We need to move closer."

She pulls her arm out of my grasp and moves over and down the hill out of the safety of the bushes. I follow slowly behind her as she puts her hands in the air, showing we aren't a threat.

"I wish to speak to your pack leader. We mean no harm." Her voice is strong, and no fear shines through her words.

A young man I recognize answers first as he steps forward, "And who are you?"

"My name is Celine." She nods in my direction, "And that's my brother Cole. We have important information for your Alpha. We also have the only thing that can heal his daughter."

The blonde-haired man moves closer before the young man to his side stops him and says, "Easy, Logan."

The blonde man, Logan, turns to his friend, "Troy, she said someone was coming. This must be them."

"It could still be a trap."

"Are you willing to risk her life by not listening to her? When has she ever been wrong?"

Troy's eyes turn sad as he listens.

My sister lowers her arms, turning to me. "Give me the amulet."

I pull it out of my bag and hand it to her without question. As she closes the distance between her and the men, my mind goes over what the men said.

"She said we were coming?" I ask.

Logan nods.

"This will heal her, but we need to work fast." Celine steps up and places the amulet into Logan's outstretched hand.

He looks down at it in amazement. "This must be what the journals were talking about."

My eyes open wide as I move closer, "You have the shifter journals?"

Logan looks to Troy and the other two men at their side but stays silent. He says nothing as he turns, walking into the cave as Troy looks from me to my sister.

"Follow us. We will take you to Aaron."

Chapter 25

Julian

I sit next to Amberly's unconscious body, feeling helpless. She said someone was coming, but what if they get here too late? I can feel her life slipping away. With every tick of the clock, her soul sinks deeper into the darkness, and soon, I fear no one will be able to reach her.

Logan quickly enters the room and I feel his nervous energy as it hits me in the face. My hand tightens around Amberly's. I turn my head to see him and Troy standing at the door to the room.

Logan speaks first, "We have visitors."

My heart drops as Aaron moves into a standing position, just as two unfamiliar figures move into view. The girl has her onyx-colored hair pulled back into a ponytail, revealing her bright, lime green eyes. Her complexion is pale, almost as if she hasn't seen the sun in years. Looking at the male, he has the same complexion and hair color, but his hair is short and messy on top of his head. His eyes are a hazel green. From how they are standing, I know they are the ones Amberly said were coming.

I can smell the male's uneasiness, but the female wreaks of determination and darkness, which makes me stand on high alert.

Logan gestures to the newcomers, "This is Celine and Cole, and they've come to help. They brought the amulet we need to heal Amberly."

My eyes widen in disbelief. I drop her hand, standing and taking a step forward.

"Where are they from?" I ask skeptically.

Troy answers, "They left Vladimir's group."

"Was that before or after we killed him?" I snarl, looking at them angrily. They are the reason we're here in this situation.

The girl, Celine, steps closer. "We've come to help and to warn you."

I laugh. "Warn us? About what?"

"Vladimir was only the beginning."

Troy chuckles beside her, "I think we can handle what's left of his group."

Celine's cold eyes land on him, her face solemn as she continues. "I know you've heard about the seven."

Aaron's hands turn to fists as he moves closer. "What about them?"

She turns her gaze to him. "You know the evil and good seven are meant to fight. It's been foretold."

Aaron nods.

"You may not like what I'm about to say, but I need you to trust it is the truth."

"And why should we trust you? We know nothing about you," I growl.

"Because we risked our lives just coming here and choosing to help you, but we know it's the right thing to do," Celine canters.

Aaron moves closer to her. "What do you need to tell us?"

For the first time, Celine's eyes fall on Amberly, and it takes everything in me not to step into her line of sight.

With a deep breath, Celine looks from Amberly to all of us. Her next words come slowly. "Her grandparents aren't as dead as you were led to believe."

Tension fills the air around us the moment the words leave her lips. I know what's coming next will change our lives in a way I only hope to protect Amberly from.

"What do you mean?" Aaron chokes out.

Her eyes lock with his. "They left and joined Vladimir all those years ago. They've been working with him all this time."

Shock is evident on his face, and Troy whispers, "But why?"

Celine shrugs, "They believed in his cause. They never thought their daughter should have been with you, Aaron. When they followed her into the woods that night, they had already planned to kill you, but then they heard she was pregnant. That's when they made the choice to kill you both. They didn't believe in mixing bloodlines and considered Aidan and Amberly an abomination."

I move to stand next to Aaron, "So you're saying they believe we should all stick to our own kind and be ruled over by someone like Vladimir. Someone who can control us and keep us in our place, and that all humans should be wiped from existence."

"Yes," she replies.

Aaron's voice holds great sadness. "But their grandchildren are from mixed breeding; they are their blood."

For the first time, Celine's expression turns sad.

"They don't consider them their blood, and they disowned their daughter the moment they learned about..."

Her words drift off as she goes silent, causing Aaron to avert his eyes.

"Once they learned about me," Aaron whispers, turning away from the group.

Celine nods.

The room remains silent for a long moment before I take the amulet into my hands. As devastating as this news is, we have a purpose.

"We don't have time for this right now. Amberly is getting weaker with each passing moment. How do I use this?" I ask, cutting through the tension and sadness that fills the room.

Angela, who remained silent and in the shadows this whole time, moves to my side. "Here, let me."

I willingly hand the amulet to her, watching as she looks it over. The rest of the group continues to discuss Amberly's grandparents and the reality that they are coming for us with the rest of the seven and an army of demons and other creatures.

Angela moves closer to Amberly and turns the amulet until it clicks and sharp needles exit the backside. Each one is about an inch and a half long.

The amulet itself is round and blood red in color. It's rather plain looking, considering what it's supposed to do. I watch, fidgeting with my fingers as Angela places the amulet over Amberly's heart.

"Here goes nothing." She whispers.

Everyone in the room quiets and turns their attention to us. You could hear a pin drop with the silence that has taken over the room. Angela pushes the amulet down in one quick motion, sending the needles into Amberly's heart, causing her body to lift off the bed and a cry to escape her lips.

The second Amberly seems to be in danger I push Angela aside and reach for the amulet.

Angela grabs my arm, "Don't!"

"It's hurting her!" I'll do anything to ensure she's no longer in pain.

"It's her only hope. She will die if we don't let the amulet do what it's meant to."

I know in my heart there is no reason to argue, but it's hard for me to sit back and watch as Amberly suffers. I turn and slump back into my seat, sinking down to place my head in my hands.

Troy's voice fills the quiet room. "What do we do now?"

Celine answers.

"All we can do is wait."

Chapter 26

Amberly

Something sharp pierces the skin over my chest, sending fire rushing through my veins. Still in a haze, I try to silence my screams, but the pain is excruciating. A liquid substance emerges from the sharp points now piercing my skin, leaving a burning inferno in its wake.

Sweat coats my body, and every inch feels like it's sitting inside the flames of the hottest fire on the hottest day of summer. I attempt to move, trying to escape the heat, but my body is heavy. Julian places his hand on mine, and seconds later, the tingling moves up my hand and down my arm, lessening my pain.

"I'm right here. I'm not leaving you. Come back to us. Come back to me," he whispers to me.

His words ignite a new need inside of me.

I need to wake up.

The inferno caused by the liquid moves down my legs, and once it hits my feet, the heat dissipates and is replaced by an icy sensation freezing me. That liquid was burning off the poison inside me. I feel the rest of it leaving my body as the cold hits my veins.

"Wake up, Amberly," Angela begs.

I breathe out, and with this breath, I feel the last of the poison leaving. In its place is a newfound energy and strength. I open my eyes, taking in all the worried faces surrounding me.

"Hey, guys, what's new?" I say, trying to lighten the mood.

One by one, their heads fly up, eyes locking on mine. Tears fill their eyes and run down some cheeks as their worried faces turn to ones of relief and happiness. Everyone laughs before pilling themselves on top of me.

"Guys, you're squishing me," I squeak, covered by the ones I love.

* * *

With a nervous laugh, I offer my hand to Celine. "It's nice to finally meet you. Thank you for saving my ass."

She smiles nervously before taking my hand. "I'm just glad it worked because if it didn't, I think your pack here would have eaten us for dinner."

We laugh together, but her brother Cole remains silent. I sense his unease filling the air around us. I want to make them feel at home, leaving the past where it belongs. A fresh start for all of us, and with them on our side, our chances of winning the final battle only increase.

I move to stand in front of Cole. "It's nice to meet you."

He smiles but stays quiet, causing Celine to bump his shoulder with hers. "Don't be rude."

His eyes focus before he takes my hand, shaking it lightly. "I'm sorry, but can you blame me for being on edge?"

"Not at all. I understand completely and take no offense to it, but I promise you're safe here."

"Maybe. For now." He replies while his eyes scan the room filled with my pack.

I frown. "Together, we stand a better chance at coming out of this alive, and if we do, we will have a better future waiting for us. United we will stand, and divided we will fall."

Julian turns me to face him and wraps his arm around my waist, pulling me close and kissing me on the forehead.

"I couldn't have said it better, little wolf."

I nudge him with my body, "Who are you calling little?"

"I thought it was obvious." He smiles down at me.

I lightly poke him in the chest. "I'll happily remind you that I'm only an inch shorter than you."

"An inch is an inch, my love. It counts."

I look at Celine, smiling. With a sigh, I say to her, "Men, am I right?"

She laughs. "It's a good thing we need them."

Julian turns as he offers his hand to Celine. "I wanted to personally thank you for coming. I know it couldn't have been an easy choice. But because of you, Amberly is alive, and I am in your debt."

Celine reaches for his hand, shaking her head, "You owe us nothing."

Julian's eyes lock with mine. "That's where you're wrong." He turns back to Celine as his hold on me tightens. "I owe you everything." He looks to Cole, "Both of you."

Cole finally relaxes. "I was only along for the ride," he mutters, laughing.

Julian nods with a smile.

Celine's face turns serious as she looks from Julian to me. "I know you just woke up, but we do need to talk about what's coming."

I place a hand on her shoulder. "And we will, but first, let's eat and get to know one another more. Then, I would like to bury our dead and say goodbye. Once we have done that, have had a night of peace and are well rested, we can touch the subject of the next coming war."

Chapter 27

Amberly

My legs barely keep me erect as my heart aches inside my chest. I fight back the tears begging to be set free, and my breath turns shallow. Watching John, Dean, Troy, and Logan lift my mother's lavender-robed body onto the pyre, my vision becomes blurry, and my legs threaten to pull me to the dirt ground. Grief wraps its hands around me, cutting off my air as I choke on a sob that fights to make its way up my windpipe. I extinguish the flames that threaten to swallow me whole, taking a step forward.

Julian grabs my forearm lightly, making me turn to him.

"You don't need to do this."

"Yes, I do," I choke.

I walk to the front of the pyre that now holds my mother. Grabbing a pyre log, I place it over the multicolored blaze, lighting it on fire. Aidan moves around the altar counterclockwise three times, sprinkling the wood with holy water before coming to stand next to me. His gaze holds a sadness that I know matches my own. He may not have known our mother very long, but I know his heart feels her loss just as mine does. He moves his hand in my direction, and I place the flaming log in his grasp. With his free hand, he takes mine, and we turn to face the altar.

This is how ancient Greeks were said to have buried their dead. Although we aren't Greek, my father once told me this was the way of the pack. Anyone who fell in battle or was beloved by the pack would be honored with this ceremony. No one in the pack put up a fight against doing this for my mother. She wasn't a wolf, and this wasn't the witch way, but I know this is what my mother would have wanted.

Everyone in the pack felt my mother's love. She welcomed them all into our family as they did her. When we put it to a vote, it was unanimous to honor her with a pyre funeral.

Part of the tradition was that the oldest male would light the pyre. If I'm being honest, I'm happy Aidan is here and agreed to do it because as much as I'm holding it together, I don't think I could light my mother's body on fire. I hold my breath as I watch Aidan move around the altar. Each time he touches the burning log inside the pyre my eyes close. When I open my eyes for the last time, I see the fire beginning to catch under my mother's body. Once Aidan finishes and places the burning log in his hand into the pyre, he moves back into place next to me and our father.

The voices of our pack, the witches and warlocks, sound behind me in unison.

"May you find peace in the afterlife. For death is not the end, and we will meet again. Until then, rest and know you are loved."

Upon the last word, my knees give out, and the floodgates in my eyes that I've been fighting so hard to keep closed fly open. Julian, Troy, Logan, Aidan, and my father are beside me an instant before my ear-piercing cry rings through the night sky.

Julian wraps me in his arms as I sob loudly into his chest, gripping his shirt in desperation as his hand gently moves the hair away from my face.

"I'm right here, little wolf. I've got you," he whispers.

My mother's dead. She's gone.

I should have saved her.

I could have saved her.

I've never felt a loss like this before. When I thought my father was dead, it hurt. But I never knew him. I felt like a part of me was missing and would never be found because I never knew the other person who made up half of who I was. When Julian was dead, the grief swallowed me and pulled me into the darkness, and I knew it was only a matter of time before I lost myself.

But this... This is different.

They say no death feels the same, and now I can attest to that.

The loss of a friend isn't the same as the loss of a parent, and losing a parent isn't the same as losing your partner.

My mother's death, her leaving this world forever, has darkened my world. I don't know how I'm going to pull myself from the edge of the abyss, but I know I have to.

Chapter 28

Julian

I hold Amberly close as she sobs and convulses in my arms. We sat at the foot of the pyre for hours, waiting until Amberly's cries tapered off. She cried, screamed and howled for hours before her body became too weak to hold her eyes open. I peer down at her when she turns quiet, finding that she has fallen asleep in my arms. I look at Aaron. He nods before patting me lightly on the shoulder. I gently place one arm under her legs and move into a standing position. My eyes look back at Aaron, my pack, and lastly, the pyre as the flames dance high into the night sky, taking with them a soul that was meant for so much more in this life than it was given.

As I make my way to Amberly's room, I glance down at her tear-stained cheeks, and the sight causes my heart to contract. I know there is nothing I can do to take this pain from her, but I would give anything to do it. Losing a parent takes a piece of who you are. It doesn't matter how old you are when they are ripped from your world; the effects are always the same.

Who you become starts with your parents. They show you how to navigate the world, your emotions, life, and everything else. Without them, the world around you darkens in a way that can never be mended, no matter how hard you try. I should know; I've been trying for nearly twenty years now.

Making it to her room, I carry her in and gently place her on her bed. I slowly back away from the bed and quietly close the door with a faint click, hoping not to wake her. I grab the blanket from the foot of her bed and place it lightly on top of her sleeping body, then take a seat in the chair next to her. A moment later, a moan of pure heartbreak passes Amberly's lips as she moves to her side. Her eyes open slightly as the trapped tears escape down her cheeks.

"Where am I?"

"In your room," I whisper.

I move the strands of hair away from her face as her body trembles from a suppressed cry.

"Where are my father and brother?"

"Still outside."

She begins to move into a sitting position. "I should be out there."

I place my hand on her shoulders, pushing her back down to the bed with little effort. "No, they agreed. You need your rest."

Her lips quiver as she holds in another sob. "I should be there. She would want me to be there. She needs me, they need me."

"Amberly, they will be fine, and you've done everything she would have wanted. She would be so proud of you."

"I let her die," she chokes out, her red, puffy eyes locking with mine.

My heart breaks as I look down at my mate. I move into the bed next to her, pulling her close to me as she releases a small cry.

"No, my little wolf, you didn't. You did everything you could. In war, there are losses, and I wish I could take this one from you, but I need you not to think for one second that this was your fault."

"I could have saved her."

"Not without losing a piece of yourself, and she wouldn't want that," I whisper.

"I don't know what to do now. I'm broken inside, and I don't know if I have the strength for the fight ahead," she whispers into my chest.

"We will figure it out together."

She tilts her head back to look me in the eyes, "You promise?"

I smile lightly, "I promise. I will sit with you every night and come and hold you while you cry. I will listen and be your voice of reason when you need it. I will help you through every second. But first, we need to deal with what's coming."

She releases a small sigh and whispers, "You mean the war."

I nod, knowing it's the last thing either of us wants to talk about, but I also know we can't dance around the subject. The sooner we plan for it, the sooner we can mourn our losses.

"It's closing in. I can feel it. But I also know that once we make it through this final battle, life will be a lot brighter."

"You mean if."

Her matter-of-fact tone sends a chill running through my blood. I need her to believe we will make it through what's coming and that there is a light at the end of this dark road that we've been traveling down for far too long. I need her to have a reason to fight.

I wasn't planning on asking her to marry me until this war was behind us, but I need her to know we have something worth fighting for and that our future is right around the corner.

And that my future is her.

"Amberly, there's something I've been wanting to say," I fidget with the hem of my shirt, "or ask you, I should say."

Propping herself up on her elbow, she wipes away the remaining tears before looking at me.

"Another day is never promised, and we have to make the most of what we are given. I was lost before I met you. The day you agreed to come back to the cave with me changed my life, and since then, you've given me purpose. I never want to live a day without you, and I fight every day to be worthy of the love and light you bring into my life."

Amberly smiles, and my heart contracts. Her smile is all I ever need in this life. Seeing it now, when her world is so dark, makes me know we are destined for each other.

"Julian."

"Yes?"

"You're being weird," she laughs.

I rub the back of my neck, praying for the right words.

"I'm sorry, I just want to get this right."

Her brows furrow in confusion. "Get what right?"

What if she says no?

That thought hadn't occurred to me until just now. I don't know what I would do if she didn't want to be my wife, my mate, for the rest of our days. I want my future to only be with her, to one day have pups of our own and grow old together. I never once thought about settling down until her, and I need her to know there's nothing I want more than her and our future together.

"Spit it out. You're making me nervous," she said, looking at me with wide eyes.

"Amberly, I want, I mean." Why was this so hard? "What I'm trying to ask is, will you marry me?" I finally was able to get the words out, my nerves still on high alert.

Her eyes shine as her smile disappears. Her silence darkens the room around us as my heart beats loudly in my chest, waiting for the one answer that could change my life for better or worse. We're young, but when you find your mate in a pack, it's for life. Some find them even sooner than we have. I want everyone to know she's mine, and I'm hers.

"I…," she grows silent once more.

I remain quiet, hoping she will think before giving her answer. She will be the pack's leader soon enough, and she will need an alpha by her side to rule. I know she is new to our ways, but this is something she will need to move forward with once her father is ready to step down. The thought of anyone else standing at her side makes my blood boil.

"Julian, I think right now isn't the best time for this conversation."

I take her hand in mine, "I think it's the perfect time."

"We could die tomorrow; nothing is certain, and I don't want to rush into this when it's something that should be thought over. My father was planning on marrying my mother, but now that future is gone." She pauses, squeezing my hand as she gazes into my eyes. "I don't think it's the best time to do this. And when we choose to, I want it to be a moment of happiness for everyone around us. I don't want my feelings to be clouded with the darkness of my loss. I want to feel every second of joy in those moments with you."

"If I learned one thing from the hell we've endured, it's take nothing for granted, and if you love someone, let them know every day. Because tomorrow isn't promised." My nerves have subsided, and now, I'm filled only with love for this woman in front of me.

"And if we are to die in the coming battle, I would like to go knowing I had you as my wife. No matter how short of a time. I would die happy knowing you were mine in every way, and we had something most people don't find in their lifetime."

My words cause her to pause, but I continue.

"If you're uncertain because of us, that's one thing…"

She cuts me off with a smile. "No. If there's one thing I'm certain about in my life right now, it's you. I want nothing more than to start our lives together, as crazy as it sounds," she laughs.

I grin, "Hey, why does it have to be crazy?"

"Because we are too young to even consider marriage," she laughs.

My heart skips a beat, but I don't let that stop me. I need her to know that if she wants this as much as I do, then there is no reason we shouldn't do it. The thought of her wanting to be mine as much as I want her to be mine has the wolf inside howling.

"We may be young, but we have been through more than people three times our age. We are older and wiser at heart, and that's all we need. I want to marry you; I've wanted to from the moment I saw you kiss Logan."

A small groan leaves her lips, which causes me to smile.

"I knew at that moment that I never wanted you with anyone else. That seeing you with anyone would break me in two. My days begin and end with you, and now I want to have it all. I want *us* to have it all. I think we deserve that much." I squeeze her hand lightly, waiting for her response. "So?"

Her smile widens across her face, causing my heart to leap inside my chest.

"The moment you asked me, I didn't need to think about it. My answer is yes." She leans in close until our foreheads are touching, "Yes. I'll marry you."

Chapter 29

Aaron

Smoke and fire fill the air around me, causing my eyes to sting. Tears run free down my cheeks as I stand frozen in the dirt, watching as my heart and future burn to ashes in front of my very eyes. This time, there's no question if it's lost to me forever; she's really gone.

My heart leapt with joy when I exited the cave to see her standing in the forest, knowing that my life would change forever, for I had once again been united with my love, my mate — something I never expected to happen. The day I thought I lost her turned my world into an empty abyss, and no matter how hard I fought to free myself from it, there was no escape. Not until I became responsible for a handful of young pups, my pack. When I rescued them, I became responsible for someone other than myself again. I may have lost my love and my own pup, but this was another family I had created, and I couldn't turn away from them.

If it wasn't for Angela, Julian, Dean, and John, I don't think I ever would have found a way out of the darkness. But now they are grown, and I fear nothing could save me from the impending grief I will soon find myself in. With nothing to focus on, the way I had to when they were young, there is nothing holding me in place. Nothing to keep me standing. My children are grown, and though they may need a father, they don't need me in the way I need right now.

"Aaron, I'm so sorry for your loss."

Consumed by the flames burning through my heart, I didn't hear Johnathan take his place next to me.

"Thank you."

"She was an amazing woman, and she will not be forgotten. Her name and story will live on for many generations to come. Take solace in knowing she will never truly leave us."

I turn to him, my blurry eyes resting on the wise man beside me, who is also fighting against his own grief.

"Your words are kind," I whisper to him.

"And true. Not only is she the mother of the most powerful creatures to walk this earth, but they will also be responsible for ending the tyranny and life this world has known. They alone will bring peace to these lands. She will be known not only for their place in history but for the strong woman she was and how her sacrifice made our freedom and peace possible."

His words, though meant to make this loss lighter, only make the darkness move in closer around me. I nod my head and focus back on the fire.

"I'm sorry to talk about this now, but time is running low. I think it's time to send for reinforcements. The naturals, the angels and fairies, would be the best to reach out to."

"If they haven't lent a hand before, what makes you think now will be any different?" I question him.

I follow his line of sight to my son, sitting alone, looking broken and lost.

"Because now the prophecy is taking place."

I turn my gaze back to him.

"What prophecy is that exactly?"

"It's in the journals. It tells of a lost son that no one knew of returning to the light. And that with him, death and loss will follow," he says, looking sadly at the pyre in front of us. "The loss will create unity like the lands have never known and with it, the end to the darkness and separation between the supernatural worlds."

"Do you really believe these journals?" I ask skeptically.

He nods. "Yes. For things I have read in them have already come to pass."

"Could just be a coincidence."

"Too many things have been accurate for it to simply be a coincidence."

"Like?"

The minute the word leaves my mouth, I wish it hadn't.

"First, the birth of your children. You and your mate being separated and finding each other all these years later. Also, a forbidden love between the ultimate power and a shifter, the return of your son, the death of an evil leader, and lastly, the loss we have recently endured."

"You're telling me all of that is in the journal?"

He nods.

I sigh before replying, "If you think they will join us, I will send out scouts before the night is over."

Julian nods. "I think that would be wise."

Chapter 30

Julian

My inner wolf wants nothing more than to run free with joy at our mate agreeing to marry us. I walk into the cold night air to see everyone still gathered around the pyre. Angela's sad eyes locate me first as she places a hand on Logan's shoulder before whispering a few words and heading in my direction.

"How is she?" She asks once she makes it to my side.

"As good as she can be."

She nods in understanding.

"I wish I could do more to help her," she whispers.

I reach for her hand, giving it a squeeze. "Just being there for her is enough."

She turns her gaze toward me, and her eyes lock with mine. "Why are you here? You should be with her."

"She's sleeping, and I need some fresh air."

Angela's eyes widen as she moves closer to me, giving me a quick sniff before I can swat her away with my hand and a laugh.

"What are you doing?"

Her eyes open wide as she looks at me. "What aren't you telling me?"

I smile with a shrug, "Nothing."

"Your scent tells me otherwise," her nose crinkles with her words.

With a scowl, I reply, "How many times do I have to ask you not to smell me?"

She shifts back with a smile, "You do it."

"True, but not to you." I laugh.

She shrugs. "Sorry, but my wolf could sense something was off with you, but not in a bad way. Given the current events, I wouldn't expect anything but anger and sadness to emit from you, but that isn't what I'm smelling."

I mumble, "Well…"

She hits me in the chest, a giant grin spreading across her face. "Spill."

I glance around us to make sure no one is listening in. "I'm not sure if now is the time to say anything."

"Julian, if you don't tell me right now…"

I put my hands up in surrender and smile before pulling her further away from the group.

"I asked Amberly to marry me."

Her eyes widen, "You what?"

I nod.

"What did she say?"

My eyes travel the area before answering. "She said yes."

Angela screams in excitement before throwing her hands to her mouth and silencing herself.

"Sorry," she giggles, "but oh my God. She said yes?"

I smile.

"When will you guys do it?"

I shake my head. "I don't know, but I would like to do it immediately."

"Why the rush?"

"I don't want to waste any more time. I want us to be married before the battle comes. I want her and everyone to know how much I love her and that despite all the loss we have endured, there is light at the end of it. That we have something to fight for that is ours."

"I completely agree." Her eyes travel to the rest of the group, "When are you going to tell the others?"

"I want to make sure she's okay with everyone knowing first."

"Smart move."

I smile, "Hey, I'm learning."

One of her eyebrows rises, "Slowly."

We look at each other and laugh until our sides hurt.

"What's so funny?"

Troy's voice causes us to wipe the tears from our eyes and look up.

Logan, Troy, Amara, and Aidan reach our side, and I give Angela a stern look, causing her to smile.

"We got lost in a moment. A memory."

Logan places his arm around her shoulders, looking down at her, "A good one, it seems, from the sound of things."

Her smile widens across her face as she glances in my direction. "A very good one."

"We could all use something to laugh about," Troy mumbles from Amara's side. "So how about sharing the joke with the rest of the group," he says, looking to me.

I glance at Angela with a *'what do I do now?'* face.

Angela grabs Logan's hand before looking at Troy, "Honestly, it's been a long day, and I think we all need some rest. There will be time to laugh tomorrow, and we will need it before all the seriousness returns."

Logan looks around the group, "She's right. We'll need as much rest as possible, and I think Aaron could use this time without us hanging around."

Aidan glances back at his father, still staring at the pyre and quietly speaking with Johnathan. "I don't know what to do. Should I stay with him or give him space? This is all new to me."

I place a hand on his shoulder. "Your father is strong and will be okay. You need to take this time to deal with what happened yourself. Amberly and Aaron will be here in the morning and you will all need each other in the weeks ahead. For now, focus on what you need."

Aidan nods before looking around the group one last time, then heads back toward the cave.

I release a long breath. "Alright, everyone. Let's take it down for the night."

The rest of the group moves toward the cave entrance. Angela pauses and looks back at me, seeing I haven't moved.

"You okay?"

"Yeah, I think I'm going to talk to Aaron for a few minutes before I retire."

She nods before turning her back on me and continuing to the cave.

I make my way over to Aaron, meeting Johnathan as they end their conversation. I nod at him as he walks away from us.

"How is my daughter?" he says, his voice barely above a whisper.

"Sleeping, but she's okay."

"Good."

The flames are beginning to die, and I know it will take a lot to convince Aaron to get some rest.

"What did Johnathan want?" I ask him.

"He thinks it's time to call in reinforcements and I think he's right. I'm trying to come up with a plan where Amberly and my son won't need to be as involved in this fight."

"I don't think there is a way around that."

He runs his hand over his face, defeated. "I know. But I have to try. I've lost enough and so have they." His eyes lock with mine. "I sense you have some news of your own to share."

My heart sinks to my stomach. Amberly will kill me if I tell him before she does.

"I, um…" I start, and my nerves cause me to pause.

"Out with it, boy. It can't be anything worse than this." He gestures to the pyre with his head.

I rub at my neck feverishly. "Actually, it's good news. I just don't know if now is the time to tell you."

He turns in my direction, a small, forced smile forming. "I could use some good news."

Well, how could she argue with that?

"I…well, I asked Amberly to marry me."

His eyes open slightly, but he remains quiet. I can tell he's waiting for me to continue.

"She said yes, and I would like to marry her before the battle arrives on our doorstep," now that I've gotten it out, it feels as if a weight has been lifted.

"She's not pregnant, is she?" His tone is serious as he turns his gaze to me.

I choke. "God, no. I've wanted to ask her for a while, but with the battles and everything else going on, I just didn't. But I'm tired of waiting. I want her to know what we are fighting for. I want her to have an extra reason to give it her all. We have our whole lives ahead of us and a future we deserve. We just need to get through this final battle."

"There will always be more battles," Aaron whispers.

"True. But I have a feeling that after this one, the battles we will face for the rest of our lives will be small in comparison. Like, who left the eggs out all night."

Aaron looks at me, and we both laugh.

"So, you and my daughter are getting married?" Aaron smiles lightly.

I nod.

He moves so quickly it takes me off guard. He pulls me in for a bear hug.

"Jocelyn would have been so happy. I know you will take care of her and love her for the rest of your days. I couldn't ask for more."

Chapter 31

Amberly

Darkness fills the area around me, making my surroundings impossible to see. Dread and fear creep into my body as I stand frozen in place. I've never been afraid of the dark, but something inside me is screaming that I'm about to see something my mind isn't ready for.

In the distance, a blur of color emerges. I walk slowly ahead, knowing I'm not going to like what's about to unfold in front of my eyes. As I move closer, I see a battle taking place, and I have no doubt this is the final battle between Vladimir's people and my own. My heart pounds wildly in my chest as I watch spells, wolves, angels, fairies, and knives flying in all directions. My eyes rapidly move across the scene before me, searching for familiar faces.

I find my father battling it out with two young demons, sweat pouring down his cheeks. I scan to the right of the scene and find Troy, Amara, Logan, and Angela fighting a mix of witches, warlocks, and demons. They appear to be way outnumbered, but they are holding their own. I search the area for the two last people on my mind until they come into view. Julian and Aidan are fighting back-to-back against...

It can't be.

Is that Sage?

I squint my eyes, hoping to zero in on the scene before me, but it only becomes harder to focus. The red-haired woman is joined by four others, two women and *two men. My instincts tell me they are the rest of the foretold fourteen.*

Julian and Aidan are more than outnumbered, and for the first time, I find myself wondering where I am and who I may be fighting. I catch my silhouette out of the corner of my eye, fighting against two older people, a male and a female. I look at their faces, my heart beating with recognition. I've seen those features somewhere before.

That nose.

It's my mother's.

Those cheekbones.

They are my cheekbones.

And the lips.

My mother and I share those same lips.

What I'm seeing can't be possible. They died years ago. The older woman lands a blow, sending me to my knees and causing me to cry out from the pain as she sinks her blade deep into my shoulder. I notice my father, Aidan, and Julian get momentarily distracted as they take in the scene of me fighting against my grandparents.

I stare up into my grandmother's eyes as she pulls the blade from my trembling and exhausted body, my blood running free down my arm. I sink forward as she says something before handing the knife to my grandfather. He cleans it with his shirt, placing it back in its holster at his side. He moves closer, gripping my sweat-filled hair in his old but firm fist, forcing me to look him in the eyes as she says something I can't hear. He releases his hold, sending my hands to crash back into the earth as I pant wildly. My eyes see his fist arching back. I sit back on my knees and stare into his emotionless face.

"You don't have to do this," I whisper.

He smiles evilly as I barely make out his response, "It's already done."

He moves his now flame-covered fist forward, aiming for my chest. I know if I don't move, I will die at my grandfather's hand. I wait for the impact as the scene moves in slow motion, almost like it wants me to see what's about to happen.

My father, Julian, and Aidan make it to my side. Julian pushes me to the ground as my father sends my grandmother sailing through the air with a wolf-enforced kick to the stomach. Aidan takes my place; hands raised high as he sends our

113

grandfather into a nearby tree, but not before I see a smile on the old man's face, telling me he accomplished something I didn't see.

I look harder at the scene in front of me.

Julian shifts to the side, allowing me to move back into a sitting position. As I cradle my arm, I stare over at Aidan as he turns in our direction, his hand on the handle of our grandfather's dagger that now lies in his chest.

I gasp, my hand covering my mouth. I continue watching the vision, watching myself run to my brother's side as he falls to his knees, gasping for breath.

"Aidan, I can heal you. Just sit still," I choke out.

He places his hand on mine, shaking his head. "No."

"Don't be stupid! I can heal this," I yell at him.

"You're weak and injured. And because of what our grandmother did, your powers are a fraction of what they were. You do this, and you will die," he forces out.

His strength quickly leaves him, and I sob as he crumbles into my lap.

"I can't just watch you die," I cry, grabbing hold of him.

"That's exactly what I'm asking you to do."

"But I just found you, and we have so much life left to get to know one another." Tears are streaming down my cheeks. I can't lose him.

He places his hand on mine. "You filled my life. Before you, it was empty. I was a shell of a person. I was good because you showed me how to be. I can die knowing what I did made a difference, that I made our family proud and kept my little sister safe."

I watch as his eyes begin to dim. At the same moment, a loud explosion sounds next to me, and Julian is ripped from my side. I lean over Aidan, trying to protect him from whatever is going on around us.

"Amberly," He chokes out. "You need to protect yourself." Blood pours from his mouth. "The battle isn't over."

Tears continue to stream down my cheeks. "I'm not leaving you."

"You have to. You have to survive. Promise me."

My eyes leave Aidan's for a moment, and I see Julian running toward me as my grandmother approaches, but I have no will to fight. Julian shifts into his wolf form and runs toward my grandmother, but he's no match for her and my grandfather's magic as they join together, sending him crashing down in front of me. I gently place Aidan on the ground before turning my magic on my family.

I may not want to fight, I may be weak, but I'll be damned if I sit here and watch as they take my mate from me. Not while I'm still breathing.

I see the dagger leave my grandfather's holster and sail through the air at a ridiculous speed. I wait for the pain, but instead, I hear a yelp. I open my eyes to find Julian at my feet as he shifts back into his human form.

Anger consumes me as my vision turns red. I scream, and with the last of my energy, I send my grandparents sailing into the trees closest to us. But they don't stop there. Their bodies sink through the sturdy bark as my scream continues. They emerge from the back of the trunk and into the boulders at the base. Once I see their eyes close, my scream subsides, and I fall to my knees, spent.

With the last of my strength, I crawl over to Julian's naked form. Pulling my shirt over my head, thankful I wore a tank top underneath, I placed it over his body before pulling him close to me. For the first time, I see the blade. It's just below his heart.

"I can get it out, and then you can start to heal. Just hold on," I stutter out.

He gasps as I reach for the blade. "Don't touch it. It's laced with Wolfsbane. I can smell it."

"Okay, I'll get Logan then," I start to stand, but he grabs my hand.

"Just sit here with me. The battle is just about done," he says, his voice barely above a whisper.

I smile down at his weakening body as the floodgates in my eyes open. "Okay."

"Don't you wish you had agreed now?" he questions.

I scoff, unsure what he's talking about. "Agreed to what?"

"To marry me before all this happened."

My smile disappears. "No, because you're going to get better, and we're going to get married and celebrate our victory. You and Aidan are going to be just fine."

The vision before me disappears, sending me banging my hand against an invisible wall.

"No. I need to know what happens," I try to fight it.

"Amberly."

My heart stops as I turn to see my mother smiling at me. A blinding light

115

surrounds her.

"Mom?"

"Yes, it's really me." Her smile widens.

"But how?"

Closing the distance between us, she takes my hands in hers. "We don't have long. First, I want to tell you how very proud I am of you. You will make a fine leader when the time comes. A mother wants nothing more than to see their children happy, safe, and strong. You and your brother are the best things I've done, and I only wish I had more time with you both."

Tears run freely down my flushed face.

She squeezes my hands lightly. "You need to know the vision you just witnessed can be changed. Everyone does not need to die. As long as you open your mind and think about your next moves, you will come out victorious." She pauses briefly, resting her hand on my tear-stained cheek. "The future your father and I have always wanted for you, the future you and Julian want together will happen. It's right around the corner."

"But I saw..." I stutter.

She shakes her head, cutting me short. "You, of all people, should know that nothing is set in stone. We've changed things before. This too can change."

"Tell me what to do. I'm lost without you." I need her guidance right now. I need her.

"My sweet girl, you have the answers inside of you. Turn to yourself and the ones around you. Trust in each other, and you can never fail. Know that I am always with you. Tell your father I will be waiting for him, and our lives together do not end in death. Be there for your brother. He will need you more than he can admit. Lastly, follow your heart. Don't be afraid to love and want the things you want."

I don't have to ask her what she's talking about as the last thing Julian said to me in my vision plays back in my mind. I want to be his wife more than anything, but when I said yes, I knew we wouldn't agree on when to do it. I wanted to wait until after the battle, but maybe in order to change the outcome of the vision, I can start with this. Like my mother said, I need to follow my heart. And the one thing I know I want more than anything is to be married to my mate.

I look at my mother as tears begin to form in my eyes once more, "I wish you were here. I don't know how I'm supposed to be happy and start my future without you."

She brings her hand back to mine, holding them gently. "I will be there with you, front and center. You might not see me, but open your heart and mind, and you'll feel me there with you. On your wedding day, when you learn you'll become a mother, and when you have each of your children. I will be there for every single moment. I wouldn't miss them for anything. Death isn't goodbye, and it's not the end, my sweet girl."

A light shines deep in the distance as my body grows heavy. My mother's eyes begin to fill with tears, telling me our time is almost over. I pull her close.

"I'm not ready to say goodbye," I whimper into her hair as we embrace one last time.

"This isn't goodbye, honey. It's until we meet again." She whispers, "I love you."

"Always and forever," I mumble into her shoulder.

The light moves in around us until I see nothing else. My body weighs me down, and I feel myself move through my mother's form.

"Remember, I will always be there. Follow your heart, my love. Don't be afraid to be happy. I love you."

My mother's words are the last thing I hear before falling into oblivion.

* * *

My eyes open to the darkness of my room, sending the tears in my eyes to run freely down my cheeks as I suck in a breath, trying to suppress the sob threatening to escape my lips. I feel a warm hand holding me through the fabric of my shirt. Julian pulls me close, resting his chin on my shoulder.

"Talk to me," he whispers.

I roll over, wrapping my arms around his neck and pulling him toward me until our lips touch. A warm, electric-like feeling moves through my body, causing my sadness and fear to subside. I've never had something like I do with Julian. He calms me in a way no one else ever has. We fight like every other couple, but I find myself counting down the seconds until we make up again. My day begins and ends with him, and I wouldn't change a thing.

I always considered love something to avoid. Watching the pain that my mother went through daily with the loss of my father, I never wanted to feel that. I think that's part of the reason why I always kept Logan at arm's length and never said how I felt. I did the same thing with Julian without even realizing it until this moment. I only let him in part of the way, afraid of what would happen if things didn't work out or if I lost him. The pain I felt when I saw him kissing Amara or lying dead in front of me nearly consumed me, and in those moments, he only had a piece of me. The thought of giving him everything and completely letting him in was terrifying and crippling. But the thought of not doing it was heartbreaking. The one thing I know for sure while laying here with him, kissing him until I can't breathe, is that I can't live without him. And I don't want to.

I pull back, panting, only to find him doing the same.

My smile widens as I whisper, "I'm ready."

His eyebrow lifts in confusion. "For what?"

"I want to be your wife."

He chuckles lightly, running his fingers down the length of my arm and sending goosebumps across my skin.

"I thought we already covered that."

I shake my head. "No. I mean, I want to marry you. Now. Today."

His eyes widened in surprise. "Today?"

I nod.

"Are you sure?" he asks, his brows furrowing but his face filled with excitement.

"I've never been more sure of anything in my life."

"It's just before, you seemed..."

I cut him off. "I know. But I thought about what you said, and I don't want to take anything for granted anymore. I want to be yours in every way possible, and I want the future we've talked about. And I don't want to wait."

His smile reaches his eyes as he gently strokes my cheek, "Little wolf, you have made today the best day of my life."

I smile as he moves closer, kissing every inch of my face and neck, filling my heart with joy and laughter.

Chapter 32

Amberly

Telling everyone we planned on being married was easy enough. Somehow, the word had already spread through the cave that we were engaged. I can guess who let that dog out of the bag. So, when we woke up this morning to tell my father we wanted to get married tonight, he wasn't surprised. He even said he would expect nothing different. Angela and Amara were jumping at the bit to do any and all preparations.

For the last few hours, I've sat back and relaxed, watching everyone run around me like dogs without their heads. If I'm being honest, it's been a very funny and pleasant sight to see. No one is training or afraid, but instead, united and excited for something meant to be a happy moment.

I notice Celine and Cole off in the background of the chaos that has filled the forest atmosphere around me. I know I should probably let it go, at least until after tonight, but this might be the only chance I get to talk to her. I jump when everyone else is distracted.

I rise from my thinking rock and make my way in their direction, but not before Angela grabs me by the hand.

"Where are you going?" She inquires.

"I was going to check in on our new guests. Make sure they are doing okay," I say to her.

Smiling, she replies, "Already acting like the pack's Alpha. It looks good on you, by the way." Her face turns serious as she clears her throat. "However, we are looking at five hours and counting. I need you to go and try on the dress I left for you and let Amara mess around with that rug on top of your head."

I scowl as I place my hand on my knotty hair. "My hair isn't a rug. It's one of my best features."

We stare at each other for a moment and then burst into laughter.

"All the same, it will need some time to prepare for tonight. Don't have Amara stress over it at the last minute," she says to me, still laughing.

"I won't, I promise. Once I make sure they are doing alright, I'll head straight to Amara."

Her eyes narrow on me with serious intent. "You better, *Your Majesty*, or I will find you and carry you there myself."

We share a smile before she turns to leave, and I begin to walk toward Celine.

"Amberly, congratulations on the big night. Is there anything we can do to help?" Celine asks upon my approach.

I smile, "Actually, there is something I need to talk to you both about. But first, how are you doing? Is everyone treating you okay?"

Cole and Celine exchange a look. "Everyone has been very nice. Is everything..."

"That easy to read, am I?" I whisper.

They glance around before leaning in as Celine replies, "Sorry to say, but you are an open book. Is there a reason we are whispering?"

"Follow me." I wave my hand, motioning them to follow.

We make it to the back of the outside of the cave, which is currently deserted. I turn around before gesturing to a formation of rocks we can sit on.

"Last night, I had one of my visions," I mumble as we sit on the rocks.

"So, it's true?" Cole asks.

I nod.

"We heard you could have visions of the future, but no one was sure," he continues. "I mean, it's a very rare gift, and only a handful of our kind has been known to have it in the last century. What are the visions normally about?"

"I wish I could say they were happy visions, but so far, every single one I've had has been about death. I wish I didn't have to see them, but at the same time, I'm grateful because it gives me time to change them."

"What do you need us to do?" Celine asks.

"What was it about?" Cole inquires at the same time.

I smile. "The coming battle and some things I'm a little unsure of. I don't know how it would be possible, but I believe my grandparents were the ones I was fighting."

They exchange a look of fear.

After a moment, Celine replies, leaning in closer. "Yes, Vladimir was able to sway them to his side all those years ago. When your mother believed they were dead, your grandparents actually left with him. They thought they had killed your mother and father in the woods that day, and they believed in Vladimir's vision, so they chose to leave with him. When we all learned you were still alive, he forced them to stay hidden."

"As a contingency plan," Cole adds.

Celine continues, "So when they saw you kill Vladimir, instead of attacking, they left to rebuild."

"Rebuild how?" I ask, afraid of the answer I might receive.

"Vladimir had the rest of the seven," Cole responds. "He put them under a sleeping curse and hid them in the walls of our home. Your grandparents knew where to find them. Before we left, they had Celine break down the wall. By now, I would assume they are almost back to their peak power and should be on the move soon."

Celine places her hand on mine. "I think we still have some time." She continues, leaning back, "I've come to know Henry and Annabeth over the years, and she is more calculating with her moves. She won't come here until she is sure the seven are ready. Most of them have been in those walls for years. They will need more than a nice meal and a normal night's sleep. They will need training, guidance, and time to regain their powers, which will take some time."

"It's been a few days since you arrived. How much time do you think we have left?" I ask her.

Celine smiles, "I would say it's safe to expect at least a month before they arrive."

I close my eyes, releasing a sigh. "You really think we have that long?"

"Like I said, they aren't Vladimir. He rushed into things, he was cocky. They are strategic and don't plan on losing," she says, looking at Cole as he nods in agreement.

My heart stops as my body turns cold. "We need reinforcements."

"And you will have them," Cole says, smiling at me.

I glance at him. How can he be so sure? In my vision, I did see other creatures on the battlefield, and they appeared to be fighting on our side. But what could he know that I don't?

Celine tilts her head as a small smile forms on her face. "Did you really think we would come here, knowing what we know, without planning something?"

I remain silent, staring at them.

Cole looks to his sister before continuing. "We sent out messengers to all the villages in the area. We told them about the battle to come, what it means, and that we need their help in order to win. We informed them of the prophecy and that their freedom from the darkness that has taken over our world is only one battle away."

My heart skips a beat before I ask, "Do you think they will come?"

Celine's smile grows. "Yes, and before you ask if we think they will make it in time, I do. They want this change just as much as we do. You have given us something we had only hoped for. The prophecy was something many looked forward to. But many didn't want to believe because they feared it would never come to pass, or at least not in their time. We are fortunate that you were born in our time, and we will do what we can to ensure the rest of the prophecy comes to pass."

"Even if that means your lives?" The words escape my lips before I can stop them. "I'm sorry, I shouldn't have been so blunt. I shouldn't have said that at all. You have both risked so much already."

Celine shares a look with her brother before answering me. "If we are to fall in this battle, then so be it. It's been too long, a life in the darkness that Vladimir created and Henry and Annabeth keep alive. We want to be free, even if only for a short while. Everyone deserves to finally feel the peace that winning this battle will bring."

I nod, knowing exactly how she feels.

Mirroring my nod, Celine continues. "Anyway, thank you for checking in on us. But we know Angela runs a tight ship and would kill us early if we keep you any longer. I'm glad we had a moment to discuss everything, but now it's time to relax and enjoy this day."

"Oh, yes, my hair appointment," I say with a laugh. Moving into a standing position, I look down at the twins, "Would hate to have knotty hair tonight. Can't have Julian marrying a bride with a bird's nest on her head."

We all laugh as I exit, heading for Amara and my hair appointment, just as I promised.

Chapter 33

Amberly

"I have no idea how you've lived with this hair for so long. I would have cut it off or ended my life. I'm honestly not sure which," Amara states in complete seriousness as she huffs and puffs while moving around my head.

She rests the comb in her hand on her lips as she thinks, and her other hand supports her elbow while holding the scissors. I fear she just might cut off all my hair before the night is over.

"I've never really cared about looks. I'm more of a 'take me as I am, love me, or leave' sort. I've always just thrown it up and called it a day."

"What about when you wear it down?" She asks through bared teeth.

I smile. "I would treat it the night before with a blend that my…" I stumble over the next words. "that my mother made. And then spend about twenty minutes brushing it. Hence, the reason you don't see my hair down too often. It's too much work."

She gently runs her hand through my hair, looking at it in wonder. "Doesn't Julian like your hair down?"

My eyes connect with hers. "I never asked."

"Hair is normally one of the things men care about, and speaking from experience, they tend to prefer it down," she says matter-of-factly.

My cheeks burn.

"I think he would love to see your hair down more often. There has to be a way," she flips a section of my hair in distaste, "to tame this beast. You are part wolf, after all, and if you can handle that, your hair shouldn't cause you this much trouble."

"You would think," I laugh.

Lowering herself until her face is next to mine, our cheeks lightly touching, she whispers, "We will figure it out. Can't have the alpha of our pack looking like a ragamuffin."

Amara stands, moving the comb and scissors back to my hair. I glance at her in the mirror.

"A what?"

She laughs, "Don't worry. After tonight, your hair won't look like this ever again. I mean, being a witch, there has to be a better way to deal with it."

"A spell like that would fall under serious personal gain, and I was taught from a young age never to use my magic that way."

Rolling her eyes, she cuts a few inches off my hair. Hearing the snips, I jump forward as I watch it fall to the ground.

"What are you doing?" I bellow.

One hand holds the scissors, the other the comb, and she raises them, palms to the sky, with a shrug and sly smile.

"I made you a promise, and I intend to keep it. However, I need a little help working this miracle."

"So you're going to cut all my hair off?" I scream.

"For someone who didn't want to put effort into it, you sure are getting angry over a few inches. You still have the length. It just won't touch your butt anymore," she grins.

I sit back in my seat, sighing, "How about a little warning next time? I mean, it has to be illegal somewhere to just chop someone's hair off without a warning and some consent."

Amara doubles over in laughter at my comment. Her face turns red as she tries to breathe. I stare at her through slitted eyes, folding my arms over my chest.

"Consent! Girl, you're killing me," Amara mumbles through her gasps for air.

"I'm glad the massacre of my hair is amusing to you," I mumble at her, rolling my eyes as she continues.

Chapter 34

Amberly

L ooking at my reflection, I see a stranger. Someone I've never met before. She's flawless, beautiful, and strong. I have to look at myself for a while before I can admit this woman I'm staring at is me.

My hair is pinned up around my head with flower and diamond clips, as some strands hang loose. The back is in a half-up, half-down fashion to match the rest but comes down in a sophisticated wave. My gaze moves to my ears as my hand lightly touches the left earring. A sapphire stud that belonged to my mother. The necklace resting over my breastbone completes the matching set. The necklace has one big sapphire in the center, roughly the size of a penny. On both sides of the stone rests a single diamond, a little smaller than the blue beauty. Next to both diamonds, on each side, rests another sapphire, half the size of the one in the middle.

I've never been one for pretty or flashy things, but wearing these today feels right. They also gave me something borrowed and something blue.

My dress, the color of snow, rests against my flushed skin, making my complexion appear ghostly. Being fair-skinned has its trials, but it would be nice not to look like a dead person on your wedding day. The blending of browns and greens over my eyelids stands out against my skin, causing my eyes to be the first thing to grab your attention. I guess I should be grateful for the full-on woman look today.

My shoes, against my firm objection, are white, three-inch high heels with a beautiful silver design on the heel. It looks like branches are forming from the sole and reaching for the sky as they travel up to the top of the backs of the shoes. A round diamond pops from the branch-like design every half inch before it continues up.

The elbow-length sleeves of the dress rest off my shoulders, showing the skin down to my bosom, Amara joked as I put the dress on twenty minutes ago.

"Julian isn't going to let you down the aisle. He's going to grab you and head right for the bedroom with the way you look," she laughed.

Her comment sends my mind racing. As I peer down, seeing how my gown hugs every curve to my hips and flows out, I have no doubt that Julian's thoughts will be exactly as Amara said.

"Aren't you a vision in white?" Angela cries from the doorway.

I turn to her, smiling as butterflies fill my stomach.

"You look absolutely beautiful. Julian won't know what hit him!" She grins, walking toward me slowly.

"That's my worry," I smirk.

Grabbing me by the hands, she looks me in the eyes. "Finding you changed his world, but the moment you agreed to marry him set his soul on fire. He doesn't know how he got so lucky. He knows how lucky he is to have you. We all do."

"It's Julian and all of you that changed my life," I mumble, tears threatening to stain my cheeks as I attempt to hold them in. "The day he found me in the woods, he opened a door to a life I never knew existed. Good, bad, or indifferent, I wouldn't change anything we've been through because it led us here. I met a father I never knew I had, gained a bigger family, learned about my wolf, grew as a woman, and met my forever love. I've gotten more than most," my heart contracts, causing me to pause. "I would gladly fight a battle every week if it meant having him and this life with all of you at the end of it all. I only wish we didn't lose so much in the process of making it here. I wish…"

Her smile fading, she finishes my thought, "You wish your mother were here."

I nod.

She squeezes my hands lightly. "She is, Amberly. She wouldn't miss this." She places her free hand over my heart and continues, "Hold her here, always, and she will never leave."

Tears fill my eyes again, ready to break free at any moment. Angela pulls me in for a tight, much-needed hug before whispering, "You got this. You're ready. Dry those tears, and let's get you down that aisle."

Chapter 35

Julian

To say I'm a ball of nerves would be an understatement. Now I know what people mean when they talk about cold feet. It's not so much because you don't want to go through with it, at least not in my case. It's more like the excitement, knowing that soon, you will be forever linked to the one person you can't live without.

The hall of the cave is full and bright, with small lights hanging all over the ceiling, on the backs of the chairs, and by the assortment of lavender and maroon flower arrangements. The setup is one we will remember for years to come. The cave has never been so lit and lively. Everyone in the pack is restless from the excitement of tonight. Our pack's Alpha will be joining his daughter and their Beta in a way no one can break, and soon, our Alpha will step down, and Amberly and I will become the next to lead, making this a huge deal for all the wolves.

Then there are the witches from Amberly's home. They arrived here shortly after the last battle to pay respects to their fallen leader. They haven't left, and I don't think they will anytime soon, as their new leader is Amberly. We haven't yet discussed what will happen after this war is over. Will we stay here with the pack or return to her home? The witches need someone to lead them, and just like the wolf dynamic, witches stay with the bloodline of the leader. So their choice is Aidan or Amberly, meaning someone will have to leave.

"You look deep in thought," Troy says as he approaches me with a smirk, "We aren't getting cold feet, are we?"

With my grin reaching my eyes, I laugh, "Never. I was only thinking about a very important conversation that's coming."

Troy's smile disappears. "And what conversation is that?"

"Something Amberly and I need to discuss together before I say anything," I respond.

His eyes turn to slits as he watches me. Before either of us says anything, Logan walks up with Angela.

"It's almost time!" Angela shrieks.

Logan glances in her direction with a smile, "Someone is very excited."

Her smile disappears as she glares at him. "Of course I am. A marriage is a huge deal to a pack, and there hasn't been one in my lifetime, so this is a big deal. And Julian is like my brother. Seeing him get married to someone I have grown so close to only makes this moment more special."

Logan raises his hands in defeat. "I was only joking! Calm down, woman."

Poking him in his chest, he watches her hand cautiously as she growls, "Don't ever tell a woman to calm down, and now isn't the time for jokes."

"As you say. I'm all ears and listening loud and clear. No more jokes," Logan smiles playfully, "Can I have a kiss?"

Angela releases a long breath and takes a step back.

"I'll take that as a no," He mumbles.

"Better be more careful with that one, mate," Troy whispers as he nudges Logan's shoulder with his.

Angela turns back to face them with bared teeth, her wolf canines expanding. I move in front of her.

I place my hands lightly on her shoulders, "Whoa, hey, down girl."

She looks at me with glazed-over eyes, almost like she's confused. Our eyes connect, and the fog lifts.

"I'm sorry. I don't know what happened. I think I'm a little sleep-deprived," she says quietly.

"Yeah, maybe," I mumble.

Something is going on with her, and it's best to figure it out now before she snaps at someone. Music sounds in the background, and I quickly turn to look down the aisle and see Aaron standing in a tux at the end of it. He smiles at me before reaching out his hand, which Amberly takes a moment later.

My heart stops in my chest when my eyes connect with hers. She's always been beautiful and flawless, but at this moment, I'm in complete awe of her. I've never seen her in a dress before, but man, after this moment I hope to see it more often. She is a vision, and I have to remind myself that she's mine. She smiles bashfully in my direction before breaking our eye contact as she and Aaron begin to make their way down the aisle to where I am waiting.

It takes everything in me to stand in place and not run to her. I want to pick her up in my arms, kiss her like our lives depended on it, and carry her back to our room. I push down the urge, knowing we will have plenty of time for that later. They approach, and Aaron stops, turning to Amberly before placing a soft kiss on her hand and pulling her in for an embrace.

"Your mother would have loved seeing you in this dress. You look beautiful," he pulls away, revealing tears in both their eyes before he turns to me, "You take care of her. She is your responsibility now."

I nod as Amberly rolls her eyes, happy she isn't giving us a fight at this moment. Aaron stretches out his arm to offer me Amberly's hand. I take it willingly, and the moment our skin touches, that burning fire spreads through my hand and down my arm until it ignites my chest. Peace is all I feel at this moment.

Chapter 36

Aaron

"Amberly, having been raised with your coven, weddings are slightly different than in a pack. So, if you have any questions throughout the process, don't hesitate to stop and ask me along the way," I tell her. She nods in understanding, so I continue. "To begin, we will have each of you share your vows with one another. Then, you will address the pack before exchanging your rings. And then, of course, the kiss, cementing the bond between husband and wife. Being in a pack, we also place a mark upon our spouse."

"A mark?" She asks, unsure.

I offer a reassuring smile. "You each pick a spot on your mate and bite. It will permanently leave your mark on their flesh. This ties you together as one in the pack's eyes, as well as by anyone else who knows pack rules."

She looks at Julian, and her uncertainty vanishes, replaced by a deep longing to be united with her mate.

Turning to Julian, I offer him the ring for Amberly.

Taking it, he flips it repeatedly between his fingers as his smile grows. Looking up at Amberly, his eyes are full of happiness I've never seen in them before this day.

"Amberly, I don't even know where to begin. To you, we've only known each other a short while, but for me, I've known you almost my whole life.

From the moment I saw you in the woods as a strong young girl, bright and determined to always outsmart her friends in the newest game invented."

Chuckles fill the room.

"You stole my heart from that very first moment," Julian starts, tears of joy already forming in his eyes. "I had to know you. Every chance I got, I would go to that spot to find you. There was something about you that always pulled me in. The day I finally approached you, my world lit up in a way I can't begin to try to describe. Every moment has led us to this place, this moment, that I never dreamed I would have with you. I promise to love, cherish, and protect you all the days of our lives. There has never been another for me, and there won't be another after. You are my world, and I can't wait to start this next chapter with you."

I turn to look at my daughter, and her cheeks are wet and shiny with tears as she fights back the urge to sob.

Smiling, I offer her Julian's ring. "Amberly."

Wiping the tears from her eyes and face, she takes the ring before looking at Julian.

"You said I feel like we haven't known each other all that long, but that's where you're wrong. I may not have met you until recently, but I felt you. I always knew something was missing; something was outside my world, looking in and waiting for me. I'm so glad you found me and came to me that day. You woke up a part of me that was sleeping and gave me the life, reason, and fight I needed to navigate this world and the things coming my way. Without you, I'm not whole. I wasn't full until the day you kissed me. I can't wait to be yours forever and see where the future takes us."

Julian fights to keep his composure, but the tears in his eyes are even more evident now. I couldn't be happier to see the man he has become and to know that my daughter will always have him to look after her.

"The rings," I choke out the words, emotion settling deep inside me.

"With this ring, I pledge my love, commitment, and protection. With this ring, know that my love for you is everlasting," Julian promises as he takes Amberly's hand in his, sliding the ring into place.

As the ring slides home, Amberly releases a small happy sob before grabbing Julian's hand to do the same.

"With this ring, I pledge to be your partner in every part of our life together. I promise to never take for granted every moment we are lucky to share together. You are my other half; with you, there is nothing I can't overcome in this world," she slides the ring on his waiting finger.

"With the rings in place, now you will set the intended mark upon your mate," I announce.

With a smile, Julian takes Amberly's hand. Flipping it over to expose her left wrist, he places a small kiss there. He looks up at her, their eyes lock, and he exposes his teeth. His canines break through, exposing themselves and their intention. He lightly trails them over the sensitive spot on her wrist, never once breaking eye contact. Biting down, his teeth sink through the tender flesh of her bare wrist. Amberly sucks in air between her teeth, making a slight whistling sound as her eyes close to the slight pain. Julian pulls back from her wrist, licking the blood and cleaning the area, allowing it to begin the healing process. Placing a few soft kisses on the spot, he holds her hand as he stands up straight once more.

I nod to Amberly, as now it's her turn for the mark. She smiles lovingly at Julian before moving forward. Pulling the collar of his shirt to the side to expose his neck, she trails a line of kisses along his collarbone before resting just below his left ear. Exposing her canines, she sinks them in, causing Julian to hiss as he closes his eyes and wraps his arms around her. Everyone in the pack, including myself, averts our gaze as the moment becomes intimate in nature.

Pulling away from one another after a few moments, I whisper, "You may now kiss, cementing your bond as mates from now until death do you part."

Chapter 37

Amberly

O ur lips part unwillingly, and as we rest our foreheads together in happiness, cheers and howls sound around us. We laugh deeply together before separating and turning to our audience. Holding hands, we make our way into the crowd as the music changes. Julian swirls me around him before pulling me to his chest.

"May I have this dance?" He asks.

Giggling, I reply, "Yes, you may."

He holds me close as we move around the dance floor. Some join in, as others watch us happily from the sidelines. Julian leans in, hovering his lips on the skin of my neck and causing me to suck in a breath as my eyes close to his touch. He places a kiss on my hot flesh before moving to my ear.

"I can't wait to have you alone, Mrs. Harken," he whispers to me.

I pull away, looking at Julian in his lust-filled eyes, "Julian, wolves have very good hearing."

He chuckles softly, "Like they don't already know our plans for later. After all, it's what's known to happen after the wedding, and it's not like they don't know we've already been together."

"You're hopeless," I smile at him.

"Hopelessly in love."

"Oh my God, you are so cheesy."

"I can't help it; you bring it out in me."

"Then we have a problem."

"What? You can't take my humor for the rest of your life?" he says sarcastically.

"I don't know, you are a bit much to handle," I reply.

"You're one to talk."

He's trying to bait me, but I won't let him. I love our little moments like this, and to know we will have a lifetime of them together makes everything worth it.

* * *

We say our goodnights and head to what was once only Julian's room. Now, it's ours. He opens the door, gesturing me in. The door clicks closed behind us as I have my back to Julian. His fingertips trail down my arms, leaving fire in their wake. I close my eyes, leaning my head back until it rests on his shoulder. His lips find the bare flesh of my neck before he nibbles me lightly, causing a moan to escape my now parted lips.

We've been together before, but for some reason, every touch feels different now, more intense. The heat from his soft touch fills every fiber of my being, my body begging for more. The tips of my fingers and toes begin to tingle before it moves up to my lips. The heat trailing down my center meets his hand as it lifts my dress, sliding underneath to find my center.

Julian's raspy voice sounded in my ear, "You're so warm."

"I need you. Julian," I rasp out.

I hear the smile in his husky voice, "Your wish is my command."

Julian flips me around to face him in one swift motion, grabbing my legs. He lifts them up around his waist, cupping my ass in his hands. Kissing me forcefully, he moves us toward the bed, dropping me down as he stands above me, looking me hard in the eyes as he removes his clothing from his body. His chest rises and falls quicker than I've ever seen before. He stands there unmoving, then slowly runs one hand up my leg at a snail's pace, sending my body arching off the bed.

"Julian," I groan.

"Yes." He whispers.

"Please."

"Tell me," he growls.

"Touch me. I need you to touch me."

He grins devilishly. "But, I am touching you."

My eyes lock with his, both filled with raw desire.

"No. I need you to really touch me. Now!"

I move into a sitting position before grabbing his arm and pulling him on top of me. A moment later, our bodies embrace, every curve perfectly fitting together as pure ecstasy fills my body and my cries of pleasure fill the room.

Chapter 38

Julian

Sleep takes us quickly, and it's mid-day before my eyes part. I glance to my side to see Amberly lying on her stomach, arms tucked under her head, hair a tangled mess all around her. The sheet is draped over her, just high enough to cover her bottom half. I smirk as I listen to her light breathing.

To think, I get to wake up to this every morning. I never thought I could be this lucky or this happy.

Her eyes flutter open, taking in the light as she looks at me through cloudy eyes.

"Good morning, beautiful," I whisper to her.

With a groan, she turns to bury her face in her pillow.

"What time is it?" She grumbles.

"Time to get up, I'm afraid."

She turns her head sideways on her pillow, eyes pleading, "Do I have to?"

I chuckle, "I'm afraid so, sleeping beauty, there's a lot to be done."

"Remind me again?" She smiles.

"Well, for starters, we have a decision we need to make, and then there is training and, I'm sure, many other things. Plus, we have our so-called coronation later today."

She leans up to rest her head on her hand as her elbow sinks into the bed.

"I forgot about that. What exactly are we doing?"

"Aaron will be stepping down as Alpha, and we will take his place as the leaders of the pack. With that…" I drift off in thought.

How should I explain this to her?

"Julian?" she questions my sudden silence.

"Sorry," I shake my head, starting again. "It's a whole thing. I know you still have a lot to learn about being a shifter, but with each Alpha, there is always a new power that they receive from the ritual, and the pack itself becomes stronger from the ceremony as well. Now that it's a joined union, there is no telling what will happen as there is nothing in the history books about the Alpha's being married before the ceremony. So, only time will tell."

Amberly reaches out to take my hand in hers. "Together, we rise. Divided, we fall. This will only be a good thing for the pack and us."

I smile before placing a kiss on the back of her hand and then her forehead. "I have no doubt."

I pull back, still holding her hand in mine, as her mouth opens to speak once more.

"So, what's this important decision we need to make?"

My heart plummets into my stomach, and I release a groan. "Well, we need to decide where we are going to live."

"What do you mean?"

"Someone needs to lead the witches. You are the next in line, and now you are the Alpha here. I know it's not something we need to decide right now, but it's something we need to talk and think about before we decide how to move forward."

Removing her hand from mine, she rolls onto her back, draping her arm across her face and exposing her bare chest to my longing eyes. A growl sounds deep in my chest as I look at her.

"Did you just growl at me?" She mumbles as she removes her arm to look at me. Her expression changes as she realizes how bare she is. "Oh, I'm sorry."

She moves to grab the sheet to cover herself.

I grab it away from her. "Don't you dare," I growl with a grin.

She smiles as I move on top of her, forcing a giggle to leave her lips. "Julian, we still need to talk."

"Later," I reply.

I move my head low, kissing a trail from her mouth down to my targeted destination. I want nothing more than this moment. Nothing else fills my mind but her and my need for her.

Chapter 39

Amberly

"About time you two left your room. We were just about to send someone to pull you from the bed," Troy laughs.

"Not funny." I flush, walking toward the group.

Being outside feels rejuvenating. I know my wolf side has been craving the night air more since the wedding, and she's happy to feel the breeze brushing against our skin. Hearing the little pitter patter of the animals running around the forest is comforting. It lets me know, at least for the moment, things are calm and we are safe.

"Lay off, Troy," Logan says sternly.

"What, I can't play with our little Ly anymore?"

Logan glares at him.

Troy puts his hands up in surrender. "Fine, but really, how's it feel to be married? Our little Ly, married, can't believe it."

Julian wraps his arm around me, pulling me to his side. His warmth becoming my own, spreading down to my toes. Having him close fills me in every way a person needs to be.

"Honestly, it mostly feels the same." My reply comes slowly.

"Really? I would have thought something would have felt different, at least the sex," Troy exclaims.

My cheeks flush as the blood rushes to them at the thought of how primal

I felt last night, this morning, and even now just standing next to Julian. It's like every cell in my body is alive and firing off whenever I'm in his presence. I felt a pull and attraction to him the moment we met, but this is different.

Julian remains quiet as his eyes find mine, and I wonder if he's thinking the same.

"That's not something you ask a lady," Julian states.

"Fine, then what can I ask?"

"Nothing. You can ask nothing." Logan remarks.

"You guys are no fun." Troy pouts.

Everyone turns quiet when Angela walks up to the group. Moving slowly, her eyes smiling as they land on me and Julian. I mentally prepare myself for the next verbal playful attack.

"Hey, guys. Hope you had a fun night." Angela smirks, "But I'm afraid it's time for you and Julian to get ready for the ceremony."

My eyes widen, "Already?"

"Afraid so, time to get the show on the road."

Angela grabs my hand, pulling me out of Julian's embrace. Logan and Angela exchange glances as Julian and I do the same before leaving each other's view. We move slowly deeper into the forest, but still close enough that we aren't too far from the others if we need them. An owl hoots overhead, causing us to look at the trees with a smile. The night is alive with all kinds of sounds and little yellow eyes watching us from the shadows.

Turning toward Angela, I ask, "Is there anything you can tell me about the ceremony to prepare me?"

"Not really. It's just a simple exchange of power from Aaron to you. Some ashes are rubbed on your foreheads, and everyone consumes a magic drink to pass over the leadership and to bring forth your power. Then the pack will drink from the same glass to give them theirs."

"Julian told me that normally, the Alpha isn't married when they do the ceremony."

"That's true. I don't think I recall a time when one was married for the ceremony. Normally, they get married after they are already the leader."

"Do you think that will create a problem?" I ask her.

"I doubt it. If anything, it might be better for the pack. Maybe since there are two of you instead of one, it will make them even stronger."

"I guess we're about to find out."

* * *

Angela places her thumb inside the small round bowl, pushing it down into the ash. When it emerges, it's as black as the night sky. She moves to Aaron first. My father, Julian, and I are all kneeling on the ground with our hands in our laps. The ceremony always takes place in the same area, it's sacred to the pack. Deep inside the cave, there is a hidden spring that feeds water to a small lake. The sky can be seen from an opening high up where the cave wall is gone. Little trees and plants grow around the water's edge, and it's a beautiful sight when the moonlight hits the water, casting the light over the land and trees. The colors are a miraculous mix of blue, green, orange, and red.

Aaron closes his eyes as Angela approaches. "You have served your pack well. Now, it is time to step down and let another lead. May you live out the rest of your days in peace and comfort," she says, bending to reach for him.

She smudges the ash on his forehead in an X. My father's mouth and eyes open, but no sound comes out as his head shoots back and arms spread out wide. Aidan starts to move forward, but Angela puts a hand in the air, stopping him.

After a second, we watch as Angela moves to Julian. He closes his eyes as she draws a line down the center of his forehead with the ash. Just like my father, his mouth and eyes open as his head moves back and arms open wide. I see his eyes shift from yellow to green as my father's shift from blue to green.

Angela then moves to stand before me with a small smile. I close my eyes, and a moment later, I feel her thumb trail a line down my forehead. A warmth washes over me before a weight fills my body, causing me to do the same as my father and Julian before me. I glance at my father to see his eyes shift from green to yellow as my eyes begin to burn slightly. I close them tight, and when the burning stops, I open them to look over at Julian, whose eyes are green.

Julian smiles as he looks me in my eyes. "They're beautiful," He whispers.

I smile at him. "So are yours."

"I wish you could see them."

"Aren't they the same?" I question.

"No. You are the true Alpha. Your eyes glow blue. Mine will be green, as I am your mate."

Angela grabs the cup from the table. "Next, you will drink the elixir."

She moves again to my father first. He drinks from the cup, and his hands connect with the ground with a thud as his body shakes.

"Dad!"

"Amblery, don't move," he growls.

I look from him, to Julian, to Angela, and back again. Angela moves to Julian, and he takes the cup, drinking from it as my father had. Moving to me, she kneels, offering me the cup. I glance around the room, knowing I have to continue because we've already come this far. I stare at my father and Julian, knowing that their pain won't stop until this is over. I take the cup and fill my mouth, allowing the cool contents to run down my throat.

I wait for the pain, but none comes. I open my eyes to look at Angela as she quickly moves into a standing position with a small gasp. Before I can ask what's going on, she smiles, takes a sip from the cup, and then offers it to the next in the pack. As each person drinks, the weight is less and less, but it's replaced with strength and fire in my veins. It's like nothing I've ever felt before. I lift my hand and make a fist, then flex my fingers out, looking at both sides of my outstretched hand and then down my arm, where blue lines begin to run down the length of my arm to my fingertips. With it, I feel an undeniable power.

The last of the pack takes a sip from the cup, and as he swallows, my father and Julian sit up straight once more. A howl sounds through the cave, and it takes me a moment to realize it's coming from me.

146

* * *

"How do you feel?" Julian asks as he offers me a glass of water.

"Strong," I say, smiling before sipping of the water.

Smiling, he looks at Angela, "What do you think?"

"I honestly don't know. I've never heard of anything like that happening before," she replies.

I look back and forth at them, confused. "What are you talking about?"

Angela speaks first, looking at me. "Your eyes glowing blue is a normal part of the process, as is Aaron's turning yellow. But the blue vein-like lines that formed on your arms and then trailed down to your hands. That's not really normal."

I turn to Julian as my heart beats wildly in my chest.

"Don't worry. I don't think it's a cause for alarm. Honestly, I think it's the opposite."

"Meaning?" I question them, worry in my gaze.

"Well, no wolf has ever been part witch or mated with one. I think because you are part witch, it will affect our pack differently."

I look down at my hands, and the blue lines are nowhere to be seen. But the strength I felt is still there, and with it, an increased adrenaline and hunger for one thing. My mate. My gaze returns to him and I know he can see the lust in my eyes as he smirks.

"Soon," he whispers.

Angela smiles.

"So, how do we figure out what power we have from the union and what our pack will have to make them stronger?" I ask.

Angela answers. "It normally takes a few days to manifest. Thankfully, we have some time before we have to worry about the next battle. The change should take hold before then."

"How's my father?"

Angela moves to the side to show Aaron sitting with Aidan and the others. He's in a deep conversation from the looks of things, but a smile is wide across his face. If I'm being honest, he looks younger and lighter somehow.

"He's fine. Like I told you, Amberly, no one was ever in any real danger. This is a normal pack ritual. If anything, everyone is stronger for it."

I nod my head before turning my attention back to Julian. "So…"

He chuckles loudly. "Okay. Okay. Sorry, Angela, but I'm needed elsewhere," they laugh together. "If anyone needs us, you know where we will be."

Heat moves to my cheeks as I grab him by the hand, pulling him down the hall behind me. I hear Angela giggling behind us as we disappear.

Chapter 40

Logan

"Where did they go?" I ask Angela as she joins the rest of the group.

"Oh, you know, honeymoon stuff," she says, smiling.

Aaron and Aidan groan.

In a low, pained voice, Aaron grumbles, "Maybe it's for the best. It's never too early for pups."

Angela slaps him playfully on his chest. "Aaron!"

"What? I'm just being practical. You can't tell me with how much they are going at it that it won't happen soon enough."

"Please, tell me we are not sitting here talking about Amberly's sex life," Troy groans.

"Well, you had no problem doing it," Amara reminds him. "Honestly, I wouldn't be surprised if we didn't see them for a few days." She laughs as Troy looks away with a grimace.

"Ew," he murmurs.

"In other news, how about we get some training in while we wait? I know it couldn't hurt," Angela states.

"Sounds better than sitting here doing what we are doing now," Troy responds, and everyone begins to stand.

As they all walk to the exit, I grab Angela lightly by the wrist, pulling her close. "Just wanted to check in on you. You've been seeming a little on edge the last few days and we haven't had much time to talk."

"I'm fine. Just tired, been burning the candle at both ends lately." She smiles up at me.

"Well, I was hoping we could have a little time to ourselves later. I would love to cook you a nice meal."

"And then maybe some dessert to go with it," she replies, her gaze turning wicked before pulling me in for a deep kiss.

"Well, you'll get no complaints from me," I murmur on her lips.

"I didn't think so." She smiles as she runs off after the others.

It's crazy to think about how much our lives have changed. To think of how simple our lives once were. Part of me would give anything to go back to those days, but an even bigger part of me wouldn't trade what we have found on this new path in our lives for anything. As hard as it's been, and even though our future is uncertain, we've gained something so strong and true. I've watched Amberly become whole. She found what was missing in her life. She's become the warrior I've always known she would, and as for me and Troy, I think we've found our home here. I never thought I would love anyone but Amberly. I always thought it was us in the end. But life has shown me how much what we think is our path really isn't and how we might be meant from something greater than we have planned for ourselves.

Chapter 41

Julian

"I never thought I would say this a day in my life, but girl, you need to slow down. You're going to burn me out." I laugh, out of breath.

"I don't believe that for a second," she replies from her position on my chest.

I run my hand through her hair as she shifts to move her head higher on my chest.

"I love you, Amberly."

"I love you."

"Get some rest," I whisper, kissing the top of her head.

"Hmmm."

A moment later, her breathing becomes heavy, and I know she's out. Today was intense in every way. The last few days have been intense. I don't know where she's been getting her energy from, but I've barely been able to stand. Our marriage ignited something primal inside of her. I saw it in her eyes after we kissed, cementing our bond. Then, the Alpha ceremony only seemed to add to her need. I've never heard of it affecting anyone the way it is her, but I can't complain. Being alone with her and having this time together is something I've craved since the moment we met. She has always been my missing piece; without her I'm half of who I'm meant to be, and I can feel the difference whenever she isn't around.

Listening to her sleep brings me a peace I haven't been able to feel in a while. Here with her, no matter what's coming our way, I just get lost. In her light snore, her intoxicating lavender scent, and the warmth of her skin. Everything about her pulls me in and brings me comfort.

I can't wait for this final battle to be behind us. Our future will finally be ours, and we can create the life I've envisioned for us. I only hope she wants the same things.

Chapter 42

Angela

"Is this normal?" Logan asks me.

I stare at a group of five from our pack. Their hands shift, from human to wolf and back to human. They don't seem to be in control.

"No. It's not," I whisper.

I approach them, kneeling to look closer. "What's going on?"

"We don't know," Sara replies. "It just started happening."

I look back at Logan. "Go get Aaron."

He nods and disappears.

"It's okay. We'll figure this out," I say reassuringly.

Sara closes her eyes, and when they open again, they are glowing blue, just like Amberly's. She closes them again, and when they open once more, they are her normal yellow glow.

"What's happening to us?" She asks, fear evident in her voice.

"I don't know," I shake my head in disbelief.

Sara turns to John, standing across the room, and reaches for him. It happens so fast; if I had blinked, I would have missed it. John was about six feet away, and now he was sitting right next to Sara, holding her hand.

"Sara, what did you do?" I ask.

"I...I don't know. I wanted John next to me," she looks up at John, terrified. "And then he was," she mutters.

"Oh. My. God." I jump up and make a beeline for Aaron while screaming over my shoulder at the group, "Don't panic, everything is fine. I know what this is."

"Care to share it with the class?" John yells after me.

But I can't stop. I keep running. I need to tell Aaron what's happening before it hits the rest of the pack.

* * *

"Aaron! I figured out the pack's new power," I say, winded, coming to a halt when I get to him, Aidan, and Logan. I kneel forward, holding myself up with my hands on my knees to catch my breath.

"I'm all ears," Aaron replies.

I stand straight again. "They somehow became part witch," I spit out.

Everyone's eyes widen.

Logan is the first to speak.

"How is that even possible?"

"Well, since the Alpha is part witch and she's married, it creates a stronger union and Alpha connection," I gulp down air, my breathing slowly returning to normal. "I guess she was able to transfer that part of herself to everyone else."

"Wait, does that mean she's not a witch anymore?" Logan's expression turns to worry.

"No, she's still a witch and still has all the powers she did before. It's just the pack can access that for themselves now. The only issue is no one knows how to control it. That's why I sent Logan to find you. We need to warn them about this change and start teaching them how to control it before it gets out of control."

Aaron nods. "Angela's right. Logan, can you and Troy help me let the pack know what's going on?"

"What about Amberly? Shouldn't we tell her? She might want to help,"

Logan asks.

"I think we should leave them be," I say, shaking my head. "The group of us can handle this. Let's gather everyone outside the cave and tell them all at once, and then we can break into groups and try the simple spells first."

"Sounds like a plan," Aaron remarks.

Everyone separates, going in different directions to search for the pack members.

Chapter 43

Sage

E very muscle is stiff. I feel the ache down to my bones. I twist and turn, trying to loosen up my body.

God only knows how long I've been in this shithole.

I notice four other bodies on the ground next to me as they stir.

"I knew you would be the first to wake."

I glance up to find Annabeth and Henry walking in my direction.

"How long was I in there?" I question.

Waving her hand dismissively, Annabeth replies, "Honestly, lost track."

"How long?" I growl through my teeth.

Unaffected by my tone, Annabeth shrugs her shoulders. "I would say about a month."

My face twists with rage. "How dare he put me in there with them," I nudge my head toward the other bodies, "and for that long."

Annabeth moves next to me. "Vladimir didn't always make the best choices, but he did the best he could with what he was given."

I turn on her, my tone filled with hate. "Do you agree with what he did?" I spit the words in her direction.

"I don't agree with the reason he did it, but I feel it was smart to let you rest and rebuild your energy. You're going to need it," she says to me.

I push down my annoyance, looking around the room once more.

"So, where is he?" I ask.

Annabeth and Henry look to each other before turning back to me.

Henry clears his throat. "He's gone."

"And what's that supposed to mean?"

Annabeth whispers, "He's dead."

A mix of surprise and excitement fills my chest.

"Who did him in?" I ask.

Henry answers. "Amberly and Aidan."

My head snaps back toward them, sure I heard wrong.

"Aidan?"

Annabeth places her hand on my shoulder. I stare at it in distaste, and it takes everything in me not to remove it from my body.

"He's joined them," she says with a serious face.

I shake my head, sending her hand off of my shoulder. "No. You're wrong."

"I wish we were."

I stand and take a few slow steps deeper into the room. "When did this happen?"

"The night after Vladimir put you to sleep," Henry responds.

I try to make sense of what I'm hearing. Aidan would never have walked away from his family. He and I may not have become what I had craved for years, but we shared something. He thought of Vladimir as his father. He wouldn't leave that all behind for her.

Facing them, I see that their faces are barely noticeable in the dim light.

"It's her. She did this." The words come out with a growl as I clench my fists in anger.

"We couldn't agree with you more," Henry mutters.

Annabeth takes a step toward me, into the line of light streaming into the room, causing her face to shine bright in the darkness.

"He has been tricked by her wickedness and lies, and if anyone can bring him back to our side and make him come back to the fold, it's you," she says with determination in her voice.

"Me."

"Yes. You think the way you looked at him went unseen? The late nights you two shared on many occasions didn't go unnoticed," she says with a slight smile.

"I…" I stutter, the words lost on my tongue.

"You are our goldenrod," Annabeth says, standing tall before me. "Without you, we will lose this battle. You need to bring him back to our side, for I fear without him, we will lose many in this coming battle."

"You've got the wrong girl. Aidan doesn't give a shit about me, he doesn't care for any woman here," I spit out, shaking my head.

They share a look.

"What?"

"If he let her in, then his walls are crumbling. And you are the only one here he spent more than one night with. If anyone can get through the cracks in his armor, it's you," Henry says quietly.

I give him a questioning look. "And what if you're wrong?"

Their eyes shine in the darkness, and I know I'm not going to like the answer they're about to give me.

"Then he will die with the rest of them," Annabeth states.

I've never been one for feelings or emotions, and I've never cared for many people other than myself. Love and relationships are only a weakness. Yet, somehow, Aidan found his way in. He's the only person I grew up with that I actually give a damn about, and I have no doubt that when the moment comes, I will do anything to keep him safe.

He may not feel the same way about me, but if there is one person on this earth I would die for, it's him.

I watch Annabeth and Henry move across the room to bend over the other four bodies on the cool ground. They begin speaking in low voices to each other, but not quietly enough that I can't hear them.

"What if she can't get to him?" Henry whispers.

"Then he will die, like I said," Annabeth answers.

"Do you really think we can take him down?"

"I have watched him all these years. I know how his powers work, and I know from his body movements which attack he will be using before he does. If he does not come back to us, then he will die by my hand."

"Are you really prepared to kill our own blood?"

She looks at him for the first time. "He isn't our blood. She was not our daughter. Our daughter died the moment she mated with that mutt."

For the first time, I feel pity for the enemy.

Henry turns his attention back to the bodies as they begin to stir.

"It's almost time," he whispers.

"We will take the next few weeks to train them and wait for the demons, other witches, warlocks, and shifters to get here, and then we will take the final battle to them," she declares, her attention still on the bodies around them. "This time we will not lose."

I find myself questioning who the real threat is. Was Vladimir ever really in control, or was Annabeth pulling the strings and calling the shots all along without any of us knowing?

Henry turns to me. "You must go to their home. Find Aidan and bring him home."

I nod before turning my back on them. I know that what they're planning won't work. If Aidan left of his own volition, he will not return here, least of all for me. She got her hooks in him, and I fear there is no bringing him back from that. I've never had a family, so I don't know what it would be like to find someone who shares the same blood as me. I would like to say it wouldn't matter, that my path would stay the same. But how do I really know? All this time, I believed Vladimir. Believed he was right and that his way was right. That killing and the reasons behind it were right. But what if he was wrong? What if I've been following the wrong path all along? Vladimir lied to Aidan his whole life, so how do the rest of us know what the truth is? I can't be blind to it anymore.

I take the first steps on my journey and all these questions fill my mind. I have a huge decision to make and little time to do it. The only thing I know for sure is Amberly is my enemy, and I have no choice but to kill her. I just hope Aidan doesn't get in my way.

Chapter 44

One week later

Troy

Walking back to the cave, my legs feel like jello. Training today was brutal, but everyone is taking it very seriously, as we should be. We each had a section around the cave to practice with the group we were assigned. Thankfully I was placed with Amara, so at least I knew one person.

The training has been every day, twice a day, for the past week. For me, it was more hand to hand or hand to sword training since I've already mastered most magic attacks and defense. I helped Amara learn how to use the new powers coursing through her and she helped me with hands on stuff.

Watching the group shift into wolves was definitely a sight I won't soon forget. Amara was a beautiful white and grey mix, her strength easily noticeable under her fur coat.

Amara walks up next to me, causing me to stand up straight. I don't want to appear weak in her eyes, but the earth floor isn't easy to walk, especially with all the tree debris covering its surface.

"This last week feels like it flew by," Amara mutters.

"It's been a long one, that's for sure. I'm honestly happy it's over."

With a smile, Amara takes my hand in hers. "Me too. I was hoping maybe tonight we could do something together."

My heart flutters at her touch, something I never expected. I hoped she had felt the connection I was beginning to but I didn't want to push anything. Now with the roles reversed my fear isn't as high.

"I know the group is having a bonfire tonight," I say as our fingers twine together.

"That sounds fun, but I kind of wanted some alone time with you," she responds, her cheeks reddening with her words.

My heart skips as my body warms. "Oh. Umm, sure. What did you have in mind?"

"Maybe we can take a walk together and then come back for the bonfire," Amara offers.

"That works. I promised Logan and Amberly I would help them get the journals from Johnathan and organize them. I'm not sure how long that will take, but once I finish, I'll come find you."

"Okay. I'll see you soon," she whispers, placing a kiss on my cheek.

I make my way to join Logan and Amberly, thinking about Amara and how close we have become over the last few weeks. I hope tonight we can talk more about ourselves and I can tell her how I've been feeling. I never expected to come here and find someone I connected with or would come to care for. Let alone a wolf. But I did. I care about Amara like I never would have imagined.

"There you are." I look up to see Logan approaching me. "I was just about to come find you. Amberly is already with Julian at John's place."

"Calling him John now are we?" I tease.

"Well, it is a version of his name," Logan shrugs. "He said he didn't mind."

I slap him on his shoulder. "Okay, then. Let's get to it. I have plans to get to."

We walk off as Logan asks with a smirk, "And what might those be?"

"Wouldn't you like to know?"

We walk the rest of the way in silence as voices meet us in the hall from the ajar door.

"How many of those journals are there again?" Amberly asks.

"Seven," Johnathan replies.

"Well, that's not too bad. Shouldn't take too long to get through," she states.

"There may only be seven, but reading them will take some time, I'm afraid," Johnathan remarks, running his hand through his hair.

Logan moves to stand next to Amberly. "I can take a few and make some notes or mark pages that might be of interest or help."

Smiling, I add, "Yeah, we can bend the edges over on ones we think might be worth reading and then on ones we know will be important, we can tuck a little piece of paper hanging out of the page."

Amberly grins, "Just like we used to do for each other when we would study back at home."

I nod, my smilt growing wider.

Logan smirks, "It's definitely a time saver. This way, it won't all be on one person to read through them and make sense of it all."

"I don't know what I would do without you guys," Amberly says, taking our hands. "I'm so glad you are here with me."

I squeeze her hand, "There is nowhere else we would rather be."

Logan takes his hand from hers, grabbing a few of the journals from the stack before turning to me. "So Amberly you take three, and we will handle the other four."

Amberly grabs four from the stack, turning to us. "I should take four since this is my workload," she says as she laughs.

"Are you sure?" I ask.

"Yes. I appreciate you both being willing to help me get through them and helping me find the most important parts. I don't want you doing more work than you need to. You both have lives, too."

Logan hands me the three in his hands and grabs the last three off the table. "Well, let's get started."

Chapter 45

Amberly

I return to the room to find Julian waiting. He grabs the four thick journals from my hands, placing them on the nightstand next to the bed before turning his attention back to me.

"Looks like we are in for some late-night reading," he smiles.

"Logan and Troy offered to take more, but I didn't feel right making them go through more than me," I reply.

"I understand," he says, nodding. He claps his hands together. "Well, let's get started. I'll go grab some refreshments from the kitchen and be right back."

Julian bends down, kissing me on the forehead before heading out the door. To think I get to spend the rest of my life with a man who makes my heart beat fast with a simple glance still gives me butterflies. I smile to myself, thinking about how he has become the best version of himself. Sweet, passionate, loving, protective and my best friend. I couldn't have asked for more.

I just wish my mother had been here to see our wedding and see how happy I am.

I will defeat this final threat and fulfill my destiny. I will bring peace to our world and make sure we live out the rest of our days together.

I forcefully flip open the first journal. The motion sends the dust from the pages into the air around me, and I suppress a sneeze.

I scan the pages, searching for any keywords that could be important to us. Julian re-enters the room somewhere between the first ten to fifteen pages, but I'm in my zone. Placing sustenance next to me, he kisses me on the forehead before picking up a book himself.

We scan the books for the next two hours until Julian jumps up, moving to my side.

"I think I found something."

Chapter 46

Troy

I finish marking the last page I think may be of some importance before throwing my shoes on and heading outside. I find Amara talking to a group of women as the men place more wood near where the bonfire will be. As I approach the group, Amara's head tilts back as she laughs with open abandon.

"Dare I ask what's so funny?" I question with a smile as I reach her side.

Her eyes are watery as she looks at me, trying to push down her laughter. "We were just talking about something that happened at training today. Now that the pack has powers, it's made for some comedic moments, that's for sure."

"Magic does have a way of doing that," I say, tilting my head toward her. "But I'm still a bit confused on how this is all possible."

Amara lifts her shoulders in a shrug. "With Amberly taking her place as Alpha, and Julian and her being married, it created a stronger bond. I believe that's what allowed Amberly's magic to be shared with the pack. Although, she is the first of her kind, so maybe it would have happened regardless. Either way, it's good for us. Gives us an upper hand for the next battle and believe me, we are going to need it."

Nodding my head, I run my hand down the length of her arm to her hand as I move in closer to whisper. "Do you think we can go for that walk now?

I would really love to talk to you alone for a moment."

The twinkle in her eyes grows as she turns to the group, telling them she will see them later. Moving with me, we take our first steps out of ear shot.

"What's on your mind?" She asks calmly.

"With everything going, on we haven't had a second to talk about what happened," I say to her.

"You mean the kiss?" She asks quietly.

I slow my stride before answering. "Yes. I mean I wanted to kiss you but I kept thinking about everything you went through and didn't want to push anything. I also didn't know how you felt toward me. But then you kissed me, and just shrugged it off. I may not know where you stand but I want to make my intentions clear."

Amara remains quiet as she watches me with uncertainty.

We stop walking and I turn to face her, ready to reveal how I'm feeling.

"After this whole thing is behind us I would like to get to know you more. I want to take you on a proper date and I want to show you my home. I know I can be hard to read since I goof off most of the time, but I wanted you to know that I feel a pull toward you. A connection I can't explain, and I would very much like to dig deeper and see what we have here. If you are willing."

Amara closes the distance between us, putting her arms around my neck and moving closer until our bodies are touching.

"I would love to do all of that with you. It's a date." Touching my lips with hers, she kisses me lightly before pulling away. "And just so you know, the feeling is mutual."

Removing her arms from my neck, she takes me by the hand and smiles as we make our way back toward camp. "Now let's go make some s'mores."

Chapter 47

Amberly

"How are things going?" My father asks as he reaches my side. Sitting in the middle of the field right outside the cave opening, I look up at my father.

I sigh deeply before responding. "They're going. Julian and Troy found some important information in the journals that I hope will help. I still have a lot I need to read over."

He looks me hard in the eyes. "That's not what I was asking."

"Then I think I need you to be a little specific here, Dad." I answer with a laugh. "A lot has happened these last few days, so I'm not too sure which thing you are referencing."

A pain spreads through my chest at the thought of what is missing. I haven't truly given myself time to mourn, and who knows when I will be able to properly do so.

"That's my point. How are you holding up with everything?" He asks before taking a seat on the ground next to me.

"Honestly, pretty good considering the elephant on my chest," I say as he peers at me knowingly.

"How are you doing?" I ask, trying to change the subject. "I know the shift down from Alpha couldn't have been easy, and then with Mom…" I trail off.

He places his hand on my shoulder. "Don't you worry about me."

Rolling my eyes he removes his hand from my shoulder. I draw in a deep breath, moving my fingers through the earth where they lay.

"So, you can be concerned about me but I can't be about you? How does that work?" I chuckle.

"As a parent it's your job. We do everything we do to protect our pups, something you will see for yourself soon enough, I'm sure," he says, and the love in his eyes warms my heart.

He stands with a smile before walking back to the cave, leaving me alone with my thoughts and the heaviness of his last words. Being a parent is both a blessing and a curse. I can't imagine all the things my parents had to give up and go through once we came along. For my mother, she sacrificed everything. Her freedom, never leaving our village, even her very life. For my father it wasn't much different, I suppose. Losing the love of his life and his child would leave a hole in your heart that wasn't so easily filled or healed. Now that he's in our lives, I feel like he is trying too hard to make up for the time he missed, even though it wasn't of his own making. I couldn't imagine what it was like for either of them, both walking their lonely road alone. And I pray I never have to.

Chapter 48

Logan

The red and blue of the bonfire dance together as the night air warms around us. I watch the flames as they bounce higher before breaking away and disappearing. Voices from the group are drowned out by the crackling of the fire and the howls of the forest. Being here in this place, surrounded by friends and family, is the most peace I've felt in weeks.

"Hey, you." Angela appears, moving to my side and grabbing me by the hand.

"Hey," I respond softly.

Giving my hand a light squeeze, she smiles. "I missed you. Feels like I haven't seen you in forever."

"I know what you mean," I say, still staring into the flames. "Feels like this is the first time I've been able to sit in peace and not have something crazy happen to go running to." Removing my attention from the flames, I turn to look at Angela, who looks like the world is on her shoulders.

Bags of darkness take up residence under her eyes, telling me she hasn't been sleeping well. Her shoulders hang low, and her eyes are glazed over, adding to my concern that something is bothering her.

"Angela, what's wrong?" I ask, concern filling my words.

She looks at me, and the fake smile spreads further across her face.

"Nothing."

My facial expression shows that I know otherwise. Closing her eyes, she takes in a deep breath before opening them again and looking my way.

"I haven't been sleeping well," she rasps.

"Your eyes give that away. What's been going on?"

Her eyes dart around us, checking if anyone is in range to overhear us before she leans in closer to me. "I've been having these nightmares about the battle, and I can't shake them," she whispers.

"Do you think it could just be your mind playing with you?" I ask hesitantly.

Sadness fills her eyes. "I honestly don't know. I usually deal with stress very well."

"But this is different," I point out.

She stares at me, confused.

I offer a reassuring smile. "I know you've been through your fair share of crap, and I'm not downplaying any of it when I say it's nothing like your life has been the last few months. Before, it was one thing here and there with a break in between, but now..."

She turns back to the fire as her shoulders relax slightly. "Now it's constant. Never-ending."

"I think it's caused your mind to deal with the stress when you sleep because you can't put up a block like you can when you're awake," I say, reaching for her.

Leaning her head on my shoulder, she releases a long sigh. "That makes complete sense. I can't believe I didn't put that together myself."

With a slight chuckle, I respond, "You can't win every time."

"I can sure try," she jokes, looking up at me with a small smile. A real smile.

I look up again to see Amberly, Julian, and Aidan approach us.

"Hey, guys. Beautiful night, isn't it?" Amberly breaks up our conversation.

"We were just talking about that," I reply, happy to change the subject.

I hate that everything is taking this kind of toll on Angela, and I wish I could do something more for her. Other than being here for her to listen and help take her mind off it, there is nothing much else I can do. I'll be happy once this final battle is behind all of us, and we can finally begin living again.

Angela stands up straight, addressing Amberly. "Did your father find you earlier?"

Amberly's face fills with worry.

"It's nothing bad. It's actually a good thing for us," Angela jumps in. "Most of the pack has figured out how to use their new powers. I know you guys have been a little MIA this last week, but I'm sure you heard that we all now have powers of our own."

Everyone glances at me before turning their attention back to Angela.

"It happened the other day. Logan, Troy, and I have been training them on how to use the powers. It was rather funny to watch. Thank goodness no one was really hurt during the whole thing. The good news is that with this, we now stand a chance. Considering that most of their fighters had powers, it was hard for us to stand up against them before. But now, we have something to fight back with."

Amberly's face lights up. "And they don't know about it. We can use this to our advantage." Her eyes connect with Angela's. "I'm sorry I wasn't there to help with the training. Someone should have come and gotten me."

"Aaron didn't want us to." The words come out before I can stop them.

She looks at me, and her expression becomes confused. "Why not?"

"Well…" I turn to Angela in retreat.

Angela smiles before addressing Amberly. "Apparently, your father wants some pups."

Amberly's eyes widen before looking at Julian and everyone else. As her gaze moves to the ground, her cheeks turn red. Here is the start of a beautiful night.

Chapter 49

Julian

"Those were some good s'mores Logan and Troy made tonight," I say to Amberly as we make it back to our room after leaving the bonfire.

She smiles as she takes off her jacket, discarding it on the bed. I watch her quietly, noticing a shift in her energy. She stands with her back toward me, shoulders tense, as she moves to the edge of the bed and slowly sits. I step forward as she bends over to unzip one of her black, ankle-high boots. As she reaches for the other, I listen closely, hearing that her heartbeat has changed. I don't say a word as I sit next to her on the bed, moving her hair away from her face. I find her cheeks wet. Then, her shoulders shake lightly as she tries to silence the sobs that so desperately want to escape.

I don't need to ask her what's wrong. I grab her around the shoulders, pulling her to my chest. Laying my cheek on top of her head, I squeeze her lightly.

"Shhh. It's okay, little wolf. I'm here," I murmur as I hold her tightly.

Some time may have passed since we buried our dead, and Amberly said goodbye to her mother, but the loss is still fresh. I have no doubt that her mother crosses her mind on nights like tonight. Whether it's simply wishing she was here to join us or thinking about how she would be enjoying herself. This type of wound takes years to heal, not weeks. As her body convulses in my arms and she releases her cries, I wish I could take this from her. But I can't. All I can do is be there for her. Be her mate.

Her body relaxes as her sobs grow quiet, and I know she is calming down, at least for now.

"I'm going to run to the kitchen and get us something to drink and eat. This way, we won't have to leave the room for the rest of the night. We can just lay here, be together and talk," I gently tell her.

Amberly pulls away slowly, wiping her tear-stained cheeks before nodding at me.

I brush the last stray strand of hair away from her wet cheek. "I'll be right back."

* * *

I fill a plate with all of Amberly's favorites before placing it on the tray. As I turn to leave with the tray in my hands, I notice someone entering the room.

"Hey, Julian. You have a second?" Angela asks as she walks in, stopping to stand next to me.

"Sure," I respond. "I was just grabbing some food for Amberly and I for the night."

Smiling, Angela grabs an orange juice from the small fridge and turns to face me. "I didn't want to say anything in front of the others."

I turn my full attention to her as she takes a deep breath.

"We don't have much time left before they arrive on our doorstep." She pauses to take another deep breath. "I've been having these dreams, and last night I saw someone."

"Just one person? Who?" My voice is tinged with worry.

"I'm not sure who it was. It was a girl, and she was definitely sent by them, but that's all I know. But Julian, it's what I felt that's the problem."

I place the tray back on the counter, trying to keep calm.

"She means business," Angela sighs. "I felt death all around her, and I know

173

her intentions."

I remain quiet.

"She's coming to take Aidan back and to kill Amberly." Her voice is solemn.

My breath catches in my throat. "It doesn't matter because now we have the advantage. You can warn the others, and we can take shifts guarding the entrance. She won't get anywhere near either of them."

"I don't know if it's that simple. I don't know how these dreams work."

"I'm not bothering Amberly with this, not tonight. For now, just set up a schedule for people to be on alert, and I'll do the same. Let Aidan know so he's aware, and we will deal with this in the morning." I grab the tray and begin to head back to the room.

"I don't know if we will have until tomorrow," I hear Angela murmur as I walk away.

* * *

I refuse to let whoever this person is come into our home and hurt anyone else. Entering our room, Amberly is nowhere to be seen. I place the tray down harder than intended as I look around frantically.

"Amberly?"

"In here," I hear her call from the bathroom.

I move closer, hearing the water running, as my heart calms.

"I got you a little of everything," I call to her. "I'll place the cold stuff in the fridge and be right in."

My mind races as I think of all the ways I can take precautions against this person coming for my mate. I have to calm myself down before she senses something is amiss. She has enough on her mind, and I refuse to add to it. It can wait until morning.

Warm, wet arms wrap around my middle. Water seeps through my shirt, touching my warm body and causing me to shiver involuntarily. I place my hands on hers as she hugs me from behind, her face moving against my back.

I turn around slowly, searching for her eyes. She looks up at me, and I take her wet face in my hands before placing a soft and loving kiss on her lips. Her arms pull me closer until her wet, naked form is resting flush against me. She deepens our kiss as a low groan escapes between her parted lips. Her wolf is calling to mine, and the need must be addressed.

I lift her in my arms in one swift moment, continuing our kiss, as I return us to the fog-filled bathroom.

Chapter 50

Aidan

Being here with Amberly has changed so much of who I am. Before, I never felt the need for affection. Other than wanting Vladimir's approval, I didn't care what anyone else thought or felt toward me. Women mattered even less. I would use them for what I needed, and that was that. Now, things are different. Seeing Amberly happy with Julian awakened that part of me, but it's not just her. Seeing how she completes him, how he yearns to be near her, how they complete one another — making each other stronger for having the other — it's now something I want more than air.

Despite my change, everyone here knows what I've done. They know of my past, and those who understand or care to give me another chance are already happily paired off. The chances of me connecting with anyone here are very unlikely. Right now, I'll focus on this battle, getting us all out alive. And then I'll have the hard conversation. As much as being with my sister is everything I've ever wanted, seeing her happy has created this hole in my heart that I now need to fill for myself, and I know I can't do it here as much as I wish I were wrong. Leaving her, especially now, is going to be hard. But if I have any chance at my own pure happiness and growth as an honest and caring human being, then I need to go.

"You look lost in thought. Anything you want to talk about?" Amara asks as she appears from the shadows.

"Just thinking," I respond.

She giggles as she moves closer. "Yeah, I think we've established that," she says, sitting closer than expected. "What about?" she asks, looking at me.

I look into the dark forest. "I was thinking about life after this war."

Her gaze follows my own. "I think we all are. We won't know what to do with ourselves once this is behind us."

"I do," I whisper.

Her attention turns back to me. "Care to share with the rest of the class?"

She's wearing a smile when I look back to her. "I think it will be time for me to leave."

My words cause her to flinch. "Leave? Why?"

"I need a fresh start. Everyone here, as nice as they have been…this isn't the place for me," I respond, and I'm sure she can hear the sadness in my voice. I look back to the forest to avoid her gaze. "They may act okay around me, but really, they only tolerate me because of who I am to their Alpha. I can't make a real life or future for myself here."

Looking back into the night, she nods. "I can appreciate what you're saying. Have you talked to Amberly about this yet?"

I shake my head.

"I see. Hence the deep thought."

I nod.

"Well, it's not going to be an easy conversation. You both just lost your mother, and you only just found each other. Like you said, let's get through this fight, and when we come out on top, give it a little time. Allow us all a moment to breathe and then have the conversation with her."

"That's the plan," I say, still staring ahead.

"I wish you would stay, though, for what it's worth."

Surprised, I remain silent.

"What? Hey, that trip to find your Dad? It did a lot for our relationship," she smiles. "I got to know the real Aidan, and I can say there is a lot more to you than you let on. You're a good guy, whether you want to own that or not. Who cares what everyone else says? They will get to know you like I did, and then they will feel like the fools." She nudges me with her shoulder, but it doesn't help the sadness inside me.

"I just want to feel wanted, needed," I say in a pained whisper.

"You are."

Amberly comes to my mind.

"I know, but I want more than that. Being needed as a brother is great, but I want what you all have."

I see the shift in her eyes before she speaks.

"Oh, I see." Turning her attention back toward the night, she lowers her head. "We all want and deserve someone to share our lives with, and I have no doubt you will find that person. Just give it time. We are still so young. Amberly and Julian, they got lucky."

"And you and Troy?" I ask hesitantly.

I can see her cheeks redden even in the darkness. "I like him a lot, but who knows what the future holds. It's still new. I'm only saying give it time. Just because we have paired off doesn't mean it will last. Things change as quickly as the breeze. You have many years ahead of you, and I have no doubt you will have many girls catching your eye before you settle into the right one for you."

A branch breaks behind us, causing us to turn in the direction of the noise.

"There you are. I've been looking for you," Amberly says, winded.

I jump up, quickly moving to her side. "What's wrong?"

"Nothing, just want a moment of your time," she answers.

Amara shifts, looking up at me while placing her hand on my shoulder. "I'll catch you later. Just think about what we talked about."

I nod.

I watch as Amara disappears into the darkness, heading back to a place I wish I could see as my home.

"What were you two talking about?" Amberly asks. "Did I interrupt something?"

I turn back to my sister with a smile. "No, not at all."

Amberly looks to where Amara disappeared, and I see the wheels turning.

"Is everything okay?" I ask.

Looking at me, she smiles. "Yes, I was only thinking."

"About?"

"You and Amara," she whispers in a shy tone.

I try to hide my shock at her words, but her giggle lets me know I failed miserably.

"Come on. Anyone who has eyes and is paying attention can see it. We may have only known each other a short while, but we are twins, so even if it wasn't obvious, I would feel it," she says playfully.

My mind goes blank as I try to think of something to say to change the subject. I mean, Amara? Yes, she's nice and beyond beautiful, but she and I could never happen. Even if it were something I could be interested in pursuing, I wouldn't. The things I put her through; we could never put something like that behind us, not enough to have a real relationship bloom from the ashes. Plus, a woman like that deserves the best. Is that Troy? I'd say probably not, but that's not for me to decide.

"Am I wrong?" she asks after my lack of response.

"It doesn't matter because I would never go there with her."

"Why not?"

"You weren't there, Amberly. I'm so grateful you never got to see me at my darkest. You would look at me differently." I sigh, taking a second for the words to form. "But Amara got to witness it first hand. I did unforgivable things to her. The fact that she even speaks to me is a blessing."

"I don't think you're giving her enough credit," she says, taking a step toward the cave. "I saw the way you watched her as she left. But as a woman, I also saw something you missed."

I remain silent, standing to follow her back to the cave.

"I know she and Troy have gotten close, but I think she has feelings for someone else," she continues.

My stomach tightens.

"I think she's having a hard time figuring out her feelings."

I open my mouth, and as much as I feel this door needs to remain closed, I'm ready to talk about this. But the words get lost in my throat. My eyes see the silver flash as it passes in front of my face, not giving me enough time to react before it sinks into the flesh of my sister's back. The hilt of the dagger rests just below her right shoulder blade.

My eyes widen in shock as her scream of pain rings in my ears, and she falls to the dirt. Her howl of agony echoes through the forest. I move to her side, looking around the green darkness surrounding us.

Placing my hand around the hilt, I whisper, "Hold still," before yanking it free.

Amberly hunches forward, cradling her shoulder. "Where did that come from?" She asks in a rigid and shaky tone.

"I don't know." My eyes scan the darkness once again. "Come on, get up. I need to get you back to the cave."

Moving my arms under her armpits, I lift her up easily, placing my body in front of hers like a shield from any more danger that dares to emerge from the forest depths, and we continue to move toward the cave.

Suddenly, my left arm pops from its socket when Amberly is yanked from my arms and thrown into the nearest tree with a sickening crunch.

"Amberly!"

She doesn't respond as I run to her side, but I'm cut short by a woman with fire for hair. Shaking her head lightly, it moves to reveal her face. My breath gets caught in my throat. I stare at her, gasping for air.

"Impossible," I whisper. "I thought you were dead."

Smiling smugly, she stands up straight. "You can't get rid of me that easily."

A million thoughts occupy my mind before the words leave my mouth. "I never wanted to get rid of you."

"Could have fooled me," she retorts with a scowl, glancing over her shoulder in Amberly's direction. "Once I rid you of this distraction, you will see clearly again."

A growl forms deep in my chest. "That's where you're wrong. She wasn't the distraction. She is what cleared the cobwebs from my mind and showed me where I was truly meant to be. If you let me, I can help you."

Her grin widens in a threatening way as she laughs. "Help me? With what?"

"Sage, they have everyone brainwashed," I say with desperation seeping from my words. "The future they offer isn't a life for anyone. They only offer us darkness or death. But here…" I gesture toward Amberly and the cave. "Here, we stand a chance at a good life. I know you want the same things I do. If you didn't, you wouldn't have tried so hard with me."

Pain and hurt spread across her face but disappears a moment later. "You think we need these people for us to be together? We don't. It doesn't matter what side we're on."

"Sage, you're not listening to me," I plead. "We can't truly have something pure and good with anyone if we are with them. It would never last. Don't you want someone who understands you and wants you for you? Don't you want to build a family with someone?"

Her resolve shifts, her stance changing slightly as her shoulders lower. The shine in her eyes grows slightly as her gaze shifts between me and Amberly.

"She won't let me live. It's me or her," she says with a snarl, her desperation evident. "And I choose me."

"You don't know her! She isn't like the people we have been around our whole lives. No one here is!" I yell at her, trying to break through.

Shaking her head savagely, her stance returns to one ready for a fight.

Her eyes connect with mine as she whispers, "I'm sorry, but I can't take that chance. And I have my orders."

Her hand lifts before I can prepare myself for any sort of defense, and I'm sailing through the air at an alarming speed. I throw my hands in front of my face just in time to lessen the blow to my head. I collide with the huge stone formation with a thud. My head spins as white dots form behind my eyes.

My hands sink into the dirt as I try to move into a standing position, failing miserably. Sage leans down, resting her elbows on her knees to look at me on level ground.

"I have to bring you back with me. If I don't, she's going to kill you. I can't let that happen." Glancing over her shoulder to where Amberly lies motionless only ten feet away, she continues. "And I need to eliminate the threat."

"No," I plead.

I strain again, trying to stand but my head spins before falling back to the ground once more.

"Amberly! Aidan!"

I hear Julian before I see him, and he's not alone. Logan and Troy flank him, looking around the dark frantically. Sage lowers herself to the ground before she can be spotted.

Her eyes connect with mine, full of determination and defeat. She knows she can't take them all on by herself.

"I will be back. The rest aren't far behind me. This war is on your doorstep. Choose the right side, Aidan. Before it's too late." Her last words come out as a plea.

The sound of my name is still on her lips when she disappears from sight. My throat is dry as I stare at my sister, praying she is alright.

Chapter 51

Julian

"What the hell happened?" I ask an almost unconscious Aidan, lifting him from the ground. His body leans into mine as I pull him up.

"It was Sage," he spits out. "I don't know how she's still alive. She took us by surprise."

"She better pray that Amberly is alright," I growl.

I tighten my hold on Aidan as we push forward and enter the cave.

"She said the war is on our doorstep. I don't know how long we have before they get here," Aidan says, his voice straining on every word.

Before I can reply, Angela reaches our side with a light in her hands.

Running the light across Aidan's eyes, she asks, "How is your vision? Any nausea?"

"My vision is in and out. Head hurts like a bitch, and nausea doesn't even begin to cover it."

"Julian, take him to the wing. I'll be there as soon as I finish with Amberly." She looks to Aidan. "And don't fall asleep."

Amara runs up to us, looking Aidan over as her expression fills with pure concern. "I'll sit with him," she declares as she wraps an arm around him, lifting one arm over her shoulders.

Logan appears and takes his other arm over his shoulder, and I watch as they carry Aidan from the room. I turn to follow Angela to where Amberly was taken.

I feel her pain before my eyes can even locate her in the well-lit room. Her head jerks from side to side, face twisting in agony as beads of sweat trickle down her face and neck.

Moving into a kneeling position next to her bed, I smooth back the hair from her moist forehead before addressing Angela.

"I don't understand. Why is she in so much pain?" I ask, nearly yelling as rage begins to take me over.

Angela goes to work on Amberly's shoulder, barely glancing at me as she answers. "I honestly don't know. The knife missed everything of real importance. The good news is she's beginning to heal. By morning, there will only be a scar."

Amberly squeezes my hand as Angela applies more pressure to the wound. Angela places my other hand on the wound to hold the pressure and turns away, moving across the room to the far wall that's lined with ceiling-high dressers. Each one offers an array of different sized drawers, housing different medical items. Labels mark each drawer to make it easier to find whatever it is you're searching for.

My eyes follow Angela as she removes the items needed to stitch up a wound. Returning to our side, she pulls up a chair next to Amberly.

"I need you to make sure she doesn't move," she says in a serious tone. "We don't want her having a crazy scar when this is all over."

I nod as I lift my hand, and Angela removes the blood-drenched rag away from Amberly's wound. She doesn't move as Angela goes to work.

When she finishes, Angela brushes the hair away from Amberly's face with the back of her wrist before standing and heading over to the sink. It's a rather small cleaning area wedged between the furthest bed and a dresser, but at the end of the day, it gets the job done.

I take notice of Angela's shoulders shaking lightly. With a quick look at Amberly, I squeeze her hand and rise, making my way to Angela's side. Before she can turn away, I see the tears staining her cheeks.

"Hey," I whisper as I lay my hand on her shoulder, hoping to offer her some comfort. "It's okay. Everyone is okay."

Turning quickly, I can feel the worry and hurt vibrating off of her. Her voice breaks as she speaks. "Yeah, for now." Her hands fly up in defeat as the words spill out. "I'm so tired of patching up the people I love. I don't know how much more I can take."

I pull her into my arms as her sobs break free. I didn't realize until now just how much she's been keeping inside. Angela has never been one to break. She's always the strongest female in the pack, and seeing her like this isn't easy.

"I promise these days are almost behind us," I whisper, holding her tight as I push her hair away from my face.

Between sobs, she mumbles, "But at what cost? How many of us will be lost in what's coming next?" Pulling away, she rubs her face angrily. "I can't take the thought that all of us aren't going to walk away from this one."

I try to think of something, anything I can say to reassure her, but nothing comes. I open my mouth but the words stick in my throat as I hear gurgling noises coming from Amberly's direction. Angela and I turn to see Amberly shoot into a half-seated position before she leans over the side of the bed, retching.

I run to her side, pulling her hair back from her sweat-covered face as the fluids escape. My eyes connect with Angela, pleading. A minute later, Amberly leans up and sits back against the pillow, exhaustion evident in every muscle of her body.

Angela moves forward. "Amberly, how are you feeling?"

Amberly opens her eyes slightly before responding. "Like I've been stabbed and just thrown up everything in my stomach. So now I'm a little hungry." She adds sarcastically, "How about you?"

Angela offers a sympathetic smile. "I'm sorry, I didn't mean in the general sense. I'm just trying to understand where that came from."

"I don't know. Maybe it's my body's way of reacting to the exhaustion."

Her stomach grumbles, followed by a groan before her hands wrap around her midsection, and a grimace forms on her face.

I move into a standing position. "I'm going to go grab you something to eat and drink. I'll be right back."

Angela moves in front of me, causing me to pause. "Let me, you sit here with her."

I nod, and Angela exits the room. I sit back next to her, and Amberly and I sit in silence for a few minutes before her eyes fly open.

"Aidan!" she yells out.

Squeezing her hand lightly, I try to make my tone as calm as I can. "He's okay. A little banged up, but he will be fine."

"Who was it? It came out of nowhere," she looks up at me, confusion set in her gaze.

I shift in my chair and release a nervous sigh before answering. I know neither of us wants to hear her name ever again, Amberly more than anyone, but I know I can't keep it from her.

"Sage," I whisper.

Amberly moves so fast from the bed my head spins as my eyes try to follow her movement.

"Where is she now?" She demands.

I close my eyes before responding, "She's gone."

When I open my eyes again, our gaze connects as her body turns rigid. "She's gone, meaning she's dead?"

I shake my head.

"She got away?" Amberly's tone is filled with malice and fear. "What...how, how did she get away?"

Before I can answer, Amberly's face turns a shade of pale I never thought I'd see on someone, and then she's running for the sink. I stand, making my way to her side before she gets sick again.

"Let's not talk about this right now," I say, holding her hair and rubbing her back. "Getting you upset is only making this worse. Once you eat and rest, I will tell you everything I know."

Grabbing the towel hanging next to the sink, Amberly wipes at her mouth before looking at me.

"I just, I don't understand. Why is she now coming back up for air? Why wasn't she here with Vladimir?"

I pull her into my arms, planning to take all of her weight if needed. "I'm not sure. Aidan didn't say much about it." Her eyes tell me she's about to ask something, but I cut her off. "Let's get you back to the bed."

Her defiance is clear in her demeanor, but she walks with me regardless. We just make it back to the bed when Angela walks through the door.

"Everything alright?" She asks as she takes note of Amberly sitting back on the bed.

"Not so much," I say as I help Amberly get comfortable. Deciding it's best to leave the elephant out of the room for now, I add, "She just got sick again."

Angela places the tray of food on the small table next to the bed before returning to the dressers to pull out a thermometer.

At the beep, she removes it from Amberly's mouth, and a puzzled expression fills her face.

"Well, no fever. How have you been feeling the last few days?" she asks Amberly.

"Other than a little stressed and tired, fine. Honestly."

"Have you been able to eat and drink and keep it all down?" Angela questions.

Amberly's cheeks turn a shade of red as she looks at the tray of food. "Honestly, I've been eating more than normal, if I'm being honest. And no problems keeping it down until today."

My mind begins to turn, and only one thing comes to mind, but I know it can't be possible, so I keep my mouth shut. I'm not the doctor here, and it's best to leave the diagnosis to the professional.

Angela smiles as she crosses her arms over her chest. Moving closer to the bed, she looks at me smugly before addressing Amberly.

"Amberly, when was your last cycle?"

Her thinking face goes to work, and we sit in silence for a few moments before she answers. "I think it's actually due. Like today or maybe tomorrow. I haven't really been paying attention to it as much as I should lately."

Angela slaps me on the shoulder with a grin. "Should I tell her, or do you want to do the honors?"

My throat goes dry. We've been trying to be so careful. We want pups, of course, but we didn't want to chance something like this happening before the final battle. We knew that if she became pregnant, the strategy of the fight would have to change in a drastic way for the sake of our unborn child.

Amberly's expression changes from worry to confusion. "What's going on?"

Angela takes my silence as a hint to tell her. "Amberly, I am fairly certain that the reason for the symptoms you are having is because you are expecting."

Amberly's eyes widen as her mouth falls open. "You don't mean I'm..." her voice drifts off, the word never leaving her mouth. Angela smiles before sitting on the bed next to her.

"Yes, I do. I'm going to run a few more tests, but I feel they will all come out showing what I already know."

The words come out of Amberly's mouth in a jumbled mess. "I'm pregnant."

Chapter 52

Amberly

The oncoming battle strikes fear deep inside me. Only now, it's stronger. Almost paralyzing.

She has to be wrong. I can't be pregnant, not yet. Not with what's coming. How will I protect my pack and my unborn child? I can't sit out of this battle, but learning that I'll soon be a mother, my parental instincts are trying to take over, and a huge part of me wants to let them. Kids have never been something I thought of for myself. Being so young, I didn't expect them for at least a few more years. Julian and I were just married. We haven't had a chance to be just that, a married couple, and now we will be bringing a little one into the fold. Will that change us? Will we grow apart? I can't think about it; I won't. The moment I said I do, I couldn't wait for all the changes and firsts together, but as far as being a mom, I didn't think it would be this soon. Now everything has changed. My pack is important, just like Julian, but our child must come first.

Now, the plan needs to shift. I can't put myself front and center in this war. The good thing about this, other than the obvious, is that this is something huge that wasn't in my vision, and for that fact, I know our fates have changed. I only need to be smart about moving forward, and everything will be fine. I know we aren't all going to be able to walk away from this, and that's something I need to mentally prepare myself for, but at least now

I know we have a fighting chance.

"How are you feeling?"

I turn to see Julian closing the door behind him.

Pulling the covers higher, I smile. "Better."

He takes a few first steps toward me and smiles. "Can I get you anything to eat?"

Glancing at my now empty tray, my stomach growls. Looking back at him, I mumble, "I think I ate enough."

A smug smile forms on his face before he responds. "Well, you are eating for two now."

I sigh, shifting in the bed. "I still don't understand how this happened. We were being so careful."

Julian takes my hand as he sits on the edge of the bed next to me. "There is always a risk, no matter how careful you are." Glancing down at our intertwined hands, he whispers, "Are you not happy?"

I see stars as I quickly move my gaze back in his direction. "That's not what I mean. It's just with everything going on, this isn't really ideal."

His brow furrows. "Do you think I won't be able to protect my family? There is nothing I won't do to keep you both safe," he says lovingly.

"I don't doubt your ability to protect us, but I worry," I say, softly squeezing his hand.

Julian places his fingers under my chin and lifts my gaze to his.

"I promise I will do my best not to leave you alone at the end of this," he promises, staring deep into my eyes.

I didn't need to voice my fear. Since the wedding and Alpha ceremony, Julian and I have become closer in ways I never knew were possible. We sense each other's worry or fear before we notice it ourselves.

His words help calm the storm inside me, but fear still remains. I allow myself to lean into him, accepting his warm, comforting embrace. Then it really sinks in.

We are going to be parents.

I'm going to be a mother.

Chapter 53

Amara

Aidan's face contorts with pain as a small grunt escapes his lips when he shifts on the bed. I stand in the shadows across the room, uneasy about if I should even be here.

Angela came in shortly after Logan got Aidan comfortable on the sturdy black cot under the brightest light in the room.

I've been standing in the same spot, quietly watching as she runs test after test on Aidan.

Angela moves into a standing position, making her way across the room. Opening one of the wooden dresser drawers, she places the medical equipment back into its proper place. Closing the drawer, she moves to the towel station and grabs a small, light blue rag before turning toward the sink.

Aidan tries to move into a sitting position on the bed but winces in pain, grabbing at his head. Angela moves back to his side, offering him the damp rag.

"Try placing this on your eyes. It may help with the migraine. It will only get worse before it gets better."

Taking the rag from Angela's outstretched hand, he looks at her. "So what's the verdict, doc?"

Pulling up the wheeled chair, Angela takes a seat. "The good news is nothing is broken, and no real damage is done. However, you can expect the migraine and spotty vision to stick around for a little while."

With a grunt, Aidan shifts. "How is Amberly?"

Angela smiles, but I can easily see something hidden under the surface. "She is fine, thankfully."

Aidan places the rag over his eyes, and a moan escapes his lips, letting us know the relief the cloth offers him.

"Good. Sage will be back," he grumbles, his tone then becomes deadly, "And she will pay for all she's done."

Angela moves into a standing position. "Don't get me wrong, I'm all for justice. Killing Julian and what she did to Amberly. But there may still be hope for her."

Aidan removes the cloth from his eyes, glaring in Angela's direction. "You have got to be out of your mind. I'm fairly certain you have screws loose up there," he says quietly, pointing at his forehead. "There is no saving someone like that. She doesn't want to be saved."

Angela opens her mouth, but before she can speak, I step from the shadows. Their gaze moves to me.

"I don't say this lightly, and I'm not accusing in any way. But Aidan, not long ago, you were by her side," I murmur, moving closer to them before stopping at his bedside. "You came to us confused, angry, and broken. You didn't want to be changed, but you were." I look down at my feet nervously. "If you were able to change sides, if you could be saved, then who's to say she can't?"

Looking back up, I find Aidan's expression has changed. It's softer, the lines around his eyes and mouth no longer visible.

Aidan offers a small smirk. "I understand where you're coming from, and I appreciate it, but Sage and I are nothing alike."

Angela steps forward. "Maybe not, but you were just as deep in it as she is. You both killed and tortured people. Just because she's done it to people you love doesn't make it any different. Everyone you've ever hurt or killed had someone at home who loved them."

Angela's words stir something inside of Aidan. I watch as his face shifts, and full of frustration, he throws back the covers and attempts to stand. He immediately regrets the decision, falling back to the cot and moving his hand to his forehead as he leans over with an anguished groan.

Before I can stop myself, my hand is on his shoulder, steadying his wobbling body on the edge of the cot.

Touching him feels foreign, and I know there are a million reasons why I shouldn't even be in this room right now, but I can't make myself leave. Seeing him hurting like this causes me pain. I don't understand the growing pit in my stomach as my heart aches watching him like this. He will be fine, but part of me can't turn away.

Trying to understand this shift has been impossible. Since we returned from finding Aaron, I felt a pull toward him, a strong need to be around him. To make sure he is comfortable here. Maybe it's more than that, but I don't know. I can't put my finger on what's going on here. All I know is I feel better, more comfortable, when I'm around him.

Aidan's eyes lock with mine, and what I see in them scares me. Not in the way I would have thought. I see a longing in them, maybe even admiration.

"Why are you here?" He asks.

Flinching, I slowly remove my hand from his body as my cheeks grow hot. "I wanted to make sure you were okay."

Leaning back slightly, he chuckles. "Well, as you can see, I am in no danger. Why don't you go where you are needed?"

His words slice me open like a dagger, but I stand straight, not showing any sign of their affliction.

Angela crosses her arms. "Aidan. I think you're being a little harsh."

Aidan turns on her. "Why? Because I don't want her here? She doesn't need to coddle me. I'm not an invalid or a child, and she sure as hell ain't my woman. Therefore, there is no reason for her to waste any more of her time here."

"But, I…" I pause briefly as my voice cracks. "I'm your friend. I care about you," I whisper the last words.

For a moment, I catch remorse and pain in his eyes before it is replaced by anger. "Friend?" He says the word like it's poison leaving his lips. "Who are you kidding? We aren't friends. I have no friends, and that's the way I like it."

Discarding the rag to the floor, he stands. "And you don't care about me. You just want to make good with your new Alpha. Trust me, I get it. No hard feelings, but I don't need the fake emotions."

"I..." Palms sweating, I try to respond. I need him to know he's wrong in his thinking. I know it's the fear talking but I don't know what to do. What to say.

Taking his first steps toward the door, he counters, "Really, let's just be real with one another, okay? No need to play nice anymore. The final battle is coming, and then I'll be gone. You won't have to deal with my presence much longer."

He opens the door as I remain frozen in place. My veins are like ice. My throat is dry as the words remain stuck there.

Angela steps toward Aidan. "I don't think it's best for you to be walking around right now."

With a smirk, he sarcastically replies, "Don't worry, doc. I'm heading back to my room to sleep this off."

Then the door slams shut, and with it, my heart crumbles.

Chapter 54

Amberly

I push the door open slowly, silently praying it won't squeak. If Aidan is sleeping, I don't want to wake him. I take note of my free hand absentmindedly hovering over my stomach and place it back at my side before walking into the light of the room. Memories of talks my mother and I had over the years begin to run through my mind. Through many life situations, she always used the same phrase. I never understood it then, but now I do. The words ring through my mind, bringing a smile to my face. *It's something you can't understand until you become a mother yourself one day.*

I close the door behind me, smile still lingering.

"Amberly?" Aidan's worried tone fills the room.

I'm met with a tight hug as I turn to face him.

"Whoa, are you okay?" I ask.

The urgency of his embrace, the tightness, feels like home. I always thought about what it would have been like having a sibling. This normal connection between siblings wouldn't feel so foreign to me right now if things had been different. All the years we lost…It's sad that our first embrace would be after another near-death experience.

Silencing the thought, I close my eyes, settling into the hug with my brother. Resting my face against his stiff shoulder, I wrap my arms around his waist, squeezing back lightly. His chin comes to rest on top of my head, his arms connected around the back of my shoulders. I feel my strength growing, this simple, normal gesture filling me with something I have craved since learning the truth. Together, we are stronger, and together, we can do remarkable things. We only need to embrace our truth, our connection. It's time to truly acknowledge that we are family, brother and sister. We are blood, and there is nothing in this world that can beat our powers. We can win this war, united.

Aidan pulls back, placing his hands on my shoulders and looking at me intensely. "Yes, sorry," he finally answers. Looking me over, his face becomes one of concern. "But should you be up? Shouldn't you be resting?"

"Angela, cleared me," I shrug, grinning at her.

Placing his hands back to his sides, he looks unconvinced.

I move past him to sit on the cot. "She did find something, though."

I hadn't planned on telling anyone, not yet, and I figured it would be my father first, but something tells me to let it out.

Aidan moves to my side, sitting down slowly.

Closing my eyes, I release a long breath. "Apparently, I am expecting," I whisper.

Aidan's eyes widen. "Do you mean you're…"

I nod, the silence between us growing. Aidan stares into the emptiness between us. After a minute, he stands, pacing the ten-foot space in front of me. I nibble on my bottom lip, waiting for him to break the silence. Dread builds, causing my chest to tighten. If this is his reaction, what will my fathers be? Will he think I was being irresponsible?

I wince, glancing down to find my cuticle bleeding, a habit I thought I had kicked since leaving home. Evidence that my nerves are a jumbled mess.

Aidan takes a knee in front of me, taking my hands in his.

"She's certain?" he asks softly.

I nod in reply.

Slowly, his lips curve up, and butterflies dance in my stomach as he places his forehead on our joined hands. A small sob escapes his lips.

I watch him quietly for a moment before his eyes find mine, and I can see the shine of tears in them.

"This is great news," he exclaims before his smile disappears slightly. "Is the baby okay? After earlier, I mean?"

I smile at his concern. "Yes."

"Thank God." He squeezes my hands lightly, the smile returning to his face. "Does everyone know?"

"No. Just you, Angela, and Julian. I haven't told anyone else yet."

He nods, still smiling. "Amberly," he breathes, pausing to move to my side on the cot. "I won't let anyone hurt you or the baby. We will come up with a plan. No one will touch you."

I open my mouth to protest, but the way he shakes his head and the seriousness of his expression silences me.

"I have failed you as a brother in so many ways, but in this, I won't. You and my unborn niece or nephew, you will make it out of this. No matter what I have to do. You are my main priority."

Smiling, I rest a protective hand over my stomach. Small, but already, a life is forming inside me. Who am I to tell those who love us that they can't protect us when my own instincts are the same? My pack now comes second in my thought process. My unborn child is first, and there is nothing I won't do to protect them all.

The look of happiness on my brother's face at the news makes our future so much more complicated. Even after this war is won, how will I separate us now?

Aidan grabs my hand, noticing the strain of my thoughts. "What is it? What's wrong?"

I wipe away a tear I hadn't realized was there. Shaking my head, I smile, "Nothing."

"You don't have to lie to me, not me. I'm the one person you can always count on to be in your corner. I know it may not feel that way because of recent events, but I promise," he says. He shifts in his spot, the cot squeaking beneath our weight. His expression is sincere as he continues. "With this," he gestures to my stomach, "I will never fail you."

"It's not that."

"Then what?" He asks, brows furrowing.

Shifting uncomfortably, I sigh. "Aidan, there's been something I've been wanting to talk to you about, and now, I don't know how."

"I'm all ears," he offers with a smile.

"I've just been thinking...Being Alpha now, I have some tough choices I will have to make soon, and I'm struggling with some of them."

Remaining silent, he watches me closely.

"My place is here now, with the pack and my mate," I continue.

He nods, showing me he is listening and following.

"But I also need to think about our village. With Mom gone, they need a new coven leader. That was supposed to be me, but..."

With a deep breath, Aidan interrupts me, knowing the end of my sentence before I can say it. "Things have grown complicated, and you can't be in two places at once."

"Exactly," I smile.

He looks to the door, remaining quiet, and then his expression changes, letting me know he's come to a conclusion.

"What about Logan? He seems strong, loyal, and honest. He could take the place of you or run as a second."

"Not exactly what I was thinking," I reply, snickering. "Logan is amazing and would lead fairly, but he's not of our blood."

I look at him, praying he understands where I'm going with this. I can tell his brain is working, and after a few moments of silence, his eyebrows reach his hairline, his hands waving back and forth in front of him.

"Oh, no, no, no. You can't possibly think," he blurts out, jumping to his feet to begin frantically pacing the room. "I can't lead."

"Why not?" I offer a reassuring smile. "I think you would be great at it. You never know what you're capable of until you try, right?" Shrugging, I stand. "And our coven needs to be led by someone in our bloodline. It's the only way the protections our mother placed will hold. Plus, it's our birthright."

Aidan continues to pace the length of the room. I move to stand in front of him, causing him to stop and look at me.

Taking his hands in mine, I offer a genuine smile. "I believe in you. I know you can do it."

Aidan squeezes my hands gently before speaking again. "Amberly, before I learned about the baby, I was planning on leaving after the battle. I needed a fresh start, somewhere where no one knows the things I've done." His tear-filled eyes lock with mine. "I want to find my mate, and I know I can't here. But now, the thought of leaving you and the baby," he pauses, shaking his head. "I can't even stomach the thought. Plus, I'm no leader."

I take a step closer to him. "I just wanted to bring it up. Something for you to think long and hard on. We don't need to make the decision right now, but we will need to make it."

"Well, my vote is for Wicca Boy to do it," he smiles playfully.

"Noted," I laugh.

The door flies open, Aidan's body in front of me before Troy enters the room, breathless.

"Someone's coming. A huge group of people. They sent me to come find you," he gasps in my direction.

I glance at Aidan, looking over his shoulder at me as his body turns rigid. Placing a hand on his back, I look to Troy.

"Well, let's not keep everyone waiting," I say with a firm voice.

* * *

Aidan stands in front of me the whole way down the hall. Panic fills my body with each step. We aren't prepared for the fight, not yet. Turning the final corner to the main hall, voices reach my ears and my nerves calm almost instantly.

I take in the scene before me with a mix of surprise and awe.

"They made it," I whisper.

Conversing with my pack are angels, fae, and some others I don't recognize. I head to the group speaking with my father and Julian, Aidan stuck closely to my side like glue.

"Here she is," my father says, addressing the angelic beings at his side.

The woman has long snow-white hair, pulled back into a tight ponytail. Her battle armor is black, fashionable, and formed to her body, showing every curve. But her eyes are the first thing I notice. Beautiful shades of blue mixed with white and yellow. The iris is a slit instead of a circle like ours and humans. Along her forehead, circling under her eyes, are thin gold lines, a formation of swirls and dots. Glancing lower, I notice more on her collarbone, disappearing below her armor. Her black attire has a U-shaped neckline that rests just below her shoulders. The material trails the length of her arm down to her exposed hands, where one piece of fabric circles around her middle finger. The bodice clings, moving the length of her body down her legs, covering the tops of her black pumps. Her eyes and the gold pattern on her skin aren't the only things that set her apart from us and the humans. My eyes catch the light movement of white feathers behind her, her wings.

I can't help as my mouth drops open slightly at the beautiful sight.

"You must be Amberly," the male angel at her side says, extending his hand. "I'm Marcus, and this is my mate, Merida." Gesturing to his flank, he addresses the others. "This is Luscious, Jacob, Elijah, Israel, and Jadia. The rest of my men and women I will introduce to you shortly."

Looking at the men, their appearances are mostly the same. Most have ear-length or buzz-cut hair, but the color is the same on every one of them. Black, with white streaking the sides. Their armor is the same as well, tight around the neck, covering the length of their arms and legs. Something that resembles a 12-inch staff rests in holsters on both sides of their hips; a single leather strap across their chests reveals the hilt of a sword strapped on their backs.

The only thing different about them all is the gold patterns. Marcus has the same forehead and eye pattern as Merida, but the others have a single swirling line that runs from the side of their eye to their jawline. Their wings are slightly different from the women's as well, with a slight grey tint mixed with the white.

I extend my hand with a smile. "Thank you for coming," I say, shaking his hand.

Marcus smiles at me genuinely. "No thanks is needed. This is a war we have been waiting for. This evil has plagued our world long enough."

I feel Julian before I see him. His arm moves around my waist, pulling me closer to his side.

Marcus smiles, gesturing to Julian at my side. "Your mate took the liberty of filling us in on most of the plan." He raises his head toward the woman, who pulls out a small pouch from her back. "We hope you can use these. I feel they will help with an advantage," he explains, offering me the pouch with a smirk.

Slowly, I open it, pulling out two amulets.

Marcus gestures to the ruby-colored amulet shaped like a diamond. "This one is only to be worn by a natural being. Its power gives the holder increased energy, speed, and a power boost to any attack you put out. Lastly, it offers a thin armor to protect from most magic attacks."

Looking from Julian to my father and back to me, he adds, "I hope I'm not being too forward, but I feel this is the one you should wear in the upcoming battle, Amberly. It offers the most protection and advantage."

Before I can reply, he gestures to the other amulet in my hand. It's emerald in color, shaped somewhat like a square.

"This one has the power to heal any wound. It also gives the wearer with an unearthly strength and deflects attacks they may not see coming." He smiles at Merida. "We hoped they would come in handy."

Julian takes the pouch and amulets from my hands, looking them over before he hands them to my father.

"Thank you. We can use all the help we can get. And we want to thank you for coming here. You're just in time," my father says to Marcus.

He looks to his men before addressing us. "Did something happen?"

Aidan speaks for the first time. "You could say that."

Marcus's eyes close slightly as he looks Aidan over. The way he's staring at my brother makes me uncomfortable, and without thinking, I move to place myself between the two, grabbing Marcus's attention once more. His eyes beat back and forth between us before taking a step back and smiling lightly.

"Who is this man to you?" He asks me.

"He's my brother," I proudly respond.

Marcus's smile disappears before glancing at Merida and the rest of his men. He turns to Aaron, confusion on his face. "You had another child?"

"It's hard to explain," My father answers.

I step forward once more as Aidan and Julian grab each of my arms. "We are twins," I add defensively.

The group of angels glare at Aidan in a way I don't care for before turning to me. Marcus puts up his hand as if trying to silence his people before they utter a word. "We didn't know there were two of you."

"Neither did we until recently. Vladimir stole my brother when we were babies and wiped away the memory of him," I tell him.

Marcus's gaze lightens. "That explains it." He glances at Aidan. "I was trying to get a read from you, and well, it wasn't pure. But considering your upbringing and the situation, that would be expected."

I glare at him, moving closer. "What do you mean not pure?"

Israel answers first. "He has killed many. His soul is tainted, unclean."

Rage boils inside me as I step toward Israel, pulling from Julian and Aidan's grasp. "You don't know a thing about his soul," I growl. "Given the life he was trapped in, he had no choice. He's not that person anymore." I look around at the group. "And who are you to call anyone impure? I've heard about the things angels have done. Don't act like you are better than any of us here. We have done what we needed to survive and protect the humans. Nothing more and nothing less."

Marcus places his arm out, stopping Israel from moving forward. "Forgive my comrade here. We meant no disrespect. We were merely scanning each person in the room to make sure an intruder hadn't snuck in with us. There are rumors about how Vlidirmir works, and seeing what he did to your family, there seems to be more truth in it." Offering a small smile at me, he continues. "Our only objective is to keep you safe, and in scanning the room, that was our only intent."

Aaron steps forward. "You think someone from their side could infiltrate as one of you, the fae, or the others who just joined?"

"No. Now that we checked, we are clear of their kind. We simply had to be sure," he responds.

My father nods. "Thank you for making sure." He looks to me, his gaze pleading. "Now, maybe we should get back to the matter at hand."

Marcus speaks first, addressing my father and Aidan. "You mentioned something happened?"

With sad eyes, Aaron answers first. "We had a situation last night. One of their people attacked my children outside the cave. Thankfully, some of the pack scared her off before more damage was done."

Merida looks at me. "Do you know who it was?"

I nod. "Her name is Sage. We have a history," I growl.

Merida's eyes turn sad. "She killed your mate."

My eyes widen at her response. "How did you know?"

Merida's expression turns apologetic. "Sorry. Sometimes, we hear little thoughts from others when emotions are strong. When you said her name, I heard and felt your pain as you remembered what happened." She smiles at Julian. "Just as I can sense how strongly your mate and brother feel about protecting you," she continues. Her gaze moves to my stomach, and she smiles kindly. "Especially now."

Aaron looks at them proudly until her words register, and a confused look passes across his face. "I'm sorry, did you say especially now? They've always been protective of Amberly; we all have," he chuckles.

"Oh, I have no doubt. I mean, since she's expe-"

"Anyway," I laugh loudly, cutting her short. I look around at the group. "Sage made it very clear that we didn't have much time before the final battle was on our doorstep. I think we need to set up a night watch. Make our battle plan, get some food, and then rest. We're going to need it."

Aaron narrows his eyes at me before nodding. "I think that's a good idea. I'll take over the night duties and make sure the cave is covered. Julian, why don't you, Logan, and Troy cover food and sleeping quarters for everyone? Amberly, you and Aidan should talk over the final battle plans and then fill everyone in."

"Sounds like a plan," I offer enthusiastically.

Aidan and Julian turn to head to their duties. I'm about to do the same when my father grabs my arm.

"Not so fast, young lady," he mutters, glancing around to see that everyone else has made their exit. He looks back at me before dropping my arm. "Spill."

I give him my best *'what are you talking about'* face. "What?"

"Don't even try it. I raised many teenagers, and that face doesn't work on your old man. What's going on? What don't I know?" he pries.

"Dad, I think this can wait," I smile at him before trying to turn away.

He moves into my path. "Oh, no, you don't. Tell me right now. There may not be a later, and if it's something I need to worry about, I would like to address the issue now."

"It's not like that," I whisper.

Stepping closer, his tone becomes full of concern. "Did something else happen? Did you see something else?"

Fear fills me. I shake my head violently, both to clear the memory and also to assure him. "No. It's…maybe a good thing. Depending on how you look at it."

"You're adding to my grey here, kid."

Closing my eyes, I sigh before placing my hand over my stomach. "Dad. When Angela looked me over after what happened with Sage, she discovered something," I say, looking him in the eyes before whispering the last few words. "I'm pregnant."

The corners of his mouth lift higher than I've ever seen as he grins ear to ear and releases a laugh so loud, everyone in the room looks in our direction. Blood rises to my cheeks as I lower my head, embarrassed.

Pulling me into his arms, he whispers, "Your mother would be over the moon, as am I."

"You mean, you aren't mad?" I ask in a low voice.

Pulling back to look at me, his face is full of love. "Mad? Why on earth would I ever be mad at you?"

"Because we have this huge war coming our way, and now I'm pregnant.

205

That's not very responsible."

Grinning, he sighs. "Were you careful?"

"Yes."

"Were you trying to get pregnant?"

My face grows warm. "No, of course not."

"Baby girl, these things happen. You can try to be careful, but you aren't always successful. You and your mate found each other, you are married, you did it the right way. Your mother and I weren't married when we conceived you and your brother, but that didn't make it wrong." Squeezing my arm lightly, he continues, "I couldn't be happier than I am right now. I've never doubted you would make an amazing leader, and now you will be a mother, and I know you will do great at both things."

"But how am I going to protect it? I can't sit this war out; I won't," I say, shaking my head.

"No one is asking you to, but you need to be willing to do things a little differently than you have planned. You also need to accept that we're going to want to keep you safe, which means we're going to be your first line of defense now more than ever."

Worry bubbles in my stomach. "That's what I'm worried about."

Placing his hand on my cheek briefly before moving it to my shoulder, he adds, "There is no way to stop death from coming. We aren't all going to make it out of this one, no matter how prepared we are. The only thing that matters for the pack and the world, is making sure you and that baby make it out alive. That is the only objective."

"I don't understand. As long as we win this war, the world will be safe. My life shouldn't matter any more than anyone else's here."

Placing his hand on my shoulder, he ushers me forward, further from the group and prying ears. "There is something your mother and I discovered with Johnathan. It was before the battle with Vladimir. Your mother and I decided it wasn't the time to share it with you, and I had hoped maybe we never would." Reaching the furthest table, he gestures for me to take a seat. "Amberly, there is a bigger reason why Vladimir tried so hard to kill you. You and your brother are vitally important in this war, but you, more so. Your destiny isn't only to save this world from the darkness that has taken route. You are meant to be the mother to the next generation of children that come from two worlds. Your children will be the beginning of something bigger and stronger than we can even imagine."

Speechless, I stare at my father as he shifts in place.

"Your children are said to bring the humans and supernatural world together. They will light the way to peace and a new world. Without you, those children will never be born, and without them, our kind will always walk in the shadows. They will always be hunted by those who can't understand. Your children will breach the divide between our worlds."

My father's words ring in my ears. Now I know how my parents felt, knowing I had this destiny hanging over my head. I don't want that for my children, but I know our world finally needs the peace that's long since due. Having been in this life-or-death situation, the one thing I can do is prepare them.

Chapter 55

Sage

Standing a distance from the cave, Annabeth moves to the front of the group. "They have every entrance protected. If we attack one, the others will sound the alarm, and we will lose the element of surprise."

Henry flanks his wife, speaking only to her in a matter-of-fact tone. "We can kill them before they have the chance to alert the others."

A sigh of annoyance escapes her lips. "Do not underestimate our enemy."

Henry shrinks back, lowering his head.

Looking around at our vast group, I move toward our leaders. "Do you really think we will have a better chance at winning come daybreak?"

With a grin, she turns my way. "Yes, I believe we will." Turning back toward the cave, she continues. "We will wait until they are mostly outside the cave and then attack. This way, we catch more of them off guard, giving us more of an upper hand."

Her word is final. She turns her back on the group, Henry on her tail.

It turns my stomach to see how he just follows everything she says. She's just as bad as Vladimir was. Waiting to attack is pointless as we've already lost the element of surprise when she sent me here to get Aidan. If she wanted the upper hand, we should have all come together and attacked.

I watch as the group sets up sleeping areas and starts to get comfortable for the night.

"I take it you don't agree with her choice," Sam, one of the few to emerge from the wall with me, asks.

Refraining from answering or looking at him, I remain silent. Sam and Lisa were probably the only other two in our group I could stand. I hadn't had a chance to get to know the demons and other supernaturals that had joined our ranks before I left, but I doubt there are many I will be able to stand being around.

Sam is a simple creature, much like myself, and he has a deep taste for the kill. It's obvious in his eyes, the lust for the hunt. His raven bangs touch his pitch-black eyes, revealing everything there is to know. Maybe it's his Comanche blood that makes him ruthless in battle, who knows, but I'm glad he's on our side. As for Lisa, she's a quiet, petite little thing of African American descent, and when I say she's wicked fast with her spells, I mean I barely hold my own. Who knows, between the three of us, we might have a chance of taking out a nice chunk of their main lines before we fall in battle.

Sam moves next to me, looking out toward the cave and the six bodies guarding it, waiting, watching.

"I don't agree with her plan either."

Turning my head slightly his way, I raise an eyebrow.

Uncertainty spreads across his face. "I mean, I don't think waiting until morning will help us in any way."

Grinning slightly, I nod. Sam takes in a slow breath of relief. Despite how lethal he can be, he knows somewhere deep down that I could take him and win. That, or maybe Lisa is right, and he is a little sweet on me, but I don't have time to entertain such things. It wouldn't matter either way, as I have no interest in anyone other than the one who fights against us.

The thought that I may have to watch him fall in this war sends a slight pain creeping up inside my chest. I've never cared much for anyone, but somehow Aidan got through, and I can't seem to shake him. Maybe it's because I saw myself in the man he used to be. Scared, alone, deadly. But now he's no longer a mere image of myself. He has become a stranger, and I don't think there is any hope left for him. It's something I need to come to terms with, and fast, as his final hours are approaching. As are mine.

Chapter 56

Amberly

On the table in front of the group sit seven amulets, all wielding a different power. The angels gave me their two, Celine and Cole had two, the fae supplied two of their own, and then, there was the one my mother gave me when I was young. Before the enemy arrives on our doorstep, I have a hard decision to make. I've been replaying my vision on repeat in my head for the last twenty-four hours, more so since our encounter with Sage. Some big things have already changed. Our wedding, becoming Alpha, and my pregnancy, for starters. But in my vision, I'm almost one hundred percent certain none of us were wearing amulets. This may „be the last piece to the puzzle to get us out of this alive, or at least most of us. The hard part is figuring out who to give each amulet to. With only seven to go around, it won't be an easy choice.

I pick up the amulet to the far left of the table. The jade stone shining in the lights. This was one of the two Celine brought with her. It provides the wearer with armor and multiplies their strength by ten. Looking at my brother, I hold it out.

"Aidan, I need you to wear this." Looking down at the amulet, he takes it from my hands. I look around to the rest of the group. "I'm going to be giving some of you an amulet. I have put a lot of thought into this based on a vision I had. I need you to put it on now and leave it on until the battle has ended."

They exchange glances, but no one says a word before looking back in my direction.

Next, I pick up the yellow, nickel-sized, circular amulet, offering it to Julian. Its main power is healing, and I'm praying that this amulet can heal Julian from the attack I saw him take.

"Julian," I whisper when he doesn't move to take it from my hands.

His eyes silently usher me to choose another. I shake my head lightly. He sighs before taking it from my hands, placing it over his head, looking at it with disdain.

Rolling my eyes, I glance at the amulets the fae brought. The first is square, and on either side are two smaller squares, all ruby in color. The stones are so small that all three could easily fit into the palm of my hand. This amulet allows the wearer to see into people's minds. It can easily give you the upper hand in battle, as you can see an attack before it happens.

Looking at Angela, I extend my hand toward her. Without a word, she takes it from me and puts it on.

The other amulet the fae provided is like the first but with an added twist. Not only could you foresee an attack coming, but it would pull the proper spell or body deflection to stop the oncoming attack. The small green gem, triangular in shape, is beautiful to look at and easy for anyone to pull off. My eyes lock with Logan before offering him the tiny object, and like the others, he places it around his neck without a word.

Next, I focus on the two that the angels brought with them. They are by far the strongest in the group. The first one has a singular, pure white circle, the chain made from a dark brown rope. It not only offers the power to heal the wearer but also strengthens them and deflects attacks that they may not see coming.

Looking from Cole to Celine, I extend my hand once more. "This one's for you and your brother."

They exchange a look of surprise before Celine takes the object from my hand with a nod.

The other has a murky white stone with a leather strap. This is the one

Marcus asked me to wear, and since it can only be worn by someone with the natural blood running in their veins, and it is my best bet to protect my unborn child, I will be using this one. I take it from the table, placing it around my neck without a word.

Lastly, I hand my original amulet to my father, knowing he will know how to tap into its power.

"I guess that's it. Everyone has their assignments." I look around at the group as they all nod or offer a yes as their response. "I think it's time to go get our rest. We are going to need it."

I turn away from them, not ready to have a final conversation with any of them. I sense Aidan before he moves in front of me, cutting off my exit.

"I have the first watch. Come and find me when you get up, okay?" His tone isn't asking, it's demanding.

Everyone in the cave now knows I'm pregnant, thanks to my brother and father's big mouths, and because of it, everyone is on higher alert. I already can't stand the fact that anyone is in this position to begin with. As it started with me, I wish it could end the same way, but now I know that's not an option. The losses tomorrow will be with me until my final breath, but I can't focus on what we will lose, not now.

I nod, offering a reassuring smile. "I will."

He nods and begins to head for his post.

"And Aidan," I yell after him. "Everything will be okay."

He whispers, "I know," then continues heading for the exit.

Julian takes my hand in his. "Ready?"

I smile at him and nod. "Very."

Taking one last look at everyone, my heart contracts. I take in everyone's features, maybe for the last time, before we exit the hall, and they all disappear from sight.

Chapter 57

Julian

"I didn't see Johnathan or Aayda tonight, did you?" I ask Amberly as she pulls her aqua tank top over her head and into place.

"They haven't really left their room since losing Serenity. The funeral was the last time I saw them both."

Turning toward me with a sad smile, she makes her way to the bed. It's hard not knowing what to do for the one you love. I know the heartache of the loss of her mother still weighs heavy on her heart, and I'm sure learning she is pregnant has only made her miss her more. I don't know what it's like for a woman. I can't act like I do. But I know girls tend to talk with their mother about their wedding day and children, and her mother missed both. I wish there was something I could do to lessen the hurt she is feeling, as now it has become my own. Since our joining, our connection has become ten times stronger. I've been able to sense when she's scared or hurt, and slowly, the feeling becomes my own.

I couldn't be happier since learning we're going to be parents, but I know that with that comes a new kind of fear. We haven't been married very long, we are still very young, we're about to face a crucial battle, and then, there's the horrible feeling that we won't be good parents. At least I know that's my fear, but I feel it may also be hers. Sometimes, it gets hard to tell what feelings are mine and which are hers, especially when we could both be feeling the same way.

So much has changed, and I know she is overwhelmed with it all. I would give anything to take some of that off her chest.

Flopping onto the bed beside me, Amberly releases a long, overexaggerated breath into the sheets as her body becomes limp. Rubbing my hand over her back, I stare at her sadly.

"How are you feeling?" I ask.

Lifting her head from the sheets, she turns in my direction.

"Honestly, I don't even know how to answer that question." Rolling over onto her back, she stares at the ceiling. "So many things keep running through my mind. I can't quiet the noise."

"Maybe if you tell me about some of them, it will help," I offer.

Turning her head to smile at me, she nods. "I don't think it will, but talking with you is my favorite thing. Even if it doesn't get better, just knowing you are there helps." She reaches and takes my hand in hers. "I keep trying to think about life after this war. As hard as I try, I can't see it. I'm worried about what comes next. I'm scared of what and who we will lose and what lies in the wake of all the dirt and blood that's to come." She squeezes my hand tightly as I see a tear run down her face. "And I'm scared to lose you. I can't do it again, especially now." As she says the last words, her free hand moves to her stomach.

I scoot closer to her. "I promise you that isn't going to happen. I won't leave you."

"You didn't see my vision. I lost so many of you. My heart couldn't take it. I don't want to lose anyone, but you…you I can't lose. I won't survive it."

Her words cause my heart to skip a beat as my breath gets stuck in my lungs. I mean, how can I tell her I won't leave her? I will do anything to make sure I don't, but I can't promise that. Especially if it comes to her or me, I will fall before she does.

I place my hand over hers on her stomach. "I have so much to fight for, so much life left to live," I tell her, gazing into her eyes. "With both of you. What I can promise is I will do my best to be standing beside you when the dust clears."

Turning on her side, she buries her face in my chest. As her shoulders begin to shake, I rub the back of her head, holding her close as the sobs come.

She shifts her head to the side, looking up at me. "I hate that I brought all this on. Because of me, everyone is in danger, and there's nothing else I can do to protect them. To protect you, or even myself." Closing her eyes, she inhales deeply, releasing the breath as her eyes open, connecting with mine. "I'm supposed to be this incredibly strong being, and I can't even protect my unborn child from what's about to come."

I brush the hair from her face, replying with a serious tone, "You need to stop taking so much on your shoulders. You have people around you; let us take on some of the burdens you carry. Together, we will get through this." I rest my head on top of hers, a smile forming. "And once the smoke clears, we can celebrate how far we've come. We can talk about our future, our coming child. We can finally live."

"Promise?" She whispers.

"Promise."

Chapter 58

Amberly

Sleep came easily in Julian's arms last night as his words calmed the despair building inside me. Now, I'm clear-minded and ready for what's coming. Without him by my side, I don't know where I would be. Loving someone so fiercely was something I only thought was possible in books, but Julian showed me how wrong I was. He completes me in every way, making me stronger and calming the parts of me that need it.

I make my rounds, ensuring everyone is fed and on high alert, knowing that at any moment, my grandparents and Sage will make their appearance. I half expected to be woken in the middle of the night with the news, but I was thankful that wasn't the case.

Marcus, Merida, Angela, Logan, Troy, and Julian are standing at a table filled with an assortment of drinks and pastries, smiling in conversation. Calm washes over me, a smile creeping over my face as I walk over to join them.

Julian kisses me on the forehead. "How did the rounds go?"

"Good. I think everyone is more than prepared," I answer him.

Nodding, he looks back at Marcus.

"Julian was filling us in on who you passed the amulets around to last night. I feel you made good choices, and I'm happy you chose to wear that one for yourself," Marcus says while glancing at the amulet around my neck.

"I pray it will protect you and the next generation."

Grabbing Merida by the hand, he places a light kiss on it before speaking once more. "I feel it is time to return to the rest of my clan. We will see you out there."

They turn and walk away before anyone can say a word.

Troy releases a long breath. "Are we really going to just sit around and wait for the attack?"

"What else would you have us do?" Logan addresses him sarcastically.

"I don't know," he shrugs. "But sitting here is like giving them the upper hand, and honestly..."

He stops short, and I instantly recognize the look on his face.

"What?" I push.

"Ly, you aren't going to like what I was going to say," he warns.

"Since when has that ever stopped you?" I question, laughing.

He looks to Logan for help, but he just shrugs.

"I was only thinking we should be spending our time differently," he explains.

"Doing what?" Angela asks.

Troy stares at Julian before speaking. "We should be getting her out of here. Somewhere safe, her and the baby."

I step between them, cutting off any more words he may say.

"Troy, you know me better than that too even suggest that, let alone think about it," I state firmly.

He stares me down. "You are my little sister, and my first thought is always about protecting you. Sitting here like this," he looks around at the group. "Waiting for them to come to us, it's not smart." He gestures to the amulet I'm wearing. "That thing around your neck will only get you so far. We shouldn't be taking the risk. You and the baby should be far away from here."

Placing my hand on his shoulder, I offer an understanding smile. "Troy, I've always looked at you like a brother, and I love how we always bicker like family and that, at the end of the day, we have each other's backs. But I can't walk away from this fight. None of us can." I look around to see everyone nodding in agreement. "You think I want any of you here fighting?"

Troy's eyes grow sad as he looks at me, but I continue. "I don't, and if I could have it another way, I would, just like you would. But sadly, we are all in this now." I take his hand in mine, squeezing it gently. I straighten, confidence building inside me. "And there is no other group of people I would rather have by my side than who's right here with me now." I smile at everyone. "You are all my family, and I know if we stick together, we will come out on top."

I notice the tears forming in Troy's eyes and pull him in close for a hug.

"I love you," He whispers in my ear.

"I love you, too," I say to him.

"Okay, enough of the sad stuff," Angela voices. "It's time to join the others."

Pulling away from Troy, I rest my forehead against his, "We got this." I smile at him before pulling away.

He nods with a small smile before removing his hand from mine and following Logan to the exit. Julian wraps his arm around my waist, pulling me in close.

"Are you ready for this little wolf?" he asks, kissing my temple.

I stare up at him, the strength in my voice evident. "As I'll ever be."

"Let's go," he grins before pulling me forward with him.

Exiting the cave, the world is bright, even on such a day as this, and I'm choosing to take it as a blessing. A sign that things will be okay when this is all over. The way the sun shines down on the leaves forms an array of patches of bright light all over the ground. Scattered, different shapes, looking as if they are reaching for each other, trying to become whole. I raise my head and close my eyes, taking deep breaths as I bask in a patch of sunlight. The heat touching my skin spreads a calmness through my body into my soul.

"God, you are so beautiful," Julian whispers from next to me.

I open my eyes, smiling at him shyly. The feeling of the light had me lost to the world around me. For a moment, I was alone, floating in a sea of nothing but warmth and contentment. Staring into my husband's eyes, the love pouring out of his gaze grounds me even more in this moment of uncertainty and fear.

No matter what these next days hold for me and my family, this past year will always be one I revisit in my mind time and time again. All the friendships formed, love shared, connections grown, and all the happiness in our moments together. I wouldn't change my path, even if I could, because it led me to all these beautiful people, these forever moments that I will always cherish and hold dear.

Each step of life is a journey only meant for us. No one can take the path someone else is meant to have. I was meant to leave home and meet these amazing people who have become my family. I was destined to be the one to fight these battles. My path was set out long before I was a thought, and as hard as it's been, I'm choosing to look at all the positives and all the love that has come from my past. I am finally embracing my journey, no matter where it may end.

"I love you," I tell Julian.

He smiles, opening his mouth to say it back when I notice fire off to the right. A second later, someone is flying through the air, followed by a sword. I watch as the sword sinks into the leg of one of the fae speaking with my father. Everyone becomes silent, bodies tensing and ready for battle.

Without looking at me, Julian says in a stern tone, "Do not leave my side."

A fight breaks out to the right and then behind us, and before we know it, everyone around us is facing off against someone.

White wings fly above, colliding with pitch black. Angel versus demon. Colorful sparks fly, dragging my attention to our right, followed by a loud thunder-like crash. Fae versus witch. Magic and wings fill the sky as chaos unfolds everywhere.

Red catches my eye as Julian pushes me behind him with his arm extended out. Sage emerges from the center of the battle, with eight others tailing after her. I look at Julian as the muscles in his jaw tighten and his eyes dart around the group coming down on us. His plan to stick to my side slowly deteriorates as the realization sets in. Nine against one isn't possible in any scenario, and nine to two still isn't very good odds. Now, I'm in this fight whether he wants me to be or not. Even with Julian's advantage, this is going to be difficult to get out of.

The eight behind Sage are all males, and even from this distance, I can see that six of them have black pits for eyes. Four of those six are demons, their dark wings noticeable behind them. Two are dark warlocks. The others with her have no distinct markings, making it hard to know what supernatural world they come from. Either way, this fight isn't going to be easily won for either side.

Sage makes it about twelve feet from us before grinning, "Now, there is the lovely couple."

"Don't take one more step," Julian snarls.

Sage chuckles. "Uh oh, looks like the mutt has some fangs." Looking back at the group behind her, she spits out, "You know what to do."

Four of the men break formation, moving to circle behind me and causing Julian's focus to split. In that one second, Julian is ripped away from me. He lands on all fours, looking up at Sage, bearing his teeth as a vicious snarl escapes.

Sage addresses her group. "You four with me. Time to divide and conquer."

Julian's eyes are sad and pleading as they connect with mine. *Stay alive, Little wolf.*

His words echo in my mind before I answer back. *You too. Focus on the fight, no distractions.*

Hesitantly, his eyes leave mine as he looks to where Sage and her men descending on him.

Separated from everyone I love, I turn toward my foe, knowing I need to focus on each problem as they cross my path if I'm going to change the outcome of my vision. Just like I told Julian, we can't afford to get distracted. We all need to focus on what's in front of us, as hard as that can be.

My assailants move toward me with smiles on their faces. Four men against one woman. I guess it's a good thing I'm not an ordinary woman, but they aren't ordinary either. I need to be smart and calculated in every move I make moving forward. I can't get cocky in my head, but it doesn't mean I can't make them think I am. Time to use all my wits and talents in this battle.

"Come and get me, boys," I gesture with my hand, ushering them to come closer.

Spreading my legs and bending my knees slightly, I get in my defensive stance, readying myself for the first attack. The closest to me pulls a six-inch dagger with a black hilt from his pants before taking a step closer.

"So quick to join your mother, are you?" he snarls at me.

His words cause me to pause for a breath before I let the rage fuel me and move into my battle stance. Time to go on the offensive and use all the hate, anger, and sadness to my advantage.

The man with the dagger creeps closer as the other three move to flank me. Using my wolf hearing, I focus on the other men, listening for any indication of their silent attacks. My eyes never leave the assailant in front of me. My magic sees the shield he has around him, and I know this fight isn't going to be easy. But this is what I've trained for.

He lashes out with the blade, causing me to jump out of the way and into a blast of magic from one of the other men. The hit makes me trip over my feet for a moment before I correct my footing. The amulet can protect me from most blasts, but some will still get through. Since I've been standing here, I've felt their attacks from behind, though nothing has come through until now.

"Looks like she's ready to put up a fight," the one in front of me growls.

I lift my head to meet his eyes. "Damn straight. You picked the wrong girl if you were looking for an easy fight."

"Four against one. I'm pretty sure we've got this handled."

The corners of my mouth curve up into a grin.

"Your way of thinking might just get you all killed."

His face turns hard. "We'll see about that."

I turn to glance at the other men behind me. "This is your last chance. You don't need to do this. Know that you will die if you continue."

The men look at one another before laughing loudly.

I crouch down, reading my magic. "Don't say I didn't offer."

I close my eyes as I sink my fingertips into the earth beneath me, pulling on its energy for strength. I release the magic from around my body, sending it out toward my assailants. With a yell, they fly backward, landing on their backs. They don't have any added protections like I do, and if they aren't ready, my magic will get through.

I move my hands together to focus my energy and call on the elements of the earth. I feel the roots of the trees beneath my feet, connecting my mind with them, calling for them to surface.

The men begin to move back into standing positions before the earth under our feet begins to shake. They look at one another, and for the first time, I sense fear in them. As the roots begin to emerge from the soil around us, the ground moves more violently, and the man with the dagger moves forward on wobbly legs. With my thoughts, I will the roots to wrap themselves around my enemies and squeeze them until there's no breath left. Sensing an attack, I panic slightly, knowing I can't deflect it as all my energy and concentration is on the earth below me. Too much energy is being used for this attack, and if I break it now, they will be free,on and it would have been for nothing. I prepare myself for the blow just as searing pain hits me. I drop to my knees, not letting myself lose focus. I hear the men screaming as they are pulled into the air, their screams muffled as the roots and vines squeeze tighter around their bodies until I feel their last breaths.

Dropping my hands to the dirt, I release my connection to the earth. Panting, I bring a hand to my stomach, feeling the hard steel embedded in the skin just inches above my belly button. I close my eyes, biting my lip to suppress my screams as I remove the blade from my body.

Trying not to panic, I breathe in slowly, hoping to calm my heart along with the pain. I focus my senses, knowing I'm taking a risk in sitting here, but I have to know my baby is okay. I close my eyes and silence the world around me, listening inside of me. Quiet. A heartbeat. A single heartbeat. A sob sticks in my throat, fighting to the surface as the pain forms behind my eyes.

Then, I hear it. A quick and quiet little noise that sounds like butterfly wings. My heartbeats calm as relief washes over me, and my eyes open, allowing grateful tears to escape. Wiping them away, I focus on the battle once more.

My eyes turn to the four men on the ground, sensing no life left in them. War is bloody and deadly, and I don't like to think about the lives I've had to take in order to protect myself or the ones I love. I know death comes with war, but I wouldn't wish the pain of taking another life on anyone, especially my family.

I breathe in deeply before running my gaze over the battlefield to happily find everyone holding their own against the enemy. I sense their energies before I see them. Six new enemies are moving toward me.

The energy of the two on the right hits me hard in the face, and it doesn't take me long to realize they are demons. I'm definitely about to get my ass handed to me.

"You fight like a goddess," one of the male demons says.

I move into a standing position, holding in the pain.

"I'll take that as a compliment," I growl at him.

"It was intended to be," he says, flashing his teeth.

The other male demon looks at me with a confused expression. "You're backing a losing team. Save yourself and join us."

I pull my daggers from the back of my pants, throwing my arms wide as I bend my knees, readying myself for a hard fight. Knowing my magic can't hold its own against demons, it's going to be mostly a physical fight. I silently thank Marcus for the amulet around my neck.

Staring hard at the new group, I say through clenched teeth, "Never going to happen."

The second demon clicks his tongue before licking his lips, causing a shiver to run down my spine. I have no doubt that if I were to read his mind right now, he would be undressing me with it.

"Such a waste," he whispers.

"In your dreams," I snarl.

He scowls at me while looking at the other demon. "This one has a sharp tongue, Alyse."

The other nods. "Indeed, brother."

His eyes fall back to me. "I could think of better things for that tongue of yours."

I laugh. "I stand by my earlier comment."

"We will see."

A growl forms deep in my chest.

The other two witches and two warlocks watch our encounter in an annoyed manner before the two females move to flank me with smirks on their faces.

"You will be the first two to fall," I say to them with a smile.

The warlocks come at me from the front while the witches charge at my back, blades drawn. I close my eyes, focusing my energy. Bending my knees, I wait until the last second. Sensing them.

Eight feet.

Six.

Four.

Now.

My eyes fly open as I push off the ground with all my strength, sailing over their heads and landing behind the warlocks. They slide to a stop right before running each other through.

I form a fireball in each hand, throwing one at the closest warlock and the other at a witch. The witch deflects it easily, but the warlock goes up in flames, screaming. The others' eyes land on their comrade. I take the distraction, throwing my daggers at the other witch and warlock, hitting her in the shoulder and him in the leg. I pull at the daggers with my magic, calling them back to my hands.

I fuse my magic into the blades before letting them sail through the air once more. Once they leave my hands, they disappear.

The witch nursing her shoulder looks around frantically. "Where are they?"

As soon as the words leave her mouth, blood runs down from her skull as she slumps to the ground. The dagger reappears, sunk into her forehead. The other warlock and witch stare in horror as the demons smirk at me in awe.

I call back the blade just as the other lodges itself in the warlock's neck. His hands grab at the wound as he falls to his knees, the light quickly draining from his eyes.

One witch and two demons left.

The witch turns to the demons. "Are you going to help or just stand there?"

The one called Alyse moves forward, looking me hard in the eyes. I look down at my hands to find them empty; the blades have vanished. I try to bring my wolf forth, but I'm frozen.

What is he doing to me?

Almost as if he's reading my mind, he smiles sinfully.

"Are you sure you want to continue with this pointless fight?" He asks tauntingly.

I try to answer, but my throat goes dry.

Alyse turns to his brother. "Kyron, it appears she has become speechless."

Kyron takes a step toward me, playfully grinning as he rubs his hands together.

"Good, then no one will hear her scream," he purrs.

Alyse places a hand on his brother's shoulder. "Not here, brother. Let's take her away, and then we can have our fun."

The witch laughs at them. "You two have got to be kidding me."

They turn their eyes to her.

Kyron speaks first. "You cannot imagine how strong a child born of me and her would be."

The witch's laugh continues, louder this time, as she holds her stomach. "Did you not hear her before? She will never mate with the likes of you. Also, did you happen to notice the ring on a very important finger? I doubt her mate wouldn't come looking for her."

"Not if he is dead with the rest of them," Alyse replies.

"She may be strong, but her power is no match for us, not yet," Kyron states. "If we were to take her, it would only be a matter of time before she would submit."

The witch's eyes connect with mine. "I think you have the wrong girl. You underestimate her."

"We will see," he whispers.

She shakes her head, backing away. "I didn't sign up for this."

Kyron's eyes flash to her. "No, but you did sign on to kill others. To watch as their souls leave their bodies."

"I.." she starts, but he interrupts her.

"What makes killing someone less than taking away someone's will? If you ask me, I think the killing is higher on the rack, don't you, brother?" Kyron's eyes flash with malice.

Alyse nods his head in agreement. "You're free to go and kill some more since you feel that is the lesser of two evils in this scenario."

"We were called on to eliminate the threat. Not take them on as mates," she yells to the pair.

"Do you think we care?" Alyse questions. "All that matters to us is keeping the dark ahead of the light. Whether she is killed or turned does not matter, and I feel turning her will be more delicious."

Her eyes find mine, and I can see that she is torn. For the first time, my enemy feels pity for me. Something I don't welcome. I never want anyone to pity me. It's an emotion I feel the world can do without.

I watch her as her mind runs through the situation, thinking if there is any way she can help me, but I know she will find none. Demons and angels are the strongest in our world and are not to be trifled with. If I let it, the fear will cripple me, as I don't see a way out of this. One demon, maybe I could take on myself. But two?

I do the only thing I can think of while they are distracted. I reach out my mind to my brother and the rest of the group, hoping they are okay and have defeated whatever foe was in their path. I can only hope my magic is strong enough to push past the block the demons have on me and that my family will hear my thoughts and be able to come and help. Without them, my child and I will be taken away from here, and once they learn I am pregnant, I don't want to think about what they will do.

Chapter 59

Julian

S age sneers as the men circle Amberly. I try to do as Amberly asked and focus my attention on Sage, but it's hard. The four men circle around me, drawing my attention back to the battle. I need to make quick work of them so I can get back to Amberly.

Pushing my wolf forth, my nails grow five inches in length. Without warning, I sprint forward faster than their eyes can process. I rake my claws across the closest chest, feeling the flesh tear as the hot fluid runs free and screams of agony fill my ears. Without pause, I lunge for the next one and slash across their face and neck, watching as the life slowly slips away. The only noise is the gurgling of blood filling his throat, mouth, and chest. I watch momentarily before I turn to the next two. They barely have a moment to take in the scene around them before I am on them.

My claws claw the length of his back until I see muscle and bone. Shrieks fill the air as I descend on the last of the group. Grabbing his face in my hands, I look him in the eyes, releasing an angry growl. He squirms, frantically trying to get away as I apply pressure, squeezing his head between my half-human hands. My claws sink into his flesh, and I don't stop until I hear a crunch, followed by a pop, and the light leaves his eyes.

His body sinks to the ground, and I look over to see Amberly holding her own.

"Well, that was just sad," Sage grumbles as she walks toward me. "Hard to find good help nowadays."

Before I can even turn my attention back toward my opponent, I'm sailing through the air. I land hard about thirty feet away from where I was. Pushing myself up from the ground, I frantically search for Amberly. It takes me a few seconds longer than I would like before I see her. She's on the ground, but her assailants are contained in tree roots. I sigh with relief before looking around me. Sage is coming in hot, along with a group of fae. Focusing, I get my head back in the game before the selie is on me, blades drawn.

Before I can deflect the attack, the metal blade sinks into the flesh of my abdomen. With a loud growl, I push back the fae with brutal force. He sails through the air, landing on two of the other descending selie.

On my knees, I grunt as I pull the blade from my body in a swift motion. Lime, vine-like lines emerge from the wound as the pain grows. *Poison.* Frustrated, I move to a standing position, and the pain begins to dull. Glancing back at the hole in my stomach, I watch as it closes and the poison disappears. Grinning, I stare at three fae looking at one another, confused, blades in their hands.

"This is going to be fun," I whisper.

In one swift movement, I descend on them, taking a blade from the closest of the three. I spin, sinking it into the chest of the next one. Disbelief shines in his eyes before he goes limp on the blade. I remove the metal from his body, feeling the pain in my back before seeing the front of the blade sticking through my stomach. Winded, I turn on him so fast that he loses his grip on the blade, leaving it inside me. I grab his head, twisting it quickly, hearing the break before he sinks to the ground.

Falling to my knees again, I reach around, trying to grab the blade while looking for the last selie. A kick from behind makes me crash to the ground, and my face hits the dirt as a cloud of dust goes up around my face, making it difficult to breathe. The blade sinks back as the rest of my body connects with the ground.

The fae places his foot on my back, pushing me further into the earth. He leans over me, placing all his weight down on the blade. I wince as I feel the blood trickling out of my mouth and down my chin.

"You killed my brothers," he whispers, "Now I'm going to make this hurt."

I try to push him off, but he applies more of his weight to my back. I know the amulet can't heal me until the blade is removed, and I'm too weak to get him off of me. Then I remember I have something else I can use.

Focusing the last of my energy on him, I close my eyes, imagining him falling to the ground behind me. I hear a gasp, followed by a yelp, and then the weight is gone.

Still trying to get used to this whole magic thing, but it definitely comes in handy.

I pull myself up, the blade falling free from my body. I reach down, picking it up as I feel the wound beginning to close. The selie has gotten back on his feet and snarls at me before charging. I stick the blade into the ground before preparing my claws. A small dagger in his right hand sails through the air, hovering over my heart. I block it before grabbing his arm and flipping him onto his back, knocking the wind out of him as he gasps.

I lean over him, smiling. "I'm really going to enjoy this. You chose the wrong side."

Pulling him to his knees, I use my magic to hold him in place as I retrieve the sword.

"Any last words?" I ask him.

Anger flashes across his face. "Go to hell, you mutt."

"You first," I snarl at him as I sink the steel into his flesh slowly. His mouth opens wide, and a scream of pain fills the air between us. I pull it out and sink it back in as the light in his lime-green eyes begins to dim. I watch as he takes his last breath. Removing the blade from the selie's body, I pant with exhaustion as he sinks to my feet.

I'm backed up against a wall. Two demons. I can't handle them alone. Amberly's voice rings through my mind, causing my heart to skip a beat. I turn to where I last saw her, panic setting in, making it hard to breathe. After scanning the area a few times my eyes lock onto her. She's standing, unmoving, as two blacked winged figures and what I can guess is a witch stand mere feet from her.

Standing, I focus on my wolf speed and sprint in their direction.

Chapter 60

Aidan

The last of the warlocks fall lifeless to the ground around me. The last spell took a lot of energy. I glance around, thankfully seeing no new opponent approaching. I could use a second to catch my breath. This battle is nothing like the others. It's almost like our grandparents supercharged these fighters with extra juice of some kind.

Having never met them in person, I wonder if I will recognize them if I come across them. If I can put them down, then this madness will end, and the bloodshed will cease. I haven't seen anyone from the cave since I began my fight. For the first time, I'm nervous, and I feel the need to be close to my sister. If not her, then my grandparents. I need to end this.

I'm backed up against a wall. Two demons. I can't handle them alone. Amberly's voice enters my mind.

My heart begins to race as my eyes dart back and forth over the landscape and the bodies fighting on it. I search frantically for my sister, but she's nowhere. I focus my energy and begin running in the direction I feel pulled to. I'm running so fast I can barely make out the scene around me until I hear Amara scream.

I stop, scanning the field until I see her. She's lying on the ground, blood pouring from multiple wounds. One deep on her forehead, another on her left shoulder. The warlock and fae move in on her, but from the look of things, she can't stand. I run as fast as I can, charging toward the warlock at top speed. With a crunch, he goes to the ground. I turn to the fae, zipping to him with a ball of fire and energy I conjure in my hands. Upon impact, he goes up in flames, screaming. I turn back toward the warlock, focusing on using my magic to stop his heart. His mouth opens as he grabs his chest before falling to his knees and then further, his head hitting the dirt floor with a sickening crunch.

I move to my knees next to Amara. "Is anything broken?"

Her eyes shining, she looks at me. "I think they broke my leg. I'm waiting for it to heal. You seem to pop up at the best times," she shyly smiles at me.

Grinning, I reply, "Sometimes."

The cut on her forehead begins to close slowly, and my eyes look lower to see the one on her shoulder is completely healed. I offer her my hand, which she grabs and come to stand beside me.

"I have to get to Amberly. Are you okay now?" I ask, pulling away.

"Is she okay?"

"She reached out to me, she needs help."

Determination flashes across her face as she takes a step toward me. "Well, what are we waiting for? Lead the way."

Nodding, I turn, and we run in the direction I feel her energy pulling at me.

Chapter 61

Amberly

"No one is coming, little mouse," Kyron teases.

I spit at his feet as I remain trapped in place. His face twists with anger as his fist lands a blow across my cheek, causing stars to cloud my vision. The taste of metal fills my mouth.

"Hell of a punch you have there," I spit the blood to the ground. "You hit all your women, or just the ones who reject you?"

He bares his teeth, ready to land another strike, but his brother grabs his hand mid-swing.

"Enough. Let us be on our way."

Kyron nods in agreement before taking my chin in his hand and squeezing hard. "I told you I would find better use for that mouth of yours. Ready to put it to the test?"

"Enough, Kyron," his brother yells. "Grab the girl and let us leave this graveyard behind."

Kyron yanks me up as Alyse comes to stand beside us with an uncertain look on her face.

I close my eyes, pushing down my fear. I rack my brain, hoping to come up with something to stall them until my backup gets here, but I'm coming up blank.

"Let her go!" Aidan yells as he runs over the hill, Amara in tow.

Julian, Logan, Troy, Angela, and two angels follow behind them. The one female angel, known as Eva, turns her gaze to Kyron, and I know she's momentarily blocking his shimmering power.

When facing off against a demon, you always want an angel with you, as a demon's energy is weakened when an angel is nearby, and there are certain things they can't do. Zipping in and out is one of those things.

Aidan is nearly on top of us, and Julian is close behind.

Aidan glares at Kyron and snarls, "Last warning."

Alyse moves to stand in front of us. "Boy, you may be strong, but let's not get cocky now."

Aidan takes a step forward before Julian grabs him to hold him back as Eva moves closer to Alyse.

"I never thought we'd see you here, Alyse. What are you and your brother doing so far from the safety of your home?" Eva asks.

Grinning widely, Alyse turns to gesture toward me. "We came to collect." Facing Eva again, he continues, "We heard about the half-breed and grew interested." Smiling back in my direction he adds, "And I do say, I find myself quite intrigued. She has a mouth and a fire in her I haven't tasted in ages."

I feel the rage boiling inside Julian before I see him charge forward. Panic spreads through me before Eva grabs his arm, stopping his movement forward.

She addresses Alyse with an even tone. "I'd advise you against talking about his mate in that way."

Alyse's chuckle sends a shiver down my spine. "Like I care. She will be mine soon enough."

"Don't bet on it," Julian growls through bared teeth.

Alyse's expression turns cold. "Oh, I'm fairly certain," his eyes connect with mine, "she may not want me now, but she will in time."

Eva takes a step forward. "Alyse, it is unwise for you to be here, especially now. I suggest you leave before things get ugly."

"Gladly," Alyse mumbles before turning his back on the group. Placing a hand on each of my shoulders, he turns back to everyone, "You may say your goodbyes."

Julian and Aidan's eyes widen as everyone takes a step forward.

Eva speaks first. "The girl is going nowhere."

"I beg to differ. We can either leave peacefully, as you suggested," a devilish grin spreads over his face, "or we can shed a little blood first. The choice is yours."

Aidan snarls at him, teeth bared. "It will be your blood that stains the land we stand on. You best take the lady's advice and leave while you can."

Julian moves forward. "And my wife is staying. Last. Warning."

Alyse flashes his pearly whites. "So be it."

I see the flash of silver before it leaves his hand, sailing through the air toward Eva. She deflects it easily, but the second one sinks deep into Troy's chest before anyone has a chance to react.

The scene unfolds in slow motion before my eyes. Troy glances down at the dagger protruding from his chest before glancing from Logan to me and then falls to his knees. Amara and Logan move to his side as everyone else advances on Alyse and Kyron.

A scream gets trapped in my throat as I watch Amara and Logan arguing with each other as Troy's body heaves in their arms. Tears form in my eyes as I'm rooted in place, struggling to break free and make it to my brother's side. I can't watch someone else I love die. I won't. I thought I had done everything right to change this outcome, but I was wrong. All I did was change the course of events on how each person I love would die.

Eva takes flight at the same time the brothers do. Two against one, I'm not liking her odds. I stare at the other angel that was with her, not understanding why she isn't at Eva's side. Then I see it. She holds an ancient angel blade hidden behind her wings. If she was to fly, she would have to remove it and lose the advantage.

I read about the blade years ago as part of my studies. There are only a handful left, and the distinct markings on the blade are what set it apart from others the angels use. The stars and moon shine brightly on the length of the blade, making it hard to hide. It is said that this blade can kill any demon, no matter its strength. One cut, and a demon is done. It takes time to run its course, but even if they were to walk away from the battle, the angel who wielded it would know the demon wouldn't be around much longer.

The female angel stays grounded as she watches Eva tensely, her stance ready for any opportunity to use the weapon and gain the upper hand.

Kyron lands a kick, sending Eva spinning backward. Her enormous wings cause a dust storm around the group as she stays suspended mere feet above the ground.

"Athena, now!" Eva shouts.

Athena pulls the blade from between her wings, launching herself into the air with a warrior's scream and stance as she buries the length into Kyrons abdomen, his eyes going wide. She quickly removes it and slashes at Alyse. He places his hands in front of his face defensively, the blade slicing down the palm of his hand before using his wing to send Athena crashing back to the ground with a sickening crunch.

Alyse descends, hovering over his brother, who is on his knees, cradling his midsection, staring off into space with confusion on his face. Alyse moves to inspect the wound, his face working as he tries to make sense of what happened.

Alyse winces, staring at his hand, and I feel the barrier holding me in place shatter as I fall forward, hands landing in the dirt. Without a care, I jump to my feet and charge toward Troy. Alyse, paying no attention to me, lifts his brother to his feet with his good hand. Staring toward Athena, his eyes narrow to slits as I moved past him. I hear Athena scream before I notice the flames engulfing her. The heat hits me in the face before the force blasts me backward. I barely have time to react, but thankfully, I shift my body to where I land on my side instead of my stomach.

I lift my head to see Athena still engulfed in flames. Alyse watches with a sneer as Eva and the others try to get to her to put out the inferno. Eva frantically flaps her wings in Athena's direction, but it does nothing. A moment later, Athena lies on the cool earth floor, lifeless. The flames disperse as the last breath leaves her body.

Eva moves closer, pulling Athena into her arms. The smell of burning flesh fills the air, causing my eyes to water. I rub at them hastily and don't see

Alyse until he's a few feet away. Moving into a standing position, I turn to flee as Alyse is knocked in the chest with a plasma ball, sending him sailing backward a few feet. I take off in a sprint, making it to Julian and Aidan's side.

Julian pulls me into his arms, looking me over, eyes frantic, before he moves me behind him.

"Alyse, something is wrong. I'm not healing," Kyron mutters.

His brother returns to his side. "They used one of those blades. We must return home."

"Leaving so soon?" A feminine voice calls from behind us.

I sense movement, which draws my attention. My eyes peek over Julian's shoulder to find an older woman, maybe in her sixties, accompanied closely by a not-much-older male. With them, a group of male and female fighters.

"My brother is hurt. I didn't come here for your cause; we came for our own." Alyse's eyes lock on me. "But it seems now isn't the time." Returning his attention to the older woman, he continues, "This battle is of your making. We will leave you to finish it."

With the wave of her hand, the old woman grins. "Take your leave then."

Alyse's eyes fall on me as he grins. "We will meet again. You can count on that."

Before anyone can react, he and his brother disappear in a mix of flames and ash.

"Now, where were we?" The woman voices, "Amberly, won't you save us the trouble and come out from behind your mate."

I go to take a step, and I'm stopped by Julian's hand on my arm and Aidan moving in front of us.

"You can't take on all of us. Maybe it's time to rethink your plan. Leave and live the rest of your days somewhere quiet," Aidan sneers. "I would advise you to make this choice quickly."

The old woman's head flies back as a loud, sinister chuckle escapes her, and the man at her side grins devilishly. When the laughter ends, she wipes a stray tear from her eye, looking at Aidan.

"Boy, do you think we are afraid of you? You and your sister are abominations that never should have walked this earth," she sneers as her eyes turn to slits when her attention moves back to me. "We have come to set things right in the world, and we are not leaving until we do."

Gurgling noises sound behind me, causing my heart to sink. I need to get to Troy, I may be his only hope. But moving isn't really an option at the moment. We just need to get through them and the battle will end.

Heat runs down the length of my arms, stopping in my palms. The intensity grows as my thoughts about our current situation run wild. Closing my eyes, I focus my energy on creating a powerful blast, hopefully strong enough to end this quickly.

Aidan takes a step forward. "Family means nothing to you, yet you call us the abominations. This world will be far better off with Amberly in it than not," he locks eyes with our grandmother as his tone turns passive. "If you care about the betterment of our world or family, then end this now. We still have a chance. You can change, and we can be a family."

Keeping my eyes closed, I sense the sneer on her face, and feel something else as well.

"I could never let a mutt be part of my family. As far as I'm concerned, Henry and I are all that remains of our line," she barks out, her eyes filled with hatred.

I feel the energy shift before light twines behind my eyes. I open them wide, seeing the energy blast moving our way. A bright mix of white, orange, and black swirling together in a deadly motion.

Pushing Julian out of the way, I rush in front of Aidan, throwing my hands out, releasing my own energy blast to meet hers. My white, pink, and blue energy mixes with her orange, white, and black, creating one big, colorful explosion.

The energy sends everyone flying in different directions as the world shakes, and the light becomes a giant dome over the battlefield.

The impact leaves me breathless as I open my eyes, trying to adjust to the bright light that is slowly dimming. Moving into a standing position, I glance around the field, but I'm unable to make out anyone.

A flash of black moves across my vision. Taking my battle stance, my shoulders become tense. Then, a burning pain shoots through my chest, and a scream catches in my throat. Glancing down, I see an arm, but the hand has vanished. It's inside my chest, fingers wrapping around my heart. I grab at the arm frantically as a face comes into view. It's a young man, not much older than myself, and I can smell the magic radiating off of him. The young warlock smiles at me as his emerald eyes glisten.

"Not so tough now, are you?" He asks mockingly.

The pain intensifies as he squeezes his fingers around my heart, tears forming in my eyes. Then the pain stops, and his hand slips from my chest as his body crumbles to the floor.

My hand jerks to my chest and my knees go weak, but strong arms find me before I find myself on the ground. My eyes connect with my brother as he grins.

"I got you," Aidan whispers.

Placing my forehead against his chin, a smile forms on my face. The smoke and light begin to disappear as bodies become noticeable on the ground. Before Aidan and I have a chance to prepare for another attack, we are thrown from each other like rag dolls, his arms ripped from my body. I find myself now in my grandfather's clutches, his hand tight around my throat.

Everyone is busy with their opponents, but as their eyes fall on me, I see the panic in their faces. I claw frantically at his hand, but I know it won't work. I reach around and pull the angel blade that Marcus gave me before the battle from my belt. I forgot all about it until this moment. I slash the blade in an upward motion across his arm, causing him to release me with a groan.

Moving into a crouching position, I sink the blade into his abdomen, removing it again in one swift motion. He stumbles back, hand over the wound, as surprise fills his pain-stricken face. I slide away from him, still in a crouch, as he smiles. Tilting my head to the side in wonder, he opens his hand, and a beautiful milky white stone drops as he holds the leather leash. My hand automatically moves to my neck to discover my amulet is missing. I charge toward him as he waves his hand over the stone, muttering an ancient chant. Grunts and groans begin around me, grabbing my attention as I come to a stop. Everyone's amulets are glowing.

"It is done," Henry whispers.

I begin my charge toward him again, and he's too busy finishing the chant to deflect any attack. I take the opportunity and slice the blade clear across his throat, watching as the blood runs freely. With a smile on his face, he descends to the earth, my amulet along with him.

"No!" Annabeth's snarl sounds behind me. "You half-breed bitch! You will pay for that!"

Swirling toward her, I throw my hands in front of me, casting a protective charm just in time as her spell bounces off the shield, sending me back a few steps.

"You and your friends are no match for us now," she yells at us. "Your amulets are useless! No more healing or body armor. This battle is almost over!"

"I wouldn't be so sure about that," my father's voice comes from nowhere.

"You," Annabeth sneers, pointing her wrinkled finger. "You are to blame for all of this." She gestures to me, "You defiled my daughter, corrupted her. You cost us everything and now," her eyes connect with mine, "I will take everything from you."

Without my amulet, my energy is almost depleted. I throw up my arms, willing another shield, but I know it won't hold against her spell, not like the last one. I feel the hit and stumble backward. Now on my knees, I grind my teeth as I push back her spell, but only slightly. Out of the corner of my eye, I see my father shift. His wolf charges Annabeth, teeth sinking into her abdomen and causing her to wail in pain as she turns her magic on him instead.

I sink to the ground, hands hitting the dirt as I pant from exhaustion. Taking more effort than I would like, I lift my head to find Annabeth overpowering Aaron, and I know I need to get to him. Attempting to stand, I fall back to the earth. Clenching my fist, I hit the dirt, sending a mini earthquake in their direction, and just in time. Annabeth's deadly magic blow just misses Aaron.

They fall a few feet back from one another as Aidan comes up behind

Annabeth, grabbing her around the neck and allowing our father to make the final blow. And then I see it. Our grandmother uncloaks a dagger and sends it backward, sinking it into Aidan's hip. He cries out in pain before releasing her. She turns on Aidan, dagger held high, ready to strike her killing blow as the blade lights up with her magic.

I scream, "Aidan, watch out!"

With the last of my magic, I transport myself in between Aidan and Annabeth, my back toward her. I wait for the blow, but nothing happens. Then, I hear it.

A deep howl of pain and a gurgling noise. Turning around, I see the blood pouring from our grandmother's chest, deep claw marks running the length of her body. Her eyes are wide with anger as she drops to her knees, panting.

Aaron, back in his human form, staggers toward us, covered in blood. He lands on his knees with a crunch as blood pours from his mouth.

"Dad?" I cry, looking him over.

Aidan, now beside me, reaches for our father as he begins to fall to the earth. His eyes wide, he looks at us with a small smile.

"I am so proud of you both."

"Dad, don't talk like that. You're going to be fine. You can heal," I cry out.

"You know as well as I that that won't work, not this time," he says, the words straining past his lips.

"Fine. I'll heal you!" As I place my hands over his body, he grabs them.

His expression turns serious. "Don't you dare. You are drained from the battle and have your own wounds that still need healing," his voice quivers as his eyes travel to my stomach. "You need to think of your child. I have lived my life, and now it's your turn. The battle is over. You are both safe, and I wouldn't have it any other way."

"I can't lose you," I wail, tears beginning to form in my eyes.

"I will always be with you both. There is a time for everyone, and this is mine," he says, looking to Aidan. "I will finally be with your mother. You two need to look out for one another now. Be better than we were."

Aidan's eyes go blank as he looks from our father to me. "There has to be something we can do?"

"I…" The words are lost as tears stream down my face.

"Amberly," Julian calls from behind me.

I hear his hurried footsteps pounding the dirt before I feel his body heat next to me on the ground.

"Aaron," he looks from me to my brother. "What happened?"

"I wasn't fast enough. I wasn't ready!" I cry.

My father takes my hand in his. "Don't do that. Do not blame yourself. I did for your mother, and I don't want that for either of you." He turns to Aidan, "This was neither of your doing. Your mother and I made our choice, and we would do the same if given the chance again." Sadness fills his eyes as he looks at me. "Now that you will have a child of your own, you will understand soon enough." Turning to Julian, he coughs, "Take care of them. Don't let them wallow in the loss. Remember to be happy and live."

Julian nods before taking my free hand in his. "Amberly," he says, his tone somber.

I shake my head violently. "I'm not ready to say goodbye."

"It's never goodbye. It's simply until we meet again. You are ready. Lead with the grace and strength I know you have. I love you, and I am so glad I had the chance to get to know you," our father looks at Aidan, "Both of you."

His breath becomes labored and I know in a matter of moments, he will be gone, and I don't know what to do with that. The battle may be won, but at what cost? My child will have no grandparents. No one to spoil them and sugar them up before sending them home to Julian and I. Everything I went without, my child will, too, and that's not something I'm ready to deal with.

Julian pulls me close as my cries turn to sobs. I bury my face in his chest as his arms move around me, and then my father's hand slips from mine, but I don't look.

"Julian," Aidan whispers, "I'm going to…"

He stops abruptly, and I feel Julian nod his head as my father's weight is lifted away from me. Grabbing Julian's shirt, the tears flow freely and uncontrollably, and I fear they will never stop.

"Little wolf, I'm taking you home," Julian whispers before picking me up in his arms.

I hear muffled voices and crying as we make our way back to the cave. Julian stops momentarily, but I keep my face buried in his chest, not wanting to see anyone or deal with anything else at this moment.

My life from here on will be different than I ever envisioned. In some ways good, but right now, all I can see are the bad. A hollowness fills my chest as the tears begin to cease, and the weight of sleep falls over me.

Chapter 62

Julian

I walk up to the group huddled around the pyres, taking note of how many there are. After putting Amberly to sleep I made my rounds, learning who had perished on the field. Then we began making the pyres and got everyone as comfortable as could be under the circumstances. We knew we would have to wait for Amberly to join us before beginning the ceremony and saying our final farewells.

Dreading the moment Amberly will wake, I approach Logan and Angela. "Hey, how are you holding up?" I ask them both.

Logan's eyes are rimmed with crimson, and Angela's are still wet with tears.

"I still can't believe he's gone," Logan mumbles. "How are we going to tell Amberly?"

Shaking my head, I sigh, "As gently as possible. She's still mourning her mother, and now Aaron, I'm afraid of what this will do to her." Glancing at Angela, I ask, "How is Amara holding up?"

Angela shrugs lightly. "As good as can be expected. They weren't together long, but feelings were growing. Aidan is with her."

I nod. Looking around the camp, everyone is working or mourning. Too many lives were lost today, more than I had thought would be.

Angela wipes away the fresh tears trailing her cheeks with a sniffle. "We thought Aaron, Johnathan, Aayda, and Troy should be placed in the front line for the pyre burning."

Nodding once more, my eyes return to Logan.

"I know we haven't always seen eye to eye, and we weren't all as close as I would have liked, but I am sorry for your loss." My gaze lands on Angela. "I can only imagine how you are feeling. If it had been Angela..." I trail off.

Logan looks at me for the first time. "Thank you."

"I'm going to go check on Amberly. Is there anything you need here before I do?"

Angela shakes her head as Logan moves into a seated position next to the pyre containing his long-time brother.

* * *

My head hangs low as I enter the candlelit room to hear the light sounds of breathing. I find Amberly still fast asleep, her hands tucked under her face, which holds a light smile. I release a long breath before sitting next to her.

"Little wolf, it's time to wake up," I whisper, softly rubbing her back.

With a small moan, the smile disappears as she shifts to her back, rubbing her eyes sleepily.

"What time is it?" She mutters.

"Past dark. It's time love. Everyone is waiting."

I watch as her face changes, lines deepening with sorrow as the memories of today unfold in her mind. Her lips begin to quiver as she covers her face with her hands, muffling a small sob.

With a heavy heart, I take her in my arms. "I'm here little wolf. I've got you."

After a few moments, Amberly settles down, and I brush the hair from her moist face. "There is something you should know before we join the others," I whisper.

Worry fills her features. "What is it?"

Clearing my throat, I look away from her. "The death toll was higher than expected."

Pulling further away from me, she asks, "How many?"

"Nearly two hundred," I murmur. "Johnathan and Aayda were among them, and…" I stop, afraid to say his name.

She sits in silence, waiting for me to continue. When I don't, her eyes widen slightly before asking.

"Who else?" Her shoulders tense, waiting for my answer.

Looking her in the eyes, I breathe in deep. "Troy."

Tears fill her eyes once more as she turns away, standing from the bed. She paces the room as her breathing becomes labored.

"Oh, my God. I…I forgot all about… How could I forget?" She stops, bringing her hand over her mouth. "How could I…" She looks at me as the tears run down her face. "I never made it to his side. I never…" She falls to her knees, crying out the next words,. "I never got to say goodbye."

I move to her side on the floor, placing my hand on her knee as her body shakes from her sobs. I don't know how to comfort her. All this loss would be too much for most to bear, and I don't know how she is still mobile. I worry about all the stress she is taking on because of this and hope it won't affect the baby, but right now, I can't make less of her feelings, and she needs to go through the normal process of grieving all that she has lost.

A mother.

A father.

A brother.

She has lost all her family in less than a year. I am thankful she still has Aidan, as well as the pack. She will have all the support and understanding she needs, but right now, she needs to feel this and I need to let her.

Her head shoots up, startling me.

"I need to see him."

Nodding, I push the hair from her face. "You will."

She moves into a standing position, looking down at me. "No, I need to see him now."

Without another word, she storms out the door, leaving me to follow behind.

Chapter 63

Amberly

I don't stop running until I'm standing outside the cave, lines of pyres staring me in the face. I make my way over to where Logan is sitting as my gaze lands on Troy. He looks as though he is sleeping, dreaming peacefully. At least that's what I will choose to think in this moment.

"Amberly," Logan calls to me, his voice breaking.

My eyes fill with tears as I take my last steps toward our fallen brother. I reach out, pushing the hair off his forehead, and lean down to place a kiss on his cool skin. Closing my eyes, I begin to weep for another loss. A loss I could have changed.

"I can bring him back," I cry out.

Logan's tight grip on my forearm pulls my attention away from Troy.

"No," he says sternly. "I won't let you. He wouldn't want you to and you know that as well as I."

I look from him to Troy and back again. "But…"

"No buts," he cuts me off. "This is the price of war, and if it were anyone else, this would be something that couldn't be changed. Even though you have this gift, it does not mean you should use it." He looks to Troy before continuing. "Having a gift like ours isn't always good. Remember, magic always comes with a price, and sometimes that price isn't worth paying." With moist eyes, Logan stares at me. "We can't lose you, Amberly, and if bringing him or Aaron back meant losing a piece of yourself or possibly hurting the baby, you know they wouldn't do it. No matter how small the risk. Bringing them back would be a dishonor. They went down as heroes and it is time we give them the hero's farewell."

As much as his words hurt, and as hard as I want to fight against him, I know he is right. Saying goodbye to the ones we love is a part of life that no one can escape. We are born to die, and death comes for us all. No one is ever truly ready for it, but it's something we can never stop. I only wished I would have had more time. I will never hear Troy's voice again, never feel the anger I got from his playful tricks, never feel his embrace. I won't see the man he would have grown to be and my children will never know their uncle, just like they won't know their grandparents.

As if reading my mind, Logan smiles. "We will keep their memories alive. Your child will know their crazy, bullheaded uncle and the strong and passionate leaders their grandparents were. They will never be left behind or forgotten."

I nod as I look around to all the grieving faces. "It's time," I whisper.

* * *

Watching the flames, my heart breaks, and I know it will never be whole again. Saying goodbye has never been my strong suit, but I always thought I would be much older before having to say my final farewells to the many people I've laid to rest this past year. There is nothing I wouldn't give to change the course of events that have taken place, but I know Logan is right, and it's time I let myself feel the dull ache and begin to mourn.

Another tear rolls freely over my warm cheek before I turn to Julian and whisper, "Take me to bed."

He nods before taking my hand in his, leading the way to our room. I look back one last time as cries and smoke fill the night air.

* * *

The light shines bright, sending a sense of peace to wash over me. I breathe it in deep, welcoming it. Closing my eyes, I listen to the calming sounds circling in the air. The breeze is quiet and cool, the birds singing above, and then...footsteps. Opening my eyes, the light dims, slowly revealing three forms moving toward me. Sensing no threat, I stay where I am, letting them come to me.

Onyx hair catches my eye, causing my heart to skip a beat.

"Dad?" I whisper.

I'm embraced tightly as the light calms and my mother and Troy step into view. My eyes sting as tears fight to come to the surface. Pulling back from my father, my mother pulls me close, and we squeeze each other tightly as soft sobs fill the space around us. She moves away, pacing her hands on my cheeks and smiling at me before turning me toward Troy.

"Hey, sis," he offers with a smile.

I run over to him, embracing him tightly. "You weren't supposed to leave me, you ass."

"It wasn't in my schedule, but we both know how we aren't always in control," he laughs. Pulling back, his smile grows. "Though we may not be with you physically, know that we will always be there in spirit."

Tears spill down my cheeks. "It's not fair."

"Since when has life ever been fair?" He asks.

My mother steps forward. "We don't have much time. We had to let you know that we are fine and that we are happy. Finally, we are together." She looks at my father, continuing. "But more than anything, we want you to know how proud we are of you."

My father places his hand on her shoulder as they look at one another.

He looks at me, smiling. "Your mother and I have waited a long time to be together, and now we can. We wish we could be with you and your brother, but destiny had another path in store for us."

Squeezing my hand, my mother adds, "You and your brother are not to hold onto this. Mourn and be done with it. Live your lives and be there for one another.

This is what we need from you. Do not let our passing dim your light and do not for one second blame yourself for this, do you hear me?"

I nod.

Pulling me close once more, she whispers, "Good. Lead with the strength and love you hold inside. Keep us alive there, and we will always be with you."

"I'm not ready to say goodbye," I cry.

"It's not goodbye, it's simply see you later. We will see one another again. Until then, live. See the beauty in every moment. The good, the bad. Soak it all in, take nothing for granted. Can you do that for us?" she asks me, stroking my hair.

I nod.

"Good, because we will want to hear about all of it," Troy says from behind us.

My mother moves away, revealing tears in her eyes.

My father pulls her close to him before addressing me. "It is time. Be at peace sweetheart. Know that we are always with you."

My body turns heavy as my family moves away from me.

I whisper back, before it's too late, "I love you, too."

Chapter 64

Amberly

The next morning comes fast. I'm now the Alpha, and it's time to step into the role. Making sure everyone was comfortable was the easy part, and now it's time for the next step.

"Morning," Marcus says as he and his people approach.

I nod. "I trust you slept well."

"We did, despite the events," he responds.

Closing my eyes briefly, I nod. There is no time to mourn, not yet.

"We will be taking our leave from you soon. We simply wanted to thank you for your hospitality and to let you know if you are ever in need, we are here," he says to me.

Merida moves forward before I can respond. She takes my hand lightly in hers. "You have changed our worlds in ways you do not know. Peace will finally spread across our lands and we will be united." She glances to Marcus before locking eyes with me, continuing. "And soon, the human world will know of us in a way like never before. You alone will bridge the gap, giving us all a new life, and I personally want to thank you."

Speechless, I squeeze her hand before Marcus reaches for her. "It is time we make our way home." Looking at me he continues, "We will be here when the time is right. Take care of the little ones."

Before I can utter a word, they turn away and Aidan is standing in their place.

"How are you this morning?" He asks.

"Better," I whisper.

Gesturing to my stomach, he asks, "And the baby?"

"Fine," I smile. "I was actually going to come looking for you." I walk to the exit, Aidan following alongside me. "We need to talk about what I mentioned before."

His eyes become distant as he looks straight ahead. "You mean about me taking over the Wiccan village as leader."

I nod. "We can't wait much longer. They've been there alone long enough and they need to know what's happened. With all the changes coming, I need someone I can trust."

Breathing in deeply, he looks over at me. "How soon would I need to leave?"

"A few more days here won't hurt, but I would like to have you set up there by the end of the week. I need you to get to know the people there, and help Logan get comfortable again." We make our way over to the rock bench by the fire pit and I take a seat. "It's not going to be easy for him going back there. I will also need you to get to know the others, and pick three you choose to stand in your stead when you aren't around."

He looks at me confused, opening his mouth as I raise a hand to stop him.

"I want you back here in a few months. I will need you once I am further along in the pregnancy and I would like you here when they are born, at least for a little while," I smile.

Aidan's eyes widen with uncertainty. "They?"

My smile grows as he takes a seat next to me. "I had my suspicions, but it wasn't confirmed for me until a few moments ago."

Nervous energy radiates from Aidan as he shifts uncomfortably next to me.

"I'm having twins," I whisper. "Marcus confirmed it."

Running his hand through his hair and down his face, he looks at me. "Twins! Oh, man. Well, you're in for it if they are anything like us," he chuckles.

Laughing, I nudge him with my shoulder. "Speak for yourself."

His smile falls slightly as his eyes scan over the forest before coming back to rest on me. "I'm really going to miss it here and miss being with you." Shifting slightly, he continues, "Once I find someone I can trust to lead, I will come back. And once the pups are born I would like to be here more than there, so I will find a way to make it all work."

Laying my head on his shoulder, I whisper, "I have no doubt you will."

* * *

"How did it go?" Julian asks as I enter our room.

"As well as can be expected," I say before removing my shirt and heading to the bathroom.

Calling from the bed, he asks, "And how are Logan and Amara holding up?"

Pain pulls at my heart but I push it back down.

"As good as can be expected. Amara is trying to keep it together but I feel it's more for mine and Logan's benefit. She cared for Troy. I have no doubt in that, but I feel it would have eventually burnt out."

"Oh," I hear him murmur.

Pulling my night shirt into place, I lean against the threshold of the bathroom door, looking at Julian as he sits on the edge of the bed.

"I learned something today," I add with a smile.

"Tell me." He looks at me playfully.

I take a step toward him slowly, my grin growing. "Turns out, we are having twins."

His eyes widen as he moves into a standing position. "Are you sure?"

I nod.

"Well, we are going to have our work cut out for us on the first go around it seems," he says with a laugh.

Reaching me, he wraps his arms around my waist, looking me in the eyes.

"How did I get so lucky?" He asks. "You are everything I could have ever wanted and then some. I'm sorry I was so pig-headed and blind to it in the beginning, and I thank you for giving me another chance." He kisses me on the forehead before pulling away. "I don't know where I would be without you. You have saved me in every way a person can be saved."

Placing my hand on his chest,I stare at him with all the love I hold in my heart, *I wasn't the only one who did the saving.*

His smile returns with a small chuckle. "If you say so." Looking down at my stomach, slowly and hesitantly, he places his hand there, jumping lightly once his hand is in place. Eyes shining, he looks at me, "I can't wait to meet our pups." Moving his hand to cup my face, he continues, "You are going to be the best mom."

Kissing him makes my heart feel full for the first time since the loss. Things aren't going to be easy, but I can't wait to see what the future holds for us. Now that everyone is settled, I can take this time to finally mourn. We all can. And then we have a fresh start. I can see it so clearly now, the life that is to come.

Chapter 65

Five years later

Amberly

"Luna, not so fast!" Julian calls to our daughter as he runs to her side. Four and a half might as well mean six with how quick and sneaky her and her brother Lucas can be. They definitely keep us on our toes.

Lucas runs over to me, throwing himself into my arms. "Momma, Uncle Aidan coming?"

Smiling, I nod. "Yes, that is why we are outside. We are waiting. He will be here soon."

"Here to stay!" Lucas claps happily.

"Yes, to stay." I smile, looking at the horizon.

The last few years have brought so much peace to our lands, and finally, we are able to move forward. My coven has chosen to join the pack and live together as one. All the supernatural villages are on the move, creating new homes all within one click of our cave. Once everyone is settled into their new homes, we will set up one day a week to get together and celebrate our new way of life.

The humans are another story. There has been talk of more of them venturing into the forest, and some are even hunting our kind. Rumors of the deaths of fae, angels, and even the other shifter packs have traveled over the lands, causing an uneasiness during our time of celebration. I have agreed to look into the truth about the disappearances in the upcoming weeks, but for now, I have asked everyone to focus on what we have built. Also, to stay away from the borders.

If there is any danger to our kind, it has only been a few miles inside the borders. So here, we are safe. Which is another reason we are all moving closer, stronger, together.

Today, we feast, and tomorrow, we plan.

"Momma, they're here!" Lucas cries as he jumps from my arms.

Aidan's gaze lands on Lucas, running up the hill toward him. Aidan smiles as he bends down, ready to catch the blonde hair, blue-eyed, stocky cub into his welcoming arms.

"Uncle Aidan!" Luna screams as she catches wind of Lucas's beeline up the hill.

Luna runs after Lucas as Julian returns to my side with an embrace. Aidan scoops up Lucas with one arm just as Luna makes it up the hill. Grabbing her with his other arm, he lifts them off the ground and continues his descent down the hill toward us. Along the hill line, my people appear.

"Hey, sis," Aidan greets me before putting the cubs back on the ground.

Their pouty faces look up at us as we hug.

"It's been too long," I whisper, holding him tightly.

Pulling back, Aidan looks to Julian and extends his hand. Julian shakes it with a smile.

"We were expecting you yesterday, what happened?" I ask.

Aidan looks over his shoulder as a familiar face steps into view.

"Amara," I whisper.

"Had to make a stop along the way," Aidan says as he looks back at me.

Smiling, I nudge his shoulder with mine. "Did I call it or what?" I say in Julian's direction.

Julian rolls his eyes as Aidan looks at us confused. With a shrug, Aidan wraps his arm around Amara's waist as she reaches our side.

Julian looks around at the group of witches and warlocks before landing on Amara and Aidan. "Our family is now complete."

"Speaking of family," Amara smiles, "we have some news."

Julian grins, my eyes pleading for him not to speak out loud, at least not yet. No one in the pack knows we are expecting, and I would like to tell the kids before anyone else that they are going to have a little brother or sister.

Aidan takes Amara's hand in his before saying, "We were married a few weeks ago and we will be expanding the family with another little pup in a few months."

Smiles widen all around as everyone embraces. Julian slaps Aidan on the shoulder before wishing him luck with the new adventure, and then they begin laughing with one another.

"What's so funny?" Luna asks.

Rubbing her head lightly, I smile. "Uncle Aidan and Aunt Amara are going to have a baby."

Luna smiles, clapping excitedly. "I can't wait!"

Luca rolls his eyes. "I hope it's a boy." He mumbles as he looks at Luna, "We need more boys."

Luna sticks her tongue out at him before running off. Shaking my head, I congratulate them once more before taking my seat nearby.

I watch as the kids run around playing with their uncle as Logan and Angela join the group. Everyone is laughing and smiling, and my heart feels full with how much my life has changed these last few years. I've done my best to keep my promise to my parents and Troy, and I will keep pushing forward for a strong, safe, and united future for my family. What's coming next is uncertain, but I know that together, there is nothing we can't overcome.

We're safe for now, but soon, we will have to face whatever is lurking in the dark and killing our kind. Soon, life will change for my family once again, but not right now. Now, we get to just be together and enjoy our time, and for that I am thankful. These are the moments I will soak up and remember for years to come.

Coming Soon

How You Can Help

Please, don't forget to leave your review, they help more than you know. If you enjoyed this series head over to Amazon and check out my other work. If you liked this series and wanted more of the characters, keep following me, there might just be something more down the line.

I will also be offering small stories in my newsletters. If you want to sign up head over to my Instagram @lauralukasavageauthor and the linktree in my bio has the signup for that as well as my youtube channel and anything else you will need.

Thank you again for taking the time to read and review. Looking forward to seeing you next time.

www.ingramcontent.com/pod-product-compliance
Lightning Source LLC
Chambersburg PA
CBHW070749280626
47162CB00018B/2786